It's Murder Wenlock

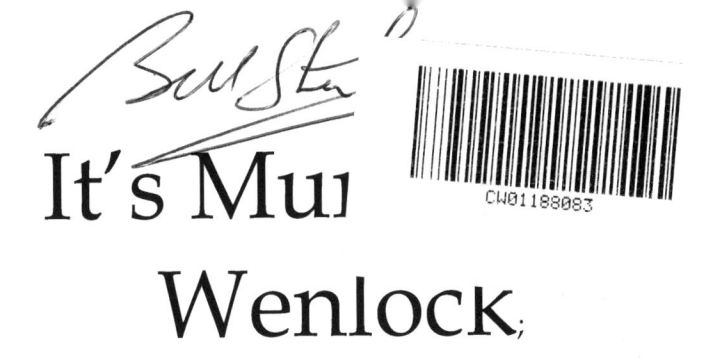

It's Murder in Wenlock Copyright © 2019 William (Bill) Stenlake

It's Murder in Wenlock By Bill Stenlake
All rights reserved. No part of this book may be reproduced, distributed or transmitted in any form, by any means without the prior consent of the author.

All characters in this publication are fictitious and any resemblance to persons, living or dead is purely coincidental. Some places named in the book exist and are real and some do not exist and are not real. The placement of all things geographical is relevant to this story only and as such should be deemed fictional.

Book Cover Photo: ©Esben Hansen /Dreamstime.com

Other books by Bill Stenlake:
- HOLLOW MILL
- THE KEEPER
- KENAN'S LEGACY
- CORNERSTONE
- THE GRAND MASTER
- DETECTIVE BRAMLEY BOOK 1
- RANDOLPH
- VOICES IN MY HEAD
- LOWARTH TOLL
- THE CORIDAE KEY
- BRAMLEY BOOK 2
- THE MANNACHS
- DIMENSIONS
- THE ROOTS
- A PAIR OF SHORTS
- THE WATCHER
- THE KEEPER TRILOGY
- IT'S DARK IN WENLOCK
- RODDY JOHNSTONE

It's Murder In Wenlock By Bill Stenlake

Forward:

I used to live in a street where there were about 17 houses. Some were semi-detached and rest were detached. The street was in a good part of the town. But it is about the people I am reminded of, as I start this book.

Some of the residents I would rarely see, as they drove everywhere. I never passed them, walking in our street. Some of the residents I would know by sight. If I passed them in the street, we might give each other a nod, or maybe a short hello. There were others I knew slightly better and quite possibly I would stop for a chat. That would be the extent though of my dealings with them. Then there were others who we socialised with in some fashion. Maybe when there was a Christmas or Birthday gathering or the like, there would be a do in one of the houses. But, and here comes the thought I always had. On any day, each and every one of these people would get home and go into their house and no one would have any idea what they were doing. They could be doing anything in the privacy of their own home; even people in as nice a street as ours was!

The other thought that passes through my mind, just before I write the first chapter, is this: However nice you think you are as a person, there will always be someone who doesn't like you, or what you do, or stand for.

Neither of the above may be relevant to the story, but then maybe they will. Read on:

Chapter 1 Not in Wenlock

The house isn't in bad condition when Bob buys it. It isn't that great either. It has the look of a house that has had just the bare minimum spent on it over the years. That probably applies to the last owners more than before. They hadn't got any money to spare on upkeep. Or at least that was the way they allocated their money, with upkeep definitely bottom of the spending list. Tired, that is what it is, in need of a complete update.

But then that is why it appealed to Bob. He got the house at a good price and now he is ready to lay into it. He will start with his plans to not only bring it up to date, but to extend it while he is at it.

The downstairs rooms are an odd shape, well one of them is. There is something like a 3 foot by 3 foot space that appears to be lost. He can't see why that is; it is just not there. Well, not accessible. He will investigate that when he starts working on that room.

To be fair the floorplan shows the room as the shape it is, so it is something longstanding that has caused this. He just knows there must be a reason for it. He has worked in enough houses to know that much.

The day comes when he gets round to it. He has started work on the extension. The foundations are in, but now he has to wait before he can start to lay the bricks. He has to wait to let the concrete set and also he has to wait for the rain to stop. It started almost as soon as the concrete mixer arrived and it hasn't stopped since. Anyway it doesn't matter. It is an ideal time to investigate the lost space.

The first thing that surprises him is that under the plaster on the wall, he finds wood. That isn't what he expected to find. It hadn't sounded like wood when he had checked the wall. He carefully removes all of the skim of plaster. That reveals what used to be a door. The question he has is: door to what? His guess is a cupboard, but he can't get the door open. The handle has been removed. Whoever did this has banged some hefty looking nails into the door, to make sure it stays shut.

Bob is not to be deterred though. He is more determined than ever to find out what is behind the door. There is no easy way to get the wood off. A drill, to make a big enough hole to get the jemmy in, is the answer. From then on it is just a case of breaking the door off in pieces. The very first piece reveals a shallow cupboard but it is not the full depth. Behind that it is solid.

Once the door is finally removed he starts to wonder if he would be wise to have someone with him when he does the next bit. There is no reason for him to think that, other than the feeling he has inside of him. That is that the back wall has been put there for a reason and that reason is not going to be a good one, for him.

He stops for a drink while deliberating, and also having a rest. He wants to carry on, but he just can't, on his own. Something isn't right here; he can feel it in his bones. He takes his mobile and selects a number to ring. A quick conversation means that he has to wait a while for his friend to turn up. In the meantime he tidies the bits he has broken off from the door; the door that is now in bits on the floor. He sweeps them up and shovels them into a black sack, which he places at the edge of the room. He has a funny feeling that he should hold onto them, at least until he has broken through the brick wall behind the shelves.

Stan arrives quite promptly and Bob shows him the reason he has decided to break through the wall. They remove the shelves first. They pick a point on the wall to make a start at and Bob takes the first go at dislodging the first brick. There is only a thin skin, so they find out. Whoever it was who put this up certainly didn't want the idle explorer to pick their way through the wall. Taking it in turns at having a go at the wall, little by little they make inroads into the blocks. Once they have a hole to work from it isn't long before they break it right down, except they don't get that far.

What they see at the first shine of a light into the space behind, is enough for them to stop. It is enough for Bob to have his worst fears confirmed. Someone has filled in the gap with rubble, but it hasn't filled it quite as much as they expected to, he thinks. You can still see enough of what they were trying to conceal. It is enough for them to lay down their tools and for Bob to use the phone again. This time the call he makes is to the police.

Within an hour the place is literally crawling with people. Bob is no longer allowed in his own house. It has been declared a crime scene. There is no doubt that it is a body that Bob has revealed behind the brick wall. The only things that need to be determined now are, whose body it is, how long it has been there and who is responsible for committing the murder. There is no doubt that murder has been committed. Why else would someone go to so much bother, to secret a body away behind a nailed in door and a cupboard back block wall.

As far as Bob is concerned, the only positive that can be taken from this situation, is that there is no one looking in his direction as to being the perpetrator of this crime.

The investigations roll on their way. Bob is excluded from his house for the foreseeable future. The identity of the body is going to take some time. As far as everyone locally is concerned, there is no one who has mysteriously gone missing, in living memory. Yes, the house has changed hands a few times, but the owners have been living at the time of sale; at least that is what the information reveals at first look.

Chapter 2 Out of Wenlock

Several weeks go by before Bob is allowed back into his house. By that time his feelings about it have changed somewhat. What had looked like a good opportunity to make some quick improvements to the house and add on good gains to its value; now seem a distant memory. Improving a house and selling it on is one thing, but when you have a long lying corpse being discovered in the same property, it makes the attractive side of any deal go sour. Just the fact that someone may have been murdered here, sends the value rocketing downwards, unless you find some kind of weirdo who wants to buy it for that specific reason.

Bob hasn't been able to do much with his plans. He really wants to demolish that entire section of the house, but that is impractical. He decides to do the next best thing. He removes what used to be the cupboard and makes it part of the room. He manages to get friends and family to assist him, in finishing the extension as quickly as possible, with the intention of selling the place on as quickly as he can.

The investigation into the hidden body hasn't made much progress either. There are no records of a missing person, either now or going back years, to fit the victim's profile; male and middle aged. There just aren't that many missing persons in the area anyway.

There is nothing to identify whose body it is. There are no teeth in the skeleton that could allow identification from dental records. The only things that they can be reasonably sure of are that the victim was male and maybe middle aged.

The previous owners to Bob have been interviewed and investigated. As was known anyway, their reason for selling the house was because they couldn't afford it. They hadn't changed the house. They are still living locally, in rented accommodation. They were horrified to learn they had been living with a corpse in the living room. The Jones family have no unexplained gaps in their history. The body does not appear to be anything to do with them, but an open mind is being kept.

The Dobbs family owned the house before the Jones family. They maintain that the room was in the current shape when they bought the house. They had nailed the door up and plastered over it when they moved in, but that was all they did in that room. They had never even questioned the fact of the lost space at the back of the cupboard, as hadn't the Jones family. They too were uncomfortable once given the knowledge of what they had been living with while they owned the house.

They were slightly harder to track down, as the reason for them selling the house to the Jones family, was because they were separating. Martin Dobbs is still living reasonably locally, just a mere ten miles away. He ex-wife Debbie has moved farther afield, living back at home with her parents. Her children live there too. Martin had directed the police to where she is living. Once again there was no one that either of them, or their families, could point to as being missing. It didn't take long to eliminate them from the enquiries too. That meant going back a bit further. That is where things got slightly more difficult.

Records show that the previous owner of the house was one David Petrich. He was a male and broadly in the age range of the deceased. But David Petrich has emigrated. Or rather he has gone back to the country of his parent's birth; Poland. His parents had moved to Britain during the Second World War and stayed afterwards. When his parents died, David stayed on in the house, but apparently was not that well a person. They found from medical records, that he struggled after losing his parents. About a year after they'd died he had to give up his job, in an engineering factory.

Even though the factory had been a victim of the recent downturn, detectives still managed to locate a number of people who had worked there. One or two actually remembered him. They told the detectives that he had often spoken about moving back to Poland. They can't remember that happening, as he wasn't working by that time, but he had definitely talked about it.

A little more digging was required, before they could move on their interest beyond him. Locating the estate agent that he had used to sell the house was the easiest task to achieve. He had used one locally. They remember that he had put the house on the market almost as soon as he had stopped worked. They also agreed with what the detectives had already been told; that he was intending to go back to Poland. They couldn't remember about the inside of the house, but then that is not surprising, as it is some years ago and they have seen many thousands of houses in the meantime. They do remember that at some time through the selling procedure that he moved away. The house had not sold instantly. To be fair it wasn't the cleanest and the decoration had needed updating. It was never going to be a quick and easy sale. At what stage had he moved away? They can't remember now, but it was still a few months after that when the house eventually sold. David had appointed a solicitor to deal with the sale before he left. Maybe they should speak to them. The detectives moved there next.

The records have long gone, as have most of the partners who worked there. Luckily though there was still one solicitor there from the day. Luck would also have it that he had dealt with David Petrich. It takes a bit of time for him to remember something about it. There was nothing remarkable really, to make it easy to remember. But he did recall a few things, after some deliberation. David had definitely come into to see him before he moved away. He was not going straight to Poland, if he remembers correctly. He had given the solicitor the power to sign on his behalf, when the house was sold. The funds were deposited in David's account as per instructions. There is nothing there to be suspicious about. That is the conclusion of the solicitor and the detectives.

The bank came next, but they drew a blank at that one. Any account that David Petrich had back then, has been long closed and the information is long gone. That also is not helped by the fact that the bank he had used has now amalgamated, or been taken over by another bank. Still there doesn't appear to be anything amiss. But there is no David Petrich they can find in the UK, not that they expected to, and enquiries as to where he might be if he did go back to Poland; are still ongoing.

That takes them further back in time, to the owners of the house, before the Petrich family bought the house. That is quite a short search, as they have long been deceased. Their descendants are all accounted for and the search sort of peters out for a while. Either some new piece of evidence needs to surface locally, or maybe they will get some feedback as to where he is, in Poland. That is if he is still alive. He wasn't a particularly well man when he gave up work, so he may not still be alive. But there appears to be little doubt that he was alive when he sold the house and moved away.

By the time these enquiries have been made and no conclusion has been reached; Bob has the house finished and ready to go on the market again. How long it will take to sell, with its recent occupancy history, is another matter.

Chapter 3 Bill in Wenlock

Much Wenlock is quiet today. It has been a while since the episode with Anne. Bill still gets some inquisitive looks whenever he takes a stroll downtown. He lives in the town and he goes into the centre quite often, if not most days. But some folks just can't get things out of their systems. It is that kind of a place. Some people have nothing better to do, than to chew over old stories, old mysteries, talk about folk and generally are disruptive to the normal daily running of life. To be honest Bill finds it quite tiresome at times, that some people have nothing better to do. Maybe it has something to do with factions, He doesn't know. He is not part of any faction, as far as he is aware. He is just one of the ones who get talked about.

Now he is not quite sure when the thought came to him, but at some point he found himself looking at a house. It was quite near to the town centre, and needed doing up. The thought was that he needed to find something to produce a better income, than the money was doing in the bank. Added to that was the comment from the estate agent. He was encouraging him to look at the house. He said that loads of people had been to have a look at the house, but the layout was putting them off. He said that none of them could think of a way to get round the main problem.

The main problem being; at the first turn on the stairs the ceiling was particularly low, so that when you went up the stairs you had to bend down at the turn to get past. The lowness being caused by something Bill has only come across since he came to live in this part of the country; the flying freehold.

Basically what we have here; is a piece of the next door house coming over part of this property. It is quite odd really and he has no idea how anyone ever let it happen in this instance and why it would have to happen in the first place. But none of that really matters, as we have the situation and if he is going to go any further with this viewing, he needs to find a way to get over the problem.

Bill ignores it to start with and proceeds up the stairs. It is not the best of layouts, even on the first floor. There is a room to the front, at the top of the stairs and a small passageway to the left, going towards the back of the house. Down there we have a small room on the left and then an odd shaped bathroom, facing over the back garden. The window also overlooks another joy he has yet to look at in this house. That is the very rickety looking extension/come lean-to, at the back of the downstairs.

That is enough of that for now. He returns to his investigation of the rest of this floor. There is one more room on this floor. It has a window to the side, overlooking the car park.

The house is listed as a 4/5 bedroom. Bill has found only the two so far, plus the small room by the bathroom. He assumes that is being counted as a small bedroom too. So he starts up the next flight of stairs, to the top floor. These stairs are far from ideal too. Yet another issue to add to the list of alterations this place is going to need, to bring it into modern day use.

The top floor is very bare. There is an open space, with a gap going past a chimney breast, which then opens out to another open space. These two are what comprise the last two missing bedrooms. This too is going to present a challenge.

Let alone the problem of the corner of the stairs, Bill is not surprised that so many have looked at this place, but no one has come up with an offer as yet. All he appears to be doing is adding to the list of challenges. He hasn't even looked at the downstairs yet. He'd come in through the front door and looked straight away at what he had been told was the real problem. Maybe the other viewers hadn't even ventured upstairs, to find what other challenges were waiting for them.

Bill makes my way back down to the bottom of the stairs. He doesn't like the hall passage. It is slightly claustrophobic. He opens the sliding door and steps into the living room. He knows straight away that this room would benefit from the extra open space the hall passage would provide. Why is he thinking this, as he hasn't made up my mind about the place. He hasn't even seen it all yet. Bill moves into the next room. It could be the dining room, or a study.

It is at this point the agent drops another little bombshell.

'The post office has a right of way through here.'

'I beg your pardon.' Bill says

'I've been told that the post office has a right of way through here. The post office is on High Street as you know, but before the car park was put in and the road brought through at the bottom of the garden, this was an archway and used by the post office, to gain access to their yard.'

'Hasn't it been rescinded then?'

'Apparently not, so I am informed by the solicitors dealing with the estate.'

That is something else to add to the ever increasing list of things to consider. He is starting to understand why the asking price is so reasonable. It is going to cost a lot, to sort all of these things out.

The kitchen when they get to it is as expected, dated and very basic. They open the back door and venture outside. Well of course, they are not outside. They are now in the covered area, which Bill saw from the bathroom window. There are a few units on the floor. Then there is the old outside toilet, which has been encompassed into the covered area. Then there is the bit to the left which appears to have been added at a later date. The floor is different here and if anything the wall is even more rickety than the rest of it. He mentally adds this to his list.

Now they go outside. The garden is enclosed. There is a stone wall, along the side between the garden and the car park. And the same wall goes across the back of the garden too. Beyond the wall is the access road to the car park. Hopefully the post office use that way in these days, rather than clamber through the dining room window of this house. He makes a mental note that it would make a big difference, if an access could be made for a car or two, to park in the back garden. That though may not be easy to achieve, as this property lies in a conservation area.

He has seen it all. He now needs to look at the main problem again. If Bill can't see a way past that, then the other problems will sink into insignificance, as they won't be relevant. But he already knows what needs to be done. Obviously the stairs need to be changed, but that is easier said than done. The bottom section before the turn needs to come back and be lower and the second section needs to be longer. The problem with doing that comes in two areas. At the top of the stairs, if you extend the staircase, it will now come across the door to the first front room. That means the door has to be moved further along the wall. That is, he supposes, not too hard to do, as the wall is a stud wall; or something like that.

The main problem is at the bottom of the stairs. In the living room, the upper section of stairs goes up along the wall between the living room and the kitchen. By extending the upper section of stairs, that would make the stairs come across part of the doorway into the kitchen. The doorway of course can be moved, but it will be a massive job. That is because the wall between the living room and the kitchen is something between two and three feet thick. That is really going to be an expensive thing to change. He is guessing that is what the stumbling block has been, to anyone making an offer.

Bill thanks the agent and they part, him going back to his office and Bill going back home, to talk about what he has seen with Kate. He has ideas going through his head, about what could be done with the place, but he needs Kate to be with him when they view it again.

Chapter 4 Bill in Wenlock

They don't want to appear to be too keen. They don't think they are in danger of someone rushing in and making an offer before they are ready to, if that is the direction they decide to go in. Bill discusses what he has seen with Kate and they decide that they will arrange to view the property again, but not today.

Bill finds that his mind is taken up with the property and he spends a disproportionate part of the night when he should have been sleeping, thinking about it. The result of that, is a short discussion over breakfast and while they are walking the dogs. They walk past the property, first the front and then the back, on their way home. The outside of the property is actually in quite good condition. It is only when you view the inside; that you become aware of all the issues that have to be solved by the next owner. It doesn't take them long to wake up to the fact, that they both know already that they are going to own this property. That is before they have even taken a second look.

The second look is taken without the attendance of the agent. When they ask to view it again, he just gives them the keys and tells them to take their time, before returning the keys back to him. They do take their time and between them, they come up with the outline of a plan which they could instigate, if and when the property becomes theirs. The reason for their confidence is quite simple. They have something that no one round here has access to. Well, it is not really something, it is someone. They have a Dave. Dave says to them; that if you can think it, then he can do it. Bill has thought what they can do about solving the issues of this house. He is going to be counting on Dave to make it happen; he will.

They walk straight round to the agent and tell him that they are going to make an offer. It is at this point that they find out the truth. They are not the first to make an offer. But the offers that have been made, are both well below the asking price. On one hand they can understand that, but on the other hand, they think the offers have been really a bit unrealistic. The property has been priced according to the amount of work that is going to be needed, to bring it back into good use.

The asking price is an 'offers over' one. They have a quick discussion and agree that their offer will be £5000 over the minimum asking price. They think that is fair enough and certainly well above what they have been offered so far.

The agent says to leave it with him and he will come back to them with an answer. They are hopeful the answer will be a positive one, but in that they are going to be disappointed, at first at least. The call they get a few hours later, comes with what they consider to be an unrealistic response, almost akin to the unrealistic offers that have been placed before. In their heads, Kate and Bill are thinking; that at least they have fulfilled the requirement, by offering more than the asking price. That, however, is not what the vendors think. Well that is the message that comes back to them, via the vendors' solicitor and the agent.

In fact the reply comes back with more or less the figure they are looking for. Apparently there are three beneficiaries and they each want a set figure, after all costs have been deducted. Adding that up, including what they think roughly the estate agent fees will be, plus the solicitors' fees for carrying out the conveyancing; then Bill thinks the price they want is almost £25000 above the original asking price.

'They are not going to get that from me. If that is the figure that they are looking for, then they should have put the asking price at least £20,000 higher.' That is what he says to Kate on hearing the news.

He talks it over with Kate and they both agree that they are not happy with the response. They don't actually want the property that much in the first place. Now that the vendors have stated their terms more or less, they decide they are going to respond with theirs. They prepare their wording, before ringing the agent back with their response and counter offer.

"The asking price was set by you. If you wanted more, then this price should have been set higher, in which case we would not have viewed the property. You asked for offers over the asking price you did set and we have offered £5000 over that asking price. To be honest we are not that bothered if we buy the property or not. You have a choice. You accept our offer or reject it. We will not be raising our offer."

The agent thought that fair enough. He wasn't pleased at what they had come back with either. He can see the opportunity in front of him, to get the property sold and get his commission in. He can also see that, in the knowledge of the figures they have come back to him with, his task is going to be even harder to achieve, if Kate and Bill don't buy it. He doesn't manage to get the offer through on the spot. The solicitor he needs to talk to is busy with a client. The agent is unwilling to leave the message he has, in the hands of his secretary.

They walk away, uncertain about which way this is going to go. They have to admit, they would like the challenge of converting this property, but they are not going to be that disappointed if they don't get it.

They don't get an answer that afternoon and are not surprised at that. They don't get an answer the next day either and are not sure what to think about that. It is a Friday and that means they won't get an answer until Monday now. That is a bit annoying. But there is nothing they can do about it. The thought goes across Bill's mind, that maybe they are trying to play games with them. If that is the case, then they have called them wrong. It won't work.

The weekend passes quickly enough, as they have several things planned. Although the matter doesn't go completely from their minds, it certainly is not dominating their thoughts.

Monday morning sees them getting a phone call, almost as soon as they are back from walking the dogs. Bill and Kate are slightly surprised to learn that their offer has been accepted. Thankfully, it would appear that over the weekend, common sense has prevailed. It is better to accept what is on the table, rather than hang out for who knows how long, to get an extra few thousand each. Well, that is their take on it.

The result is that they have themselves a property to do up. Obviously they can't start yet. The laboriously slow process of conveyancing has to be gone though. Bill wastes no time in contacting their solicitor. They have to go through the usual dance, of him setting out a fee and them accepting that, along with their terms and conditions. Then Bill has his say, that the solicitor has no need to justify his fee, by the amount of time he spends doing the conveyancing. They want it done as soon as possible and as long as he does the conveyancing properly, they don't care about the value, or not, of his fee. Bill and Kate just want it concluded as quickly as possible.

For a change things proceed at pace and it is only the matter of a few weeks before the property becomes theirs. Looking at it in the light of day, as the new owners, they can start to actually go round the place, room by room, deciding exactly what they need to get done. They also decide that they need to get the stairs done first. This is going to cause the greatest mess, but more importantly, it will make the whole process of all the work that needs to be done on the upper floors, that much easier to process.

They have got this far and yet still haven't introduced the property to Dave. True to form he is very practical about it, when he does come to see what they need doing. He doesn't even bat an eyelid at moving the kitchen door.

They have to set a few things in place before they can start. They are not only going to be making structural changes to the stairs, but also all over the house internally. On top of that they are going to make the structure out back more solid. To do all this they have a couple of conversations with the planning officer. They find they can do what they need to with permitted development. Of course they will have to have the building inspector in, to approve what work they do, so they set that up and pay the required fees.

With all that done, they are ready to go. All they need is for Dave to finish the job he is on. Then he can bring his small team over and get started on the work.

Chapter 5 Bill in Wenlock

It is only a few weeks later that he turns up, ready to get stuck into this series of challenges. In the matter of only a few days, not even the first week, the old stairs are down. The wall of the upstairs bedroom has been removed. The wall between the living room and the kitchen has been taken down about three feet over, ready for the new doorway. Paul has already started work on the new staircase. He is Dave's brother and is a carpenter. He is going to build the staircase, rather than buy one off the shelf. Bill can see this is not the first time he has built one.

So, with several skip-loads of debris already taken away, a new empty one arrives, ready for the next piece of demolition. That is going to be the destruction, not that it is going to take too much effort, of the outside area beyond the kitchen. Up to this point, Bill has been thinking this is all going quite well. In fact he has been surprised and happy at how much has been achieved in such a short time.

He decides to give Dave a hand, to get rid of the existing structure. Paul is busy working on the staircase and Kev is busy shuttling back and forwards, packing the debris into the skip, when they have it ready for him. It doesn't take much at all to demolish this extension, other than the outside toilet, which had been constructed of brick. All that leaves them with is the concrete bases. He says bases, because there are two different bases. The one outside the back door and in the outside toilet, are completely different from the other bit of floor to the side.

They have decided that they need to come up, so that they can dig them out deeper for the new floor to be put in. It is as they are doing this, that this swift progress comes to a stop, more or less in an instant. The instant is reached about an hour after they have started work on removing the concrete bases. Dave is working on the more solid one and Bill is working on the much less solid one, to the side. He has been chipping away at it and getting quite sizeable chunks coming away at a time. It is as one of these chunks comes away, that he notices it reveals something in its wake.

Bill doesn't get the feeling straight away that what he has found should certainly not be there, but then a minute later he realises something. He immediately calls Dave over and he looks at it, but obviously without the same feelings that Bill has. Bill lets him into his fear, as to what they may have uncovered. Bill can see he is not convinced, but Dave does tell him to chip away carefully, until he is sure of exactly what it is he has uncovered. He goes back to his work and Bill tentatively continues to chip away at the floor. He is not sure what he has come across, but his head tells him it is part of an arm, secreted under the film and cloth. He spends the next 10 minutes chipping away minute pieces of floor, ever expanding the area he has already revealed.

He now has a bigger area uncovered, of maybe just less than 30cm long. All there is to show for his efforts is a piece of film covered material. It is the same material he had revealed initially, just more of it. He still has the feeling that what he is going to find when he opens up the cloth, is not going to be good.

What he really wants to do is to call the police. Then he can stand back, to let someone else make the discovery. By that he means; to reveal what is hidden under this cloth. His second choice would be to have Dave come over and actually be by his side. But he doesn't think that is going to happen, unless his curiosity gets the better of him and he comes over. Bill knows that he has noticed he has stopped.

He reaches into his pocket and locates the small penknife that his Dad used to own. He flicks the blade open and with a quick look over his shoulder first, he pulls a piece of the film and cloth slightly upwards and slits the cloth. He holds the cloth up and slices along the full length of what he has revealed. He lays his knife down beside him and takes a deep breath, before pulling the cloth apart. There is a smell, which he had not expected, but which is not a surprise really. It is not a surprise, because his feelings have been justified. Any way you look at what he has uncovered, it is part of a limb and by the size of it, an arm or part of an arm.

'Dave, have a look at this!'

It doesn't take him more than a few seconds to be at Bill's shoulder. He holds open the cloth and he peers through.

'Oh shit! You were right. I guess that is going to stop everything for a bit.'

Bill stands up and retrieves his mobile phone from his other pocket. Less than a minute later he has made the call. Dave and Bill have retreated into the house. Paul and Kev stop what they are doing too. All they have to do now is to wait for someone to arrive. That doesn't take long.

The first to arrive is a police patrol car. Bill takes the officer out back, to show him what they have uncovered. He does not touch the cloth and he tells Bill not to touch the cloth again. If Bill says there is part of a corpse in there, then he is prepared to believe what he says. He tells Bill to go back into the house and wait there. He gets onto his base, to advise what is there. There are already a team of people on their way. The crime scene team have already been despatched. A detective is also on the way over.

Fifteen minutes later, the place is swarming with police. The road outside has been closed. You can't move for police vehicles anyway. Bill, Dave, Paul & Kev have been shepherded into the dining room and been told to wait there, while they assess the situation. It isn't long before they are interviewed separately, as to each of their involvement in the discovery of this body.

Kevin and Paul are told they can go, pretty much straight away. Dave is the next to be allowed to leave. Bill is not.

Bill tells Dave that he will let him know when he can resume work here in the property. They are not allowed to take any of their tools with them. The entire property is a crime scene at this stage. Dave and Paul don't appear to be too bothered about this though. Bill has been allowed to phone home, to let Kate know that he won't be home for a while. He is not permitted to tell her what has happened, although he already knows Dave is going to call in at the house on his way home. That is despite being told that he can't say anything of what they've unearthed, to anyone.

A detective with a face that Bill knows comes in to see him. It is the detective he met before and had dealings with, over the Anne situation.

'Did she tell you about the body here?' are the first words out of his mouth.

He shakes his head in response.

'Have you seen her since that business all finished?'

Again he shakes his head, and then gives a slight nod.

'Recently?' he asks.

'No. But I have sat on the bench under the Corn Exchange and then she has turned up a couple of times. But that is all. She hasn't said anything. This is something different, I am sure.'

'I hope this one isn't going to disappear if we leave it for a minute?'

Bill just smiles at this one.

'So tell me how you come to be here and how you came across the body.'

While he has been talking, Bill can hear the sounds that have been coming from out the back for the past hour or so. That is the sound of one or more people chipping away at the floor, pretty much as he had done. He knows they have uncovered more and that there is no doubt there is a body under there, a whole body at that. That much information has been relayed to him.

Bill tells Andy that he has bought the place to do up, and that they are going to make the extension a more solid structure. He also tells him that he can contact planning and building control at Shropshire council, to confirm that is what he has told them what he is intending to do.

Who owned the house before you, is his next question. Bill tells him it was a probate sale. He can confirm that with the estate agent and the solicitor. No doubt Bill's solicitor will put him in touch with the vendors' solicitor. They will be able to give him any information, as to who lived here and for how long etcetera. He is happy enough about that. I think he is happy enough that Bill has nothing to do with all this, other than being the person who found the body.

They keep Bill around for maybe another hour or so. It is at that time, they have fully uncovered the body of the woman who has been buried beneath the floor. There is no reason to keep Bill there any longer. They are going to be there for hours, before they even consider moving the now exposed body from its position in the ground.

Bill gives Andy a front door key. Andy tells him he will be in touch soon, to update him. Please do not say anything to anyone, particularly the media. He agrees to that of course and then he is let out and he makes his way home. It is less than five minutes' walk away. Somehow Bill feels quite drained, after the happenings of the day.

Chapter 6 In Wenlock

The population of Wenlock is ever changing. There are the usual reasons for this, with people moving to and from the town because of work commitments. Then there are also the natural changes that occur, because of houses becoming empty due to the owner dying. With the relatively high average age of the residents, there are proportionately more house sales due to death than in most places.

Three of the properties that came up for sale within the matter of a few months, were probate sales. The fourth one that changed hands within that same period; was because the owner, who had previously been letting the property out, decided to sell the property after he had a bad experience with letting it out.

The four houses were bought by four couples, coming from different areas of the country, and in the case of one couple from the neighbouring country, Wales.

One thing these four couples have in common; is that they don't go out to work. Although they are not all of retirement age, there isn't one of them who does go out to earn a living. There are other similarities between the couples, such as none of them are life-long partners. In fact none of the four couples have been with their partner/spouse for very long. All four of them have been together for less than five years.

The first of the couples to move into their new home are Leonard and Lucy. They have moved to Wenlock from London. They are both in their early 60's. They have been together less than 12 months. Leonard was a civil servant in the city and he has taken early retirement, after he met Lucy. They both decided that they would like to move out of the bustle of London and retire to somewhere more peaceful. Both of them had knowledge of Much Wenlock, after the home Olympics in London in 2012.

Lucy was single when she met Leonard. Lucy did not work, but lived on her own funds. She never talks about where she has acquired them and Leonard has never asked. Lucy barely talks about her life, previous to meeting up with Leonard. Leonard has never pushed her on that score either. In return, the only information he offers her, is that he has been married in the past, but his wife had run off with someone, years ago. Neither of them is particularly bothered about not knowing much about their partner's history. That may appear to be odd to some people, but it isn't an issue to them. They both, for reasons of their own, are happy to be in a new relationship and both value the person in front of them, not what their individual history might be.

The couple move into a house in Barrow Street. Not untypically the house requires some updating, as the previous owner had been resident there for the best part of forty years. There is no major structural work to be done, but there is replacement work involved; namely the bathroom and the kitchen. On top of that, the entire house needs redecoration from top to bottom. The result of that is that Leonard and Lucy barely venture out into the town for the first few months. They are busy trying to get their new home into a condition that suits their expectations of their first home bought together.

The second of the couples who move into Wenlock are Martin and Maggie. They have moved to Wenlock from somewhere in Wales. They are both in their 60's too, but they are much nearer to being 70 than 60. In fact Martin may have already reached that milestone. Of the four couples, they are the ones who have been together the longest, nearly five years.

Martin says he has been in sales and management for most of his latter career. He doesn't mention what he did in the early part of his career. He is very fond of titles and uses the title of director for one of his past jobs. The fact is; that the title of director in job titles these days, is not what it used to be. Companies appear to use this title, to give their employees an air of importance.

Maggie has had an array of jobs throughout her life, particularly early on in her working life. None of them have been exactly taxing jobs, but she does work hard when she works. There have been periods though when she has not worked. She hasn't explained to Martin how she managed to live, when she was not working. Unlike Leonard and Lucy, both Martin and Maggie have children. Martin sees his very rarely and does not remain in contact with them. Maggie does not see her children much, as Martin is very critical of them. He took an instant dislike to them on the first occasion they did meet up.

Also unlike Leonard and Lucy, Martin and Maggie have bought somewhere together previously. I am not sure what they thought they were going to achieve, by moving into the middle of nowhere in Wales. They soon found that the idyllic thought of living in a pretty and remote place, also comes with drawbacks, particularly if you are not used to living in the countryside. They tried their hand at a few things. They tried to create a market garden, but found very quickly that the climate was against them. Their knowledge of what is required to succeed in that area was sadly lacking. Willingness they indeed showed, but the effort was wasted, due to lack of adequate planning. They tried their hand at livestock, but again their inexperience and knowledge was to let them down.

Add to all this; the reaction from the locals at this couple who had moved to live in their midst. They found their efforts most amusing. In general, Martin and Maggie were the laughing stock of locals talking together. The amusing thing in that; was the fact that they were oblivious to what everyone was thinking or talking about. They still thought they were the bees' knees, at everything they tackled. Eventually they decided that the country life was not for them and so sold up and moved to Wenlock. They sold up at a lower price than they had originally paid for their house in Wales. As a result they had less to spend on the house in Wenlock. Houses are more expensive in Wenlock than in some other parts of the county. The house they bought is just off the High Street. It is the least expensive house of the four couples. It is also the newest house and has the least work needed to suit the new residents.

The third couple to move into their new home in Wenlock are Brian and Jackie. They are in their early 60's. Brian spent the first 30 years of his career in the forces. He had originally joined the army, but then he said his talents were spotted and he was moved into a more elite unit, after about five years of his service. He says very little about what he did for the rest of his forces career, saying that it is still subject to the official secrets act. Whether that is true or not, is open to debate. When he left the services, he spent some time travelling the world and getting what he did in the forces out of his system. He has never been married and has not really been in any meaningful relationship, until he met Jackie. Even then he was not too keen to get involved, but he found that nature took its natural course and he couldn't help himself from being attracted to her. When he told Jackie about what he had been doing since he left the forces and where he had lived, he was very vague. He was almost evasive, but she took it to be that there was just something, or someone else, he didn't want to talk about. They met in the Peak district, where they were both out walking. He was on his own, whereas Jackie was part of a walking group. Her group was stopped when Brian came across them. Jackie had stumbled and twisted her ankle.

Amazingly enough, not one of the walking party she was part of, had brought their mobile phone with them. Brian had his and although he initially could not get any signal, he did walk a short distance away until he did so. He summoned the necessary help and then helped Jackie to get back to road, where they were met by an ambulance. They kept in touch, well Jackie instigated that, and things moved on from there.

Jackie had been in an abusive relationship early on in her adult life. She had managed to escape that, but it has left its scars and she hasn't been in a relationship since. She has involved herself totally in her work. Her job was working as a teaching assistant in a school.

There was something about Brian, when he came to the rescue on the moors; that got to her. There is little doubt that she felt the feelings between them way before he did. She was the one who arranged for them to go out for a meal. She was the one who suggested; when the time came, that they move to a new area. It was Jackie who did the research about where they move to. It had to be in a walking area, as they both like walking, but not in a place that is too busy with walkers. Shropshire came out as the place she found for them to move to. There is little doubt that she pushed the move through too. Brian wasn't exactly keen to move there, but he folded to her choice, in the end.

The house they moved into is in one of the roads just off Racecourse Lane. The lady who used to live there had actually kept the house looking very modern. The problem Brian and Jackie have, is that it is too modern for them. They spend their first weeks getting the house into the decorative state that they want, for their first home together. Brian does the majority of the work. In fact in the first few weeks, the only places he visits are the DIY outlets in Shrewsbury. He doesn't fancy shopping in Telford. In fact he doesn't venture into Wenlock at all during this time. He always makes an excuse to not go out, even in the evenings when they have finished work for the day. Jackie thinks nothing of it. They have been together for about 2 years and she is used to this.

The last of the four couples to move into Wenlock, is David and Barbara. They have moved to Wenlock from Surrey. At least that is where they met. They are only just turned 60, literally just a few months before they decide to relocate to Shropshire.

David rented a flat in Epsom when Barbara met him. Whatever it is he does, he says that he works from home and needs to have an internet connection. All that Barbara knows about what he did, maybe still does, is that he says he provides information to individuals and companies. He says that it has given him a decent living. He admits to having been married before, but does not really want to expand on that. He has no children, or at least never talks about them, if he does have any. He also admits to having moved around a bit, but Barbara thinks nothing of that, because she knows that people who live in rented accommodation do sometimes have to move house quite regularly.

Barbara is a bit of a wild spirit. She admits to having a lot of relationships, but none of them have lasted very long. She has always got bored and moved on when she feels she needs to. She admits to having lived in many different parts of the country. She tells David that she has never had a career as such, but has managed to get enough money to survive, wherever she has chosen to live. She says that some people take a dislike to her instantly and think she is creepy. Her response is that they are just jealous of her. Surprisingly enough, she has been with David for nearly three years. She has never been happier and moving to another part of the country with the person she is with, is a first for her. Saying that, it is David who chose where they would move to. It would not have been her first choice, but she has to live with the fact she told him to choose where they would move to. She would not have chosen Shropshire, or Much Wenlock.

Their new home is one of the new houses opposite the school. Again, like some of the others, there is not a lot to do in their new home. Of course, as is, it is always the case that the décor is not to their taste. Barbara is the one to get stuck into this. She makes it last much longer than it really should have taken. David is the one who has to go shopping locally, when they need supplies from the town. Barbara has said that she will do all that, when the work that needs doing is done.

So the four couples have now moved in to their new homes.

Chapter 7 In Wenlock

Although they all moved in at different time, it is at about the same time that the four couples are ready to expand their lives and start to do things, other than bring their respective houses up to scratch.

One thing that all four couples noticed on one of their earlier trips out into the town; was the gathering in the square on a Monday morning, at about ten o'clock. It doesn.t take a rocket scientist to work out that this is a walking group. A question here and there in the shops; reveals to them that this is a weekly event and that there are different walking groups, depending on ability or willingness. But basically there are three groups. There is one for those who want a stretching walk, in other words a walk for the sake of walking. There is one which takes the largest group walking, which is also at a pace which allows easy socialising. Then there is one for those who want to walk, but cannot necessarily walk that far in distance. All needs appear to be catered for.

So it happens that our four couples turn up for the walk on the same Monday morning, for the first time. They have turned up hoping that this will also give them a new insight into the local countryside. But also, it may be the catalyst in integrating them into the local community and introducing them to other people.

It may not have been ideal that the four couples found themselves standing together, as the group congregated in the square. But by the time they realise that they are all newbies, it is too late. It would have been too pointed to change the situation and whom they were standing with and possibly walking with.

The group starts to walk off. This morning they start by walking down Wilmore Street and then into Sheinton Street. At the corner by the main road, they take a right and walk up Station Road and into the Gaskell Recreation Ground and then down the old railway line.

An hour later the group returns to town and disbands. The four couples stand talking for a short time. They have been walking in pairs, with the men talking to each other and the women doing likewise. It would be truthful to say at this point, that they are not totally compatible. That is to say, that it is unlikely in the normal run of things that these four couples would socialise with each other. But then not even one of these people could be categorised as normal. None of them could be called socialites, maybe with the exception of Barbara, but then even in her case, what she does is possibly a bit of a front.

One thing that they have all committed to though, is starting a new life with their move to Wenlock. And as such, they know they are going to have to put some of their old habits behind them. Naturally this does not come easily to them, but they are determined that this is going to be the place they are going to spend at least the next few years in. It will be much easier and more pleasant, if they have a social circle to spend some time with.

Barbara doesn't want the contact to end just yet. She has enjoyed the morning walk and the interaction with another woman. She notices that a few of the walkers have gone into various coffee shops. She suggests to the others, that they should all go for a coffee too. Her suggestion is met with general, if not unanimous approval, but that is enough for the group to walk across the road and into Tea on the Square. A lot of the tables are occupied, but the large table on the left, in the window, is vacant.

The table is a lovely one and has a unique feature, at least as far as the tables in the town are concerned, in that it has flaps on the two long sides. To get to the window side bench, the flap has to be lifted. This nugget of information is passed to them by one of the other customers, as they are standing there, wondering how they were going to get through the narrow space, to access their seats.

With four of them on that bench, they manage to borrow a chair from one of the other tables, so the eight of them sit together. One of their hosts, Sue, comes over to take their order. Her working partner Jo is in the kitchen today.

They spend another hour or so over two coffees. The talk is just general banter and more about their respective houses they have moved into. That, and the varying conditions of décor and the general standard of the house they have each moved into.

When it comes to paying, they are asked if they want separate bills, or one combined one. Leonard doesn't consult the others, before he says that a combined one will be fine. The thought in his head is that they would just split the bill four ways. That is fine for seven out of the eight, but not the eighth. If Leonard had been looking in her direction, then he would have seen a most disapproving look coming his way from Maggie. But that is not the end of it. As soon as the bill is put down on the table, she makes a grab for it.

'We only had regular coffees' she says, as she looks at the items on the bill.

After a few seconds, she starts opening her purse and extracts the exact amount that she has calculated their coffees have come to. She puts that amount, to the penny, down on the table. It isn't hard to see that Martin is looking a trifle embarrassed at her behaviour. The other six are looking on, with a look of disbelief on their faces.

'I just thought we would split it four ways' Leonard says 'after all, we aren't talking a fortune here.'

'I like to pay my own way. You should have asked if we wanted the bill split.'

'Well, I apologise. If you want to do yours that way, then go ahead.'

He looks round the others as he says this. All he sees is five faces smiling knowingly at him. Maggie has her face set in a determined manner and Martin has his eyes down, avoiding looking at anyone.

Leonard reaches forward for the bill. He deducts the amount that Maggie has put down and then divides the balance by three. David and Brian chip in with their share, as does Leonard.

'Should we leave a tip?' Barbara asks.

'I don't do that' Maggie is back in again. 'The price they show is what you should pay.'

'Tight bitch' Leonard mutters under his breath to Lucy.

Leonard, Brian & David put some coins onto the table. Maggie is already getting up from her chair. Her look across at Martin, tells him he needs to move now too. He doesn't waste any time before getting to his feet too.

'Will we see you next Monday then?' Martin says as he is about to leave the tea room.

'Unless anything comes up to get in the way' Jackie says.

The others just nod. Martin and Maggie leave the tea shop first and walk over the road, to walk up High Street.

'Sorry about that' Leonard says when they have gone.

'You weren't to know. She is a bit odd.'

'It just lets you know that everyone is different. It just leaves a bitter taste in your mouth, after we have all had such a good morning.'

'Well, she hasn't endeared herself to any of us. That is a shame, as Martin seemed to be quite a nice chap.'

'It was obvious that she has done that before and that he is embarrassed by her.'

'Well, it is time for us to get back.' Brian says 'We'll see you all next Monday, unless we bump into you earlier, if we are in town for anything.'

The goodbyes are said all round and they stream out of the tea shop. Outside they go their different ways. David and Barbara go to the right down Wilmore Street. Brian and Jackie cross the road and then walk across the square. They walk through the archway by the Wenlock Smoothie. Leonard and Lucy turn left and start their walk home, along Barrow Street.

Inside the tea room their table has already been cleared and is waiting for the next customers who are going to occupy it.

Chapter 8 Walking in Wenlock

The week passes by quickly enough. Even though all four couples at one time or another make a visit or two into the town centre, they don't bump into any of the others, until the walk the next Monday morning. The walk is a different one this week. They walk along Barrow Street and then up the hill and along the edge of fields. Eventually they swing round and make their way back towards the town centre again.

Once again the suggestion is made about going for a coffee. As before, it is Barbara who suggests this. Before anyone else can respond, Maggie is in there.

'We won't be joining you. It is not something that we normally do. We can have a coffee at home much more cheaply.'

'We'll see you next week then' Barbara says, before anyone else says anything.

Martin and Maggie walk off and turn into High Street.

'I can't say I'm sorry about that' Leonard voices his thoughts without thinking.

'I know what you are saying' Lucy says 'but not everyone socialises over a coffee.'

Now she doesn't expand on that, but her words appear to the others to have another meaning. Has she got some inside info that no one else has picked up? If she has, then she isn't saying any more than that.

The six move across to Tea on the Square again and occupy the same table as they had done the previous week.

As they moved away, the man who had been in the telephone box in the square since their return from the walk; exits the box. He walks through the archway by the Wenlock Smoothie, in the direction of St Mary's car park. He had been walking to the shops to buy his paper earlier.

Passing through the square, he had to make his way through the crowd of people waiting to go on the Monday walk. He hadn't been paying that much attention, more concentrating on making his way through the throng. But when he was part way through, someone caught his eye. At first he didn't know it was someone. He just knew that something had caught his eye. He didn't stop, but he did turn to where his eyes were being drawn. There were a lot of people there, but his eyes were drawn to a group of eight people. They were standing together chatting. None of them were looking his way, but there was something about one of them that was familiar to him. He couldn't work out in that brief second exactly what it was that was familiar, or exactly which one of the eight it was.

It was just one of those moments when you think you've seen something, but you don't understand it. He carried on, through the rest of the people standing there. He then walked up to Mrs P's, to get his newspaper. By the time he walked back down the High Street, the walkers had moved off.

He didn't give it much thought, until he got home and sat down at the table to read his newspaper. His cup of coffee was sat on the table beside him. He was flicking through the paper, just reading the stories that caught his eye. Then just as he was sipping his coffee, the thought of seeing something in the square returned to him. He sat back in his chair and thought about earlier. All he could come up with; was that one of the people there, at the very least, resembled someone he had come across before. Any more than that, he was unable to come to any conclusion. He picked up his paper again, but something inside his head would not let him go back to reading his paper.

He tried to picture the people he had seen in the group of eight. It was no good; he just couldn't picture them properly.

He had been on the Monday walk himself more than once. He knew that they would return to the town centre at about 11 o'clock. He knew what he had to do. He would go down to the square shortly before 11 and wait to see the group return. Hopefully they would make it easy for him and still be grouped together.

When he did walk back to the square, he quickly realised that it wasn't going to be easy, to just stand around waiting for these people to come back. He would stand out and they would notice him, probably. On top of that, he wasn't sure what it was that had attracted his attention. He couldn't just stand there staring at them all; trying to work out what had triggered his senses. Very quickly he noticed the telephone box. He had always known it was there, but only at this moment did he realise its value, as somewhere he would be able to stand and watch, when the walkers come back. But he decided that he wouldn't go in there, until he actually needed to. He didn't know which direction the walkers had gone off in, so he didn't have a clue from which direction they would return.

He didn't just stand in the square, but wandered into the Spar shop and looked up and down the aisles, always keeping an eye on the street outside, to see if the walkers were returning. He picked up a chocolate bar and purchased it. He arrived back out on the street, just in time to see the group returning. They came past Penny Farthing and into the square. He couldn't see his group yet, so he quickly walked in front of Wenlock Wardrobe and round the corner. He slipped into the telephone box and picked up the receiver, carefully putting his finger across the bar, to stop the dialling tone.

Not that anyone was taking any notice of him, as far as he was aware. He even pretended to talk while he waited for his group to appear. The problem he had was that he wasn't really sure what they looked like, now he was back an hour later. Luckily for him, the group came into view and then stopped at the bottom of the square, for a minute or so. He had a good view of some of them, but not all of them. Once again he had the feeling that one of them was familiar to him, but now they were there in front of him and he could concentrate pretty much on them, he was still not sure what was familiar. Even more than that, he could not categorically say which one of them was causing this feeling inside him.

After maybe only a minute or so, maybe not even that long, two of the eight walked away from the group. He watched them walk towards High Street and returned his attention, just in time to see the other six crossing the road and entering Tea on the Square.

He had been in the phone box long enough. He put the receiver back down and opened the door of the kiosk. Maybe he was wrong and there was nothing about these actual people. Maybe one of them had just triggered a lookalike reaction in his head, about someone he used to know. The annoying thing on his part; was that he couldn't even place a connection to anything. He had no idea even about a time frame, when he might have met this person or someone who looks like one of these people.

Anyway he hasn't got the time to stand here all day, to try to find out any more. After all there might be nothing in any of this anyway. If only he could work out what the familiarity was, then he might be able to get somewhere. It probably isn't that important. If he leaves it, then it may come to him in time.

He walks across the top of the square and walks through the archway, back towards his home. He had given it half a thought to hang around and maybe follow one of the couples around after their coffees. But until he had a better idea what the familiarity was, he shelved that thought and action.

It is maybe two or three days later, when suddenly the roads around where he lives are swarming with police. Then he remembers where he might know the person from, or at least someone who looks vaguely similar. At first there is little information available about what all the police action is about. Like quite a few others, he goes out into the street and tries to see what is going on in St Marys Lane, just along from where he lives. They are kept back behind the blue tapes, where an officer is stopping them from getting any nearer. He isn't telling them anything about the incident either.

If he had gone out of his front door, he would have been told to go back in. The police have already been along to his house, to tell him not to go out the front way, as the street is cordoned off. To get to where he is now, he had gone out of his back door and out of his side gate and then round to the end of the road. He couldn't see anything from his back garden, as they have put a screen up, around whatever it is they are at the house for.

It is a few hours later that word gets out, that they have discovered a body, buried in the back extension of the property. He knew someone had bought it and was just starting to do it up. It is at this point he knows that the familiar person is connected with this house, where the body has been found. There has been no identity released and even the fact a body has been found is only a rumour, which hasn't been substantiated as yet.

He doesn't learn any more that day, but he does know he will have to watch the group again, when they go walking on Monday. He will try to work out which one of them is raising his suspicion, about having seen them before. With some satisfaction that he has been at least able to make some forward progress in his problem, he goes back indoors and switches on the TV, to see if the local news can add anything.

Chapter 9 Bill in Wenlock

Bill doesn't hear anything for a couple of days. He hasn't spoken to anyone, other than Kate. To make sure that he is not tempted to tell anyone what they have found, he decides to stay at home. He doesn't even go for his customary walk with the dogs, so he doesn't get tempted or drawn into any speculation. There is plenty he can get on with anyway, to keep him busy, until they can resume the work on the property. Bill is not expecting that to be soon. Who knows how long these things take.

On the positive side, there is a good chance that they will dig up the rest of the floor in the outside area. They didn't say anything about doing that. He is just thinking that they might do that, with the thought there might be other bodies to be found. That would save Bill the work of digging the floor up. He will only know if they have, when they regain access again.

Regardless of Bill not going out, it would appear that the news has got out anyway. He supposes it was inevitable that would happen, particularly in a place like this. Kate has walked the dogs for the past couple of mornings, but she has hardly met a soul.

Kate has been downtown, to get some bits and pieces they need. As happens, she gets into conversation with people, only to find that the town is buzzing with the news of the body buried in their floor.

The rumour mill is also going full pelt, with possibilities as to who it might be. There is more certainty as to who it isn't. It definitely isn't the woman who had died; whose house they have bought. She had died in hospital, according to those in the know. It isn't any of her children either. She had three of those and they are all alive and kicking. They are the ones who wanted the extra money from the sale of the property.

What is really puzzling; is that the word is that she had lived in that house for over 50 years. Her husband had died years ago, but that was in hospital too. But the really puzzling bit is this: the floor that the body was found under; was done while she lived there. It definitely wasn't there before that. How precise this information is, they have no idea. But the sources seem to be quite sure about that. The woman and her husband had the cover put over the back patio too, between the house and the outside toilet. Then, at a later date, the rest of that back extension was done. The information machine has not managed to put a date on when that was, as yet.

This is where there are conflicting stories coming to hand. Some say that it was all done at the same time, or maybe a very short time after. Others say it was done much later, after the husband had died. That storyteller said that the husband hadn't wanted to spend any money on a further covered area.

Bill's opinion is that the floors are completely different, so it can't have been done at the same time, as they would have concreted it the same. The floor where the body was found had not been put down in one piece, in his opinion. It looked to him, in retrospect, as if the floor had been done a little bit at a time. It is almost as if they had bought small bags of cement or concrete and mixed it up, one bag at a time. That is what Bill is thinking now, as he reflects on the quality of the floor. Yes it was definitely more like cement, with some stones added in for strength. It was probably anything they had to hand.

He thinks back to when they were digging out the respective bits of floor. Dave was definitely using more power and energy to dig out his floor. Bill's was relatively easy to do.

Bill's thoughts are interrupted by the doorbell ringing and the dogs barking in response to that. When he answers the door, he is not that surprised to see Andy the detective, standing on his doorstep. He invites him in and makes him a mug of coffee.

'We're going to dig up the rest of the floor' he says.

'It was all coming up anyway. In fact we are going to take up the kitchen floor as well.'

'I was going to ask you about that. I think we might be taking that up too, just as a precaution.'

'I take it you haven't come here to let me know we can resume our work on it then?'

'No, it will be another week at least and that is if we don't find any more bodies.'

'I haven't said anything to anyone, other than Kate.'

'I know. One of the neighbours has spread the word. It is not a problem, as it was bound to come out sooner or later anyway. But the one thing we don't know; is whose the body is. We have checked out the family and the owner died in hospital. Her husband died in hospital years ago. Her children are all alive and that is pretty much that. There are no reports of missing persons that fit the profile we have at this stage.'

Bill notices that he doesn't tell him what that profile is, but then it is nothing to him. He knows nothing, as they say. He has just bought a house which has a body buried under the floor out back. Bill is thinking this, but Andy is still talking.

'As far as we know, the husband was local and there is no one missing from his family. The woman who owned the house was from Wolverhampton. She didn't have much family, as far as we can find out, and she didn't have any family round here. Their 3 children are alive too. It's a real puzzle, because as I am sure you've noticed and know; the extension and that floor have been done in her time in the house. We will have to wait and see what comes back and see if we get any more clues as to the identity.'

Bill almost thinks he is going to give something away, but he doesn't, unfortunately. He is wondering why Andy is here though. Maybe it is to do with the floor, but he is not so sure. Bill is wondering if he is going to venture down the Anne route again, or maybe appeal to his perceptions. It is the latter, as it turns out.

'I don't suppose you have any ideas?'

Now that is a funny thing to ask Bill. He is well aware that Bill has just bought the place and has no connections to the previous owners. He also knows that Bill is not from round here. He used to live in Devon, before he came to Wenlock. How does he think Bill is going to know anything? He doesn't even have a clue as to when this might have been done. It could have been 10 years ago, or it could have been 20.

Bill stops and thinks for a minute, sipping his coffee as he does so. He is about to take a leap into the dark. Who knows where this has come from? He's assuming they don't know how long the body has been there.

'How long is it since the husband died?' He asks, not expecting Andy to have the answer to hand, but he has. I already know from the word that has gone round; that the floor was put in after he died. I am wondering whether he knows this. The answer is he does and he doesn't.

'He died just over 20 years ago. Although we have been told the floor is newer than that, we have no definitive proof of that. But the thinking is that the body was put there after his death.'

'On that basis then, let's assume that the body was put there after his death and he is not involved.'

'Ok, I'm prepared to run with that. Where are you going with this?'

'I'm not sure, but if it isn't family, then there is a good chance that it is someone the wife has known? So the question that has popped into my head is this? What was her name? I can't keep referring to her as the woman.'

'It was Rose, the person who owned your house.'

'That's right I remember now. I can't remember her last name.'

'I've got it here if you need it.'

'No, it's alright, I don't need it for this, but you will. Did Rose spend any time in hospital after her husband died, other than the time when she died there?'

'I don't know. Is it important?'

'I have no idea. It is just something that has come to me. I think Rose knows; knew I mean, who the body is. I'm not saying she knew the person was buried there; or even put them there, but something tells me she knew them.'

'On what are you basing that assumption?'

'Absolutely nothing, other than that thought has just come into my head. And what is more, I think you will find I am right.'

Bill can't even begin to explain to him how he knows that, but something has happened to him inside when he just said that. It has happened before and he just knows he is right.

Part 2
Chapter 10 Going Back Some in Time

'I can't remember how I got into this, but once I was there, then there could be no going back, ever.' Jay thinks, having a quiet moment. Jay is not the name that they go by now. She changed that after the first of the episodes. She changed it to something that isn't her name now either.

Jay has gone out for a walk alone. Jay is in the habit of doing this. Jay has been with their partner for less than five years, but that makes it the longest relationship of their life. Jay has never considered being in a relationship, up to the time they met. It kind of wasn't in their make up to be close to anyone, let alone have a long term relationship.

Jay's partner understands the need for time on their own. They have a similar requirement, if not quite so strong. So from the very beginning of their relationship, they always accepted that the other could and would take time out to be on their own. Most times that consisted of just being alone for a few hours. Sometimes shut away alone in a quiet place in their house, or sometimes going out for a drive, or a long walk on their own for a few hours. On a few occasions Jay has felt the need to get away for longer and has on occasion actually gone away for a few days. That has been a bit harder for their partner to accept, partly because literally, while Jay is away there is no contact. There is no pre-set time that Jay is going to return either. Jay is quite lucky that Jay's partner is quite trusting and is laid back about it.

Today Jay has opted for the long walk. Jay isn't sure why suddenly they feel the need to have to go, but the feeling is a very definite one.

Jay walks into the town centre and stands in the square. This is where the feeling originates from. That much Jay knows, but Jay doesn't know why that is the case. Jay has thought about this on the way to the square, but nothing has come to mind. Jay is concerned that someone might have associated Jay with being in Wenlock before.

That of course is something that is only known to Jay. No one else that Jay has come into contact in Wenlock knows that Jay has been here before. Not even Jay's partner knows that Jay has been to Wenlock before. That is something that Jay definitely did not own up to, prior to the move here this time. No one that Jay has spoken to socially, or in the course of day to day shopping, or visiting pubs or tea rooms, knows that Jay has been here to Wenlock before. But that may not be the case now. Someone, Jay thinks, has had a thought that there is something familiar about Jay. It is doubtful that it could be about facial features or stature even, because when Jay came to Wenlock before, it was in disguise. Even Jay's family would not have recognized the Jay that came to town the last time. So if it wasn't looks, then it must be something else. It could only really be either stance, or how Jay walks. But even thinking of stance, it is unlikely, as the disguise that Jay took on altered the way Jay stood, so it can't really be that. So it must be the way Jay walks that has been the giveaway.

Jay is just about satisfied with that summation, when the realisation comes in a blinding flash. Jay knows it is not walking, but the eyes that are the same. Jay has quite distinctive eyes.

'Damn' Jay mutters. 'I need to find out who this person is who has upset things. But I need to go for my walk first and settle down.'

Jay becomes another person and goes into a world of their own. Crossing over the road, Jay goes through the arch by the Guildhall and turns left onto the path that goes through the churchyard. Jay has thought about going to sit in the church, but has dismissed that, as there is a possibility that someone might come and talk. Jay doesn't want that. Jay takes a right turn and walks past the grave of William Penny Brookes. A minute later Jay is coming down the steps by the Priory Hall. Jay comes out onto the lane and turns right. Jay starts to walk along the lane, away from the town. The lane twists this way and that and at the mill, Jay goes over the stream. Beyond that the path is taken through the fields and eventually out at the end onto the lane, where Jay takes a right. From there it will be a matter of choice which way the walk will go.

Jay is actually feeling a bit better already. That is because Jay has the outline of a plan, to root out or at least find out, who might have rumbled them. There is a possibility that Jay is wrong, but to be honest that is unlikely. The body was found just as Jay moved to the town, too late to pull out. That is possibly what made Jay jumpy, because where the body has been found, is somewhere Jay has been before. In fact Jay knew the body was there, quite simply because it was Jay who was responsible for the body being there.

The thought comes to Jay during the walk, whether this is the only body that has been discovered. What Jay means by that, is that this is not the only body that Jay knows about. It is not the only body that Jay is responsible for burying or hiding away.

That isn't to say that there any more bodies to be found here in Wenlock, because there aren't. Well by that the meaning is that Jay is not responsible for any more bodies being buried in Wenlock. A smile comes to Jay's face while walking along. It could be possible at one time to add the word 'yet' to that. That could bring about a possible resolution to the problem that Jay thinks might be looming.

Of course that wouldn't bring the usual rewards that her burials have associated with them. And there would be risks attached, to carrying out that type of action. The ones Jay has been involved in before have been carefully planned and executed.

'Did you see what I did there?' Jay says out loud, stumbling on the path as their attention wanders briefly. Jay sniggers at the funny just made.

The path has come to an end. Jay has not been aware of where the path was leading, but subconsciously has been taking right turns when there is a choice. It is sort of inevitable that they would end up coming back out onto a road somewhere near the edge of town, but on the other side they have left from. That is the case.

Hugging the edge of the road, there is no pavement at this part of the journey; Jay stands well in when cars come along. Jay has no idea how long it has been since the walk started and to be honest, isn't quite sure which road this is, leading into Wenlock. It is not one that Jay has even driven on before. But Jay is not bothered by that. As long as the road does eventually arrive into town, there is not a problem. To be the fair the mobile phone in Jay's pocket would provide the answer, if that is deemed to be necessary, but that is not the way Jay's mind works.

The road twists and turns and starts down a gentle gradient. There are a few cars using the road and they appear to Jay to be moving quite fast, considering that this isn't a straight stretch of road. Then ahead, Jay can see the 30 sign and the first houses of the town. At the bottom of this section there is a bend and Jay thinks that this is the Broseley Road; that the last part of the walk has been on. That would be the correct thought. It won't be long to get home now, just a matter of minutes. Back home to their new home in Wenlock. Back home to their partner. And back home to having to close this part of their life away securely and not ever letting anyone else in, even their partner. It is highly unlikely that they would choose to be with someone who has done what Jay has done, to get to this stage of their life.

Chapter 11 Going Back Further in Time

I was born into a working class family. My first real lasting memory is being taken to school on my first day. It isn't the fact that it was my first day at school really, or the fact it was school I was going to. It was the fact that when I got there, holding my mother's hand, because I wasn't keen to go, that I saw that everyone else was wearing a uniform, except for me. I say uniform, but it was only a jumper with the school logo. I though, was dressed as usual, in clothes that were dirty, stained and torn in places. I had very few clothes. I remember that much too. In fact I think I dressed in the same clothes until I grew out of them, or they literally fell apart. That may be a memory that I have made up, but I do think that is how things were.

The other thing that sticks in my mind about that first day in school, and the ones that followed, is that for the first time in my life, I was told what to do. I was also expected to stay in the classroom, until I was told I could leave. That was definitely something new to me. As soon as I could walk, I went pretty much anywhere I wanted to and when I wanted to. I could be found virtually anywhere but at home, from the moment I could walk.

Our house, if you could call it that, was never locked. There was no need to, as we had nothing to steal anyway. Today you would look at it and call it minimalistic, but ours was like that, because there was no money left to buy anything. Where I slept consisted of an old stinking mattress on the floor and a blanket. The room my Mum and Dad used to sleep in was little better. They did have a bed frame and a mattress too. They had more blankets than I did. There was an old chest in the corner, where they kept their clothes. They had more clothes than I did. My Dad had his work clothes. I seem to remember my Mum wore pretty much the same clothes all the time.

In the living room there were two old rickety chairs. The only time I ever got to sit in them, was when they weren't sitting in them, but then I wasn't in the house that much anyway. We didn't have a telly, but Mum used to sit in her chair and listen to the old valve radio. Dad, as much of him that I remember, went to work in the morning and came home sometime in the evening. From the smell that I got to know later in life, I'm guessing his route home took him to the pub for several pints.

Sometimes I would sit outside the Dog and Duck, never knowing that my Dad might have been in there. I'm surprised looking back at it, that the folks who passed me and sometimes chucked me a penny or two, didn't go inside and tell him that his child was sitting outside, while he was supping his beer inside.

But then my Dad never had any time for me. To him I was a nuisance. I was something that had come along, unwanted and only because he'd got my Mum pregnant. That was something that only happened the once. I am an only child. Somehow he made sure that the mistake he'd made wasn't repeated. Mind you, I can't say that Mum made herself attractive to him after I was born.

At home we had a kitchen of sorts. There was an old table and two chairs. The sink was old and chipped, but it was big. There was only cold water and that is where we washed, when we washed. My Dad washed every morning before he went off to his work. I can never remember seeing my Mum washing herself, but then by the time she got out of bed, I was out somewhere, playing. For me to get washed, I had to get the chair and stand on it by the sink. If my Dad saw me doing that, he would give me a clip on the ear and lift me down, before putting the chair back in its place by the table.

'Chairs are for sitting on' are some of the few words I can remember him saying.

So, most of the time, the only wash I got was when I went for a dip in the pond. In winter that didn't happen very often, as the water was too cold.

So, going back to that first day of school; it was the first time it hit home to me how little we had in our house. It also came to me how far behind everyone else I was, in the manner of communication. It is not that I am thick or anything. It is just the fact that Mum and Dad did not educate me at all. The only language I had picked up was with the other children I met, when I was out on the streets.

That first day at school was hard for me. Not only was I standing out markedly as being different, but I was also the one who was getting told off all day. I didn't know that I was supposed to sit in my chair and pay attention. I was only there five minutes before I was moved to the front of the class. But that was only after I had been led away and given a jumper like everyone else had on, from the lost box. That alone made me feel wanted, but it was not enough to keep me in my place. I just wasn't used to sitting down. I wasn't used to staying in the same place for hours on end, let alone a few minutes. I would get up and try to get out of the door, but the teacher beat me to it. I would then wander over to the windows and look longingly out at the world outside. If there had been straps on the chairs of the desks in that classroom, they would have strapped me in. But there weren't and so in the end, the teacher resorted to locking the door and getting on with teaching the rest of the class. After a while, I did actually go and sit on my chair, but I couldn't follow what the teacher was trying to teach me.

The end of that first day couldn't come soon enough for me. When we were let out into the playground, there were lots of parents waiting at the gate to pick up their children. The teacher was making sure that each child in her charge was collected by their respective parent. Several times I tried to get past her, but she wouldn't let me go, as there was no one there to pick me up.

I knew that my Mum would not be coming to pick me up. She didn't bother about me at any other time, so why should she bother to come and pick me up today, on my first day at school. While the teacher went off to ring my Mum, to see who was going to pick me up, I was left in the charge of another teacher. If my teacher had looked at the details they kept for me, she would have known that we did not have a phone. It was a lot of years later before my Mum ever got a phone in her house and it wasn't in the house we lived in back then.

The teacher who was supposed to be looking after me got distracted and I got away. I didn't go out of the gates, but instead I went round to the other side of the playground, to where the sheds were. I had looked at this place earlier, when we were allowed out to play. I had started to climb up onto the roof then, but had been stopped by a lady who was out in the playground to keep an eye on us. I had no one here now, to stop me climbing up this time. I was quite nimble and soon I found myself on the roof. I quickly went to the far side and looked down. The fence was right up against the back of the shed and beyond that was some woodland, which sloped down to the river. I didn't hesitate and jumped the approximate eight feet to the ground. I was used to climbing trees and jumping down from them, so this was no different. I landed on the ground and rolled to a stop. There weren't any shouts coming from behind me, so I knew I had not been noticed.

When I did get home a few hours later, my Mum didn't comment on anything. She didn't even ask about my first day at school. But then that was no surprise, as she never asks what I have done in the day, when I go out. What she had done was make me a meat sandwich. Sometimes I got something to eat and sometimes I didn't. I was never sure if the food that was available was meant for me or not. I just ate what was there for me to see and when there wasn't any in the house, I would scavenge what I needed.

Chapter 12 Still Back Further in Time

Needless to say, the next morning I was taken to school again by my Mum. Needless to say too, that at the end of that day, I didn't even try to get out of the school gates to go home. I used my own exit over the shed roof. Nobody saw me and nobody commented on it the next day when I arrived in school.

By the end of the first week, I was actually getting engaged by what the teacher was trying to teach us. I was getting better at staying in my seat too and by the middle of the week I had even given up on trying to escape from the classroom. I was still, of course, sitting in the front row. Even though I had my jumper, I was still the most poorly dressed child in the class. That was not helped by the fact that I was wearing my jumper all of the time. I kept it on at night, as it was warm. Of course, the result of wearing the jumper all of the time, was that it was getting dirty. That wasn't helped by me jumping off the shed roof, to get out of the playground each day. The rolling on the ground as I landed certainly added to the dirt it was accumulating. On the Friday my jumper was definitely showing the signs of wear. What I didn't know at the time was that my behaviour, my manner of dress and the way I scoffed down the school dinner that was put in front of us at lunch time, had been noted. It was probably with a measure of concern, by all of those in the school who came across me.

On the Monday morning my Mum did not get up to take me to school. I was up of course. When the time came that we should have been leaving to go to school, my mum was still fast asleep in her bed. I let myself out of the house and made my way to school. I wasn't quite in the state I had been on my first morning at school, but my jumper now had a few rips in it, as well as the dirty patches. Yet again I was given a new jumper to wear. I settled down in my chair, to start my new week of learning. I had barely started to listen to the teacher, when one of the helpers came in and took me away. We went to the bathrooms, where she stripped me down and made me wash. She then gave me some new clothes to wear. She gave me pants, something that I had never worn before. I just had my shorts, my top and my old shoes as my normal wardrobe.

So when I went back into the classroom, I was almost dressed the same as everyone else. What I knew even then and I am sure they could tell, even after me just being there a week, was that how I was dressed at this minute, was not going to last. What I didn't know, as I walked back into the classroom ready to learn, was that I had already been flagged up by the school, to the local social worker.

With me coming to start school, was the first time that I had appeared on their radar. They had concerns about me of course. The way I was dressed, how dirty I was, how hungry I was when food was put in front of me and generally how uncared for I was. Unbeknown to me, my teacher had gone round to our house after school on Friday. In the light of what I have learned since then and what I know now, I can honestly say that I expect she was shocked with what she saw, when she went in to talk to my Mum.

It was mid-way through my second week at school that the social worker went to our house. She had gone after school, expecting me to be there, but of course I never went straight home. I turned up pretty much at the same time as my Dad rolled in, after a serious session at the Dog and Duck, on his way home from work. He wasn't pleased to find someone else in the house. He became abusive and threatened violence, if the social worker didn't shift her backside out of his chair and out of his house. His house was none of her business. What he didn't realise at that moment, was that it was very much her business and he had just made things very much worse.

While he was hurling abuse at the social worker, I sneaked into the kitchen and ate half of what was on his plate, ready for him to eat. He came in there while I was stuffing the food into my mouth. He shouted at me and made a grab at me, which I managed to avoid. I wasn't so lucky with the back-hand slap that followed, which caught me on the side of the head. I fell to the floor with the force of it. My Mum and the social worker ran in while he was shouting at me and witnessed the back-hand slap that. The social worker shouted 'stop' and my Mum pushed past her and started hitting my Dad.

That unfortunately had the effect of making things worse. My Dad went into even more than a rage than he was in already. He lashed out at my Mum, sending her flying back against the wall. I was still on the ground, recovering from his blow to the side of my head. The next thing I felt was my Dad's foot, as he kicked me in the side. I scrambled away as best I could, but there were only a limited number of places for me to go, to escape his onslaught. My Mum, even though he had obviously hurt her, flung herself forward and as best she could, deflected his attention from her to me. At this point I managed to scramble to my feet and darted for the door to the living room, just as my Dad dealt out another telling blow to my Mum. This time she hit the wall and went down in a heap on the floor. I just made it through the door, as he turned to see where I was again, presumably to have another go at kicking me.

Ahead of me, the frightened social worker was making for the door. She opened that as I came out of the kitchen. She went outside as quickly as she could and I made for the same exit. I could hear my Dad roaring behind me, but there was no way I was going to stop, to experience what he might have in mind to dish out.

As I got to the outside, the noise diminished behind me. In retrospect, I realise that he had turned back, to dish out more punishment to the only person left in the house; my defenceless Mum.

The social worker was screaming for help and to be fair, I noticed one or two people appear on the street, just along the road.

'Call the police' the social worker screamed.

I saw someone dash back into their house, to use their phone.

I stood by our gate. I didn't know what to do. I could hear my Dad still rampaging in the kitchen. I couldn't help but think that he was hitting my Mum even more. It probably wasn't the wisest decision I have ever made, but I couldn't stay there. What I ever thought I could do to stop him, I will never know, but I went in anyway. As I went through the living room, I could see him in kitchen. As I suspected, he was still attacking my Mum. I picked up the only thing that was to hand, which was a plate that was lying on the carpet, by Mum's chair. I ran forward and screamed as I reached the kitchen doorway. He stopped and turned, at which point I let the plate in my hand fly. I couldn't do it again even if I tried, but the plate flew through the air and caught him square on the nose, before dropping to the floor and shattering. But it had the desired effect. He started towards me. I turned and ran, with him not too far away on my heels. I darted out of the front door and towards the gate. Two men were just about to come through the gate, to see what was going on. I have seen both of them in the street before. As I appeared out of the house, with my Dad almost in reach of me, they leapt forward into his path. I veered round them and then kept going.

Chapter 13 More of Still Back Further in Time.

I kept going until I was way along our street. I only stopped when the police car shot past me, with the siren going. In the front seats, I saw two determined policemen. Their car screeched to a halt outside our house, where Dad was still in a scrap with the two men I had met up with, as I ran out of the house. Even with the policemen closing in on him, he wasn't giving up. The two men weren't exactly losing, but they were taking some punches from my Dad. The policemen waded in, and along with the two other men they soon overcame my Dad, enough to put the cuffs on him. They sat him down on the ground and then stood back from him. Someone ran inside the house, to see how my Mum was. They were out within seconds, screaming for someone to call an ambulance.

Another police car shot past me. It too screeched to a stop beside the other police car. Those policemen decamped too and the scene quickly calmed down.

The ambulance came past me about five minutes later. It was another few minutes before they came out, with my Mum on a stretcher. The social worker was standing next to her, saying something to her, but I was too far away to be able to hear anything. I took a few steps further away, as I saw everyone start to look around. It wasn't hard to guess they were looking for me. It didn't take them long to spot me. But spotting me and catching me, are two different things. I had a bad feeling about what they might do with me, so I turned tail and ran. I heard my name being shouted, but I wasn't going to stop for anyone. No one tried to stop me, although in fairness there were only a couple of people between me and the end of the street. Once I got there, then I was in my element. I spent most of my hours outside and I knew that area like the back of my hand. A quick left and then a right down a back path and I was lost to them in seconds. That didn't make me stop running. I knew where I was going to go. I had a safe place in the woods, on the other side of the field. It was somewhere I went to get out of the rain and the wind, in bad weather. There was a bank by where an old tree had come down. It had been down a long time. It was down well before I first came across it.

The plants had grown up in front of the bank and it just looked like a wall of plants. But if you went round them, there was a small space I could squeeze through and get to my shelter. All it was really was the cover provided by some of the roots of the tree, exposed when it fell down. It was just like a small cave. It was dry. It was always out of the wind and the rain. I had never been disturbed in there, even by other children in the area. I'm not saying I was the only one that knew about it, but at that moment in time I appeared to be the only one who used it. I left a supply of snacks in there, ones that wouldn't go off if I didn't eat them straight away. I had an old bottle, filled with water from the stream. My things had always been as I left them the previous time, which is what made me say no one else knew about this place.

I made it to the woods safely. I didn't run straight across the field towards it, just in case someone spotted me and tried to follow. I went round the edge of the field, keeping low and as much out of sight as I could manage. From there, I slipped into the woods, some way over from where I wanted to be. And once I was deep enough into the trees, I worked my way across to my den and darted in there. It was always quite dark in there, but that didn't scare me. Most of the time I'd used it before this, there had been some light in there. But I knew that although there was some bit of light there at that moment, that wasn't going to be the case when it got dark outside, throughout the night.

I had never done that before. I had always gone home at some point in the evening. I settled down on the bed of leaves I had brought in to make the floor more comfortable. I guessed it might get a bit colder in the night, but I had nothing to cover me. I just had the clothes I was dressed in. I decided to risk going out and seeing if there was anything I could bring find. I searched around quickly and came across an old piece of sacking. I decided it would do, and then darted back to the safety of my den. I sat there in the ever increasing darkness, listening intently for sounds of people walking through the woods. No sound like that came to my ears. I was guessing that they had no idea where I went to when I was not home. Even if my

Mum could have told them something, she wouldn't know where I went. My Dad definitely had no idea.

After some time I lay down, and as the evening progressed, I tucked the sacking over me. I was glad that I had found it, as the night got quite cool. It wasn't cold as such, but I would have been uncomfortably cool if I hadn't got it. I ate a bit of a snack I had stored there, before settling down to go to sleep for the night.

In the morning I was woken by the little streaks of light that filtered their way through to me. I was guessing that it was early and judging from the light when I ventured out, it was earlier than when I normally get up.

I made my way down to the stream and had a wash. I took off my clothes and actually went into the stream. I had no idea what the situation was at home and I had no intention of going back there to find out. But funnily enough, I did want to go to school. I knew that people might come for me while I was there, but somehow I had started to feel safe at school. I also had the feeling of being wanted, which was something I quite liked.

So, having no idea what the actual time was, I made my way out of the woods and skirted well round the area where our house was. There were only one or two people out on the streets and a few cars and vans on the road. No one paid me any notice, as far as I was aware.

When I got to the school, the gates were locked. I knew I must be too early. If I stood where I was, I would certainly have attracted some attention, so I made my way round to the woods at the back, to wait for the school gates to open. It was a while later that I heard the sounds of the first few children arriving at school and playing in the playground. I made my way round to the front of the school again and walked into the playground. There was a supervisor there, who certainly saw me, but she didn't move or particularly look at me.

At the start of the school day, I went in with the others and took my place at the front of the class. The teacher acted as normal and we started our lessons. I was expecting someone to come in at any moment, but it didn't happen in the morning. I made it to lunchtime without being found by the others.

At lunch, I managed to sneak some extra food. I knew if I went back to my den again that night, there was going to be little to eat. I managed to beg some treats from a couple of children in my class, whom I had become friendly with. They already knew that I didn't get much at home, so they willingly gave me some things. I had a packet of crisps and a couple of biscuits to take back with me that night. I didn't tell anyone what had happened at home.

Even I was surprised when I made it to the end of the day, still in school and with no one having come looking for me.

Chapter 14 Yes I am still there.

I never saw my Dad ever again. I was collared the next day I went to school. I got as far as getting into the classroom and into my seat. Then the teacher moved over to the door and the social worker who had been there when my Dad went mad, came through the door. I knew there was no point in running. I'd always known they would catch up with me.

I was led away with the social worker. The first thing she did was to take me to the hospital, to see my Mum. She didn't look well and she didn't even open her eyes to see me. I was then taken from the hospital and to a house a few miles away. The lady there said she was going to look after me, until such time as my Mum was well enough to have me back again. I remember when the lady asked if I had any other things, the social worker shook her head, but didn't say anything.

It didn't matter. This lady had a lot of clothes that fitted me. This lady had a car too and the next day she drove me to school, the same school I have been going to. For the first time I was not the worst dressed person in the class. I could tell the others had noticed. Marjorie, that was the name of the lady where I was staying, asked me nicely if I would wait for her to come and collect me at the end of the day. Gladly I agreed I would and why wouldn't I?

I had been dressed in smart clothes. I had my own bedroom, with a bed and a mattress and blankets and pillows and they were all clean. I had lots of clothes to choose from. I had food put on a plate on the table, for me to eat when Marjorie ate. On that point, she was teaching me how to eat properly, with a knife and fork and a spoon too. She had a television that I was allowed to watch. I had toys to play with, but I had to tidy up before the end of the day.

I had been there a couple of days, before I even knew that someone else lived with Marjorie. John came home on the Friday evening. He worked away from home during the week and only lived at home at the weekend. John was nice too, like Marjorie.

In the weeks I was there the first time, I learnt so many things that I didn't know before. They took me out with them when we went shopping. I had never been shopping before. I guess my Mum and Dad would have had to at some stage, but they never involved me in it. John and Marjorie did. They took me to the play park, where there were swings and roundabouts to play on. It wasn't like the one where I used to live, where everything was broken. This one was really nice.

The social worker came to see me a number of times and took me to see my Mum. The first two times she was just the same. She was fast asleep in the bed. One time when I went after that, she was awake. She still didn't look very well, but she did recognise me, I think. She didn't say anything though. It was many more visits after that, that we went to see her and she wasn't there.

I was told, a few days later, that she had been given a new place to live and that she would be having me back home soon. I have to say that didn't fill me with happiness. I liked being with Marjorie and John.

The social worker picked me up and I was allowed to take some of my clothes with me. It wasn't too far away from where we used to live, where we arrived at. They had given my Mum a flat in a block of flats. She had furniture in every room and it was all very tidy. I even had a bed and other furniture in my room. True to form though, there was little food on offer when the social worker left me there.

Where my Mum had sat before, listening to the radio in our old house, she now sat in the chair in front of the television in this one. I might as well have not been there. So, I went out and went round my old haunts. My den was still there and intact. Nobody had been in there in all the time I'd been away. When I got round to going home that evening, I found the door was locked. That was a first for my Mum. I tried ringing the bell and then knocking on the door, but other than the shout from someone close by to 'shut up'; the door did not get opened. I had to go back to my den for the night.

I went home the next day, but the door was still locked in the morning. I went away for a time and then returned. The door was unlocked this time and I went in. I questioned why she hadn't let me in the night before. She replied that you have to lock your doors there at night and that she didn't hear me, because she was asleep. I needed to get home earlier if I wanted back in.

Needless to say that I didn't that night and so on the Monday morning, I turned up at school not dressed properly, and without my school jumper. They gave me one from the lost box. I also think I saw the sadness on my teacher's face, but maybe I was imagining that.

I went home after school and decided to stay in. There was no food to eat that day, but there was a bottle of something on the side. As far as I could tell, my Mum had started drinking before I got home. She was just sitting there in front of the television.

I asked her if there was going to be any food. I didn't understand why Marjorie and John had food for me, but my own Mum did not. I made the mistake of saying that. My Mum flew out of the chair and grabbed me. She smacked me across the face and then pushed me to the floor. She started shouting at me, about being a nuisance. She said I was the reason why my Dad wasn't there anymore and that I should be ashamed about that. She then grabbed the bottle from the kitchen and started drinking from it, while still shouting at me. When she had finished the bottle, she stood up and threw it at me. I saw it coming and moved quickly out of the way, before it smashed into the wall where I'd been just a second or two before. She wasn't done though and she ran towards me, as best she could. She cornered me and smacked me on the face again. This time I could taste something in my mouth. I started to cry, but that too just made things worse. I don't know if she knew what she was doing, but she started smacking me across the face some more and when I managed to turn away, she hit me on my body instead. She had me trapped in the corner and there was no place for me to escape to.

Someone started banging on the door and a few seconds later a man came in. He shouted for her to stop, but she ignored him. He shouted behind him for help and another two people came in, a man and a woman. The men got hold of my Mum and flung her down in her chair, while the woman came over to me. My Mum was still shouting at me, while the men would not let her get out of the chair. I think if she had been able to, she would still have come back over to hit me some more.

The woman led me by the hand and we went out of the flat, onto the balcony at the front. There were quite a lot of people gathered there. I heard the gasps when they saw me. I take it there was quite a lot of blood on me, being the reason for that.

The police turned up a few minutes later, along with an ambulance. They took me in the back and then took me to the hospital. I stayed in there for a few days. A police lady came to see me, as did the social worker.

As soon as I was a bit better, the social worker took me to another house. At first I thought she was going to take me back to Marjorie and John, but she said she couldn't, as they were looking after someone else now. She took me instead to a woman called Anne. Although Anne was pleasant enough and alright really; she wasn't the same as Marjorie. I was told I would only be there for a few days, until they decided what was going to happen to me. They didn't mention my Mum once, after they had asked me what had happened. I for one was hoping that they weren't going to send me home again. That definitely wasn't on my wanted list.

Chapter 15 Next

I didn't see my Mum, after I was taken away to hospital, for a very long time. I didn't stay with Anne for long, although it was longer than the few days they had told me I was going to be there for. I got to like her a bit by the time I left. She was kind enough, just not in the same way as Marjorie. I spent the next few months going from one short term foster parent to the next. I don't think it was because of me that I couldn't stay with each one for too long, but it may have been. I guess I will never know. The one constant I had in the first year, was that I kept going to the same school. I was settled there and actually enjoyed going each day. Each one of my foster parents, in those early days, made the effort to take me there each day. They were always there at the gate to pick me up after school too.

All was going well and I was enjoying my life, even though I was being moved every few weeks or so. Everyone did things slightly differently too, but I had no trouble fitting into the respective households. Most of the time I was the only child there, but on occasion I was with other children, their children.

I can't remember exactly when it was, but it was before my next birthday, when we went into a different pattern. I was sent into a children's home for a few weeks. Life was very different in there. Although there were adults in there, we were left to fend for ourselves more. I was the youngest one in there and the others very much took advantage of that. They made me do jobs for them and I was the one who was made to get into trouble, when things went wrong. It wasn't that bad in there at first, but at times it was unpleasant.

On top of that, and the thing I hated most about going there, was that I had to change school. The home wasn't even in the same town as my old school. There was no way they were going to put themselves out, to take just me there and back each day. The school they put me into was different. I don't know how to explain it, but I suppose I didn't feel the teacher was as interested in teaching me things, as in my other school.

They were doing work I had done before and I got bored. Also, I had no one to pick me up, or take me to school each day either. The older ones were supposed to do that, but as soon as we were out of sight of the home, they would tell me to push off and make my own way. It was only a matter of time before I didn't go home one night, after school had finished. I waited as usual at the gate for the older ones, but for some reason they did not turn up. There was no adult there at the gate to make sure they had that day, which was unusual, but not unknown.

I didn't go home, but instead I wandered to the park we passed on the way to and from school each day. I made my way in and wandered around there for maybe an hour or so. There wasn't anywhere like my den in this park.

Somehow I must have exited the park by a different gate than the one I went in by. I guess I wasn't concentrating and I was just wandering aimlessly. I was thinking I was on the right way home, but when I realised I had walked for much longer than I should have been, I found that I was lost.

I just made things worse from that point onwards and it was only as it started to get dark, that someone stopped me and asked me where I lived. Owning up that I was lost ended with a call to the police, who were already on the lookout for me.

When I got back to the home, I got into a lot of trouble. The older ones just smirked at me. I almost think it was intentional, that they left me alone at the school gates. It didn't change anything about the way the older ones were with me. If it did something, it just made the situation worse. They still abandoned me on the way to school and did not accompany me back. They bullied me more in the home and in general made my life a lot worse. For the first time since I lived with my Mum and Dad, I actually had some thoughts that that life would have been better than what I was living now.

So it was; that the first seeds of my resentment towards my parents really began to grow. If I was still there, then I would be able to escape to my den if I needed to.

The adults in the home seemed to be ignoring the fact that I was being bullied. Maybe they were afraid of some of the older children in there. It got to the stage that they were almost out of control with their actions against me. The more they did and got away with, the more they tried to do. It got to the point where I was afraid to go to sleep, for fear of what trick or prank, or just sheer bad thing, they might do to me next. Even at school they encouraged others to get at me. They were more discreet about it there, but they still managed to make my life hell.

I knew that I had to do something, to change things. No one else was going to help me with this issue. I had even changed social worker with my move here. This one did come to the home, but never spoke to me alone.

It was only when they got brazen enough to hurt me, in places where the bruises were visible even with my clothes on, that someone started to realise that all was not well in my life. The fact it wasn't someone in the home that actually did something about it, worried me. I was really starting to fear for my safety there. The older ones were getting more physical. The adults there were almost making themselves scarce, when I was around.

It was one of the playground supervisors who spoke to me first. I was afraid to talk to them in the playground, as I could see some of the others looking on. The supervisor was quite smart. She could see that I was bothered by her attention in front of others. They waited until I was back in class, before someone else came to speak to me. It was the head teacher. She took me into a room and asked me about my visible injuries. I told her what was happening at the home and I could see that she was horrified. She asked if there were more bruises under my clothes. I showed her some of them. She was even more horrified.

I began to feel a bit of hope. That was until there was a knock at the door and when she answered it, there was one of the other children from the home there. They could see me, but that wasn't what they were there for. They had been sent to get the head teacher for something and a teacher had told them where we were. I was sent back to my classroom, while she went off to deal with whatever the matter was.

At the end of the school day I was taken to the staff room, where I was told to wait, as someone was coming to collect me. I passed several of the older home children on the way and I really didn't like the looks I was getting. I sort of felt safe in the staff room, as there were two or three teachers in there. I hadn't been told who was coming to collect me and to be honest I never did find out, as something else happened next.

First of all, there was the sound of a fight, outside in the playground. I rushed to the window, as did all of the teachers in the room. What we saw was a big scrap. It wasn't just two people fighting, but a whole group of boys and girls, all scrapping. There was just one supervisor there, trying in vain to break it up. Then someone hit the supervisor. The teachers turned from the window and ran for the door. I stayed where I was, looking out of the window. Teachers were streaming out into the playground and starting to pull the fighters apart.

I heard the door go behind me. I didn't turn at first, as I was gripped by the scene in front of me. Then I heard someone speak and it wasn't the voice of a teacher.

'You horrible little shit! So you've tried to get some help. That hasn't done you any good has it? You'll be sorry you started this. You won't want to be alive, when I've finished with you.'

I was thinking that I hadn't started anything, but that wasn't going to help me now. In fact I had no idea what was going to save me. I couldn't see the teachers breaking up the fight in the playground and being back here in time to come to my rescue.

He made his way quickly towards me. I knew if he got hold of me I was going to be in a lot of trouble, physically. I was scared stiff that he was going to kill me. The look on his face told me that he wanted to. There was little between him and me. The little was a coffee table. It was big enough that he had to walk round it, to get to me. I started to run towards him and he started to smile, with a wicked grin on his face.

Initially I ran straight towards him. But as he started to walk round the table to grab me, I suddenly swivelled to my left and threw myself onto the floor. I slid along the floor under the coffee table and out the other side, before he realised what I'd done. I didn't waste any time seeing what he was doing. I just needed to get out of there,

I made it to the door and darted through it. There was no point going to the right, as that would lead me towards the main exit and the playground. In my eyes, there was much more danger in that direction. It was that conscious thought that made me turn left and run towards the canteen.

I wasn't far along the corridor, before I heard the staffroom door bang behind me and footsteps running after me. I did a right and a left along the corridor, ignoring the classrooms I passed. The canteen is at the end of the building. I just hoped the door was still open. Maybe they locked it after lunch. I really hoped not. He was closing on me, so my time would be up if the door failed to open.

I got there and pushed. The door gave way and let me in. Now I was there, I did not know what I was going to do, but something inside me had led me there. My instinct for survival I guessed. I dropped to the floor and slid under the work tables. He was too big to do this. I could hear him clattering behind me, as I scrambled along the floor. I went under one unit, then out and under the next. Suddenly I knew where to make for. The back door is in the far corner. Just along from that, if it is locked, is the hatch to the eating area. I am hoping I have enough time to try the door and still have time to make it to the hatch if it is not.

He is getting further behind me, but I do not let my hopes rise yet. I am far from being out of the woods.

Chapter 16 Escape, or not?

I grabbed the handle of the back door. I knew before I tried to turn it that it was locked, as I could see the bar across it. All was not lost though, as I did have my back up plan. He saw my fruitless attempt at escape through the door. I did see this as I turned away from the door. Once again the smile appeared on his face and the grin was by far the most evil one I have ever witnessed. My fear level went up a few more notches, as I saw him pick up a knife from somewhere. He started to move to block off my escape path out of the canteen, back through the door we came through. I panicked for a minute, thinking that maybe I had got it wrong about the hatch. I glanced quickly in that direction, but tried not to make it over obvious. The news was good and not so good. The good news was that the hatch was indeed there. The bad news was that the hatch was shut. That was probably why he was looking so confident. But I still had one advantage over him; at least I thought I had. One day at lunchtime I was sent into the canteen area to undo the catch on the hatch, to open it. My knowledge of that, was what I was hoping would give me an advantage over him. Well I was hoping it would get me out of there and ahead of him again. Where I went from there was another matter. But I thought I knew what I would do; always hoping I had the time to do it. I had seen it done on the television, so if I got the opportunity, I would get to try it for myself.

I ran towards the hatch. I think he might just have realised that he may not have all my ways out covered, as he started to make his way towards me again. I jumped up onto the side by the hatch. I flicked the bolt across and opened the hatch, enough for me to clamber through. On the other side, I jumped down. My heart was in my mouth, as he was already at the hatch, but on the other side. I am small and so it was easy for me to get through. He had a much bigger task to get through. That gave me all the time I would need, if my plan was to work.

I ran towards the big window. Just before I got there, I picked up a chair and ran with it. I held out in front of me, as I leapt the last couple of feet into the window. Thankfully, I think in retrospect, the glass shattered as the chair, with me following, came into contact. I kept going, as the chair made a hole more than big enough for me to make it through unscathed. I landed in the flowerbed outside the window and wasted no time abandoning the chair and making a run for it.

Behind me, I saw, with a quick glance, that he had stopped by the window. He didn't even try to get through the broken glass. As he was much bigger than me, he needed a bigger hole to get through, without getting cut to ribbons.

I didn't run round towards the playground at the front of the building. That, I believed would only lead me back into deep trouble again. I was not going to do that willingly. If I went the other way, which I was doing, I was going to be in much more familiar surroundings, in a way.

There are some sheds by the wall this way and I was used to sheds, or more to the point I was used to climbing them. In fact I was very good at climbing. I turned the corner and I was out of sight of the window I came through. The sheds were in front of me. I hadn't actually climbed these sheds before, but in my eyes a shed is a shed, so I was going to be able to climb them. And climb them I did. By the time I got to the top, I was still alone and there was no one in sight to see me go over to the back and look down the other side to the ground. It was no higher than I have jumped from before.

I felt exhilarated as I jumped down and for the first time in the last few minutes, I felt a bit safer. I knew I had not got completely away, but I did feel I was more in control and that I was probably better at this than he was. I scampered away from the back of the sheds, across the waste land where there used to be a factory.

I knew I was going to hit the streets again soon and that would have left me a bit exposed. There was a bit of cover there where they took the building down, but I thought that it would not be a clever place to hide out. My pursuer would tell them which way I left and no doubt say that he was trying to stop me running off.

I knew I needed to get away from this area as fast as I could. I also knew that my best chance of evading capture was to get into the countryside, preferably woodland. I was at home in woodland; well at least I was before, when I had my den. The main problem I had was that I had no idea where the nearest woodland was.

I was still frightened and although I thought that I should be walking, so people wouldn't take so much notice of me, I couldn't make myself do that. I started to run and kept turning left and then right as I came to each road junction. All the time I knew I was getting further away from school and the older children from the home. What I didn't know was whether I was getting nearer any woods.

Luck, or whatever you want to call it; was on my side. I didn't come across woodlands, but after quite a long run I did come to the end of houses, shops and other buildings. I hadn't passed many people on my journey and as far as I was aware, none of them had taken much, if any, interest in me running past them.

There was nobody around me as I climbed over the fence and made it into the first field, beyond the houses. I dropped over on the other side and found myself in a ditch. I decided that was a good thing and kept in it, as I started along the edge of the field. I would be out of sight of everyone who looked in that direction. Thankfully the ditch was dry and I made quite good time. I was walking along it then, as I didn't need to run. I reached the farthest corner of this field and crawled into the thick hedge that divided it from the next field. I stopped in there for a few minutes rest.

In many ways it reminded me of the den. When I was in there nobody could find me. Sitting there in the middle of this hedge, I thought I was in a similar place. Admittedly I didn't think the hedge would keep me totally dry, but then as I thought about it I felt the ground around where I was sitting. The ground was dry, much drier than the land I had been walking on in the ditch. If the worst came to the worst and I didn't find anywhere suitable, then I could always go back there for the night.

I pushed my way through the hedge and looked at what is beyond. I saw more fields, but the nearest one did not have a hedge at the far side; it had a stone wall instead. I made my way back into the middle of the hedge again. I needed somewhere safe to stay that night, to give me time to think what I was going to do next. Here was the best thing I have on offer at the moment. To go on would take me further away, but would I be able to find somewhere as good as this? I was not going to take that chance.

I spent the next 30 minutes or so going along the ditch and diving into the hedge at times to find a better place, if there was one. I did find one a bit further along, which I thought was less obvious and had to force my way in, even more than I had to in the original place in the corner. I then spent a further 30 minutes or so, gathering materials that I could use to make my bed softer and other materials I could use to cover me, to keep me warm.

When I had finished, I snuggled down and prepared to stay there until the morrow. During my time there until then, I endeavoured to make a plan, as to what I would do the next day and where I would try to go.

Chapter 17 After escape

The night was a dry one and I slept well, as I didn't feel threatened, for a change. I woke as soon as it got light, but resisted the temptation to start on my way. I knew I would be more noticeable being out on my own early in the morning. I was feeling thirsty and a bit hungry too, but that had to wait. In the meantime I tried to work out what I was going to do once I left my hiding place and more importantly, where I was going to go.

It didn't take me long to know that I needed to get further away from here. If they found me here, then I was going to be taken back to the home. That was something that wouldn't have been good for me. I couldn't even start to imagine what evil things the older ones would have done to me, if I ever went back.

In an ideal world I would have loved to be at Marjorie's house. Even Anne, my other early foster mother, would have been a good place to be. I thought that even if I could make it back to my first school, I would be safer than here. The big problem I had; was that I only knew the name of that school. I had no idea where it was from here. I had no idea how far away it might be too.

A thought popped into my head. Would even going back to my Mum be better than life at the children's home? To be honest I wasn't sure about that. Anyway I didn't think that was really a realistic option, so I dismissed that thought, as being a waste of time.

So I got back down to thinking what the best way forward from there was. I went through what little information I had. The school name wasn't going to help me much. St John's is the name, but that wasn't going to be on any road sign. That was what I decided I needed to look for. That was based on my trips outs with Marjorie and John. If I could just see one of the names I used to see while we were out in their car, then I might be at least to be able to set off in the right direction. Then another thought came to me. They used to go out and John would drive. If they didn't know the way to where they were going to, they used a map, which they kept in the pocket, in the car door.

I started to get a little bit excited at the thought of this. If I could get a map, I could then see which way I needed to go. I knew the name of the village where Marjorie lives.

The dryness of my mouth reminded me that there were other things that needed to be seen to first. I needed something to drink and I needed something to eat. Neither of those was going to be easy to satisfy. Neither was getting hold of a map, for that matter.

I either needed to find a stream, or I needed to go back to where the houses were. I really did not want to go back to that place, so I made my plan to keep going away and hoping to come across a stream. Meeting people was always going to be problematic, as they would want to report me to the police.

I left my hedge, going out the other side from the side I came in on. I made for the other side of the field. When I got there, I found a place in the wall I could climb up and go over. In the distance, I saw there were some houses. There were only a few of them and I had to cross some more fields before I got there. It was still early, so I was guessing there would still be no one around. I went straight across the next three fields. I was now fairly close to the houses, so I went to the edge of the field and walked along the side, approaching the houses, hopefully not in their view. I went to my left and I found that I could see a road, a short distance away. There wasn't any traffic on it. In fact I couldn't hear any traffic from anywhere. I made my way over there and over that wall, onto the road. This was a dangerous moment for me. I ran, at the edge of the road, towards the first of the houses. There were two rows of houses next to each other. There were only four houses in each row. Before I even reached them, I saw something I recognized, on one of the doorsteps; a bottle of milk. It would have been too much to ask for anything to eat too, but milk would at least satisfy one of my needs. I ran forward and grabbed the bottle and kept going. No one opened their door and shouted after me. There was another bottle of milk on one of the doorsteps in the second row of houses. I took that too. At least I had something to drink.

With my prizes in my hands, I kept to the road, until I was about a hundred yards out of the hamlet. That side there were hedges running by the side of the road. I found a place to go through and then hugging the edge of this field, I moved away from the group of houses. I didn't stop, until there was another boundary between me and the houses. I found a dry place in the ditch on the other side of the hedge and settled down, to drink some, or all, of one of the bottles of milk. It turned out to be the full bottle I drank. I felt better already and even my hunger receded some. I could then concentrate on the next part of my plan. I kept a lookout for something to eat too.

It was a few hours later and when I was getting quite tired, that I saw some more houses in the distance. When I got there, I made my way closer to the road, but didn't actually go onto it. I heard a couple of cars as I approached. I stayed on my side of the hedge and approached the houses. I brushed myself down and tried to make myself as smart as I could. My clothes weren't dirty, but they were a bit ruffled. I found a place to get through the hedge.

There was no one around as I walked into the first part of this village. It was way bigger than the last place I went through. The second bottle of milk was drunk about an hour before, so I had nothing in my hands as I walked along. I had decided to walk, as running would attract more attention to me. I didn't need that. I passed a couple of streets going off to the left and right, but I kept going on the road I was on. I heard a car coming from behind me. I decided that I mustn't turn round, but just keep walking, as if I belonged there.

The car went past me without slowing down, which was a relief to me. I watched it as it turned the bend in the road and kept going. When I made it to the corner, I saw there was still more of this place. More importantly, I saw two things that gave me heart. On my side of the road, about fifty yards ahead of me, was a shop. Beyond that, at least as far away again, on the other side of the road, was a petrol station. It looked like it was at a crossroads. The reason that both of them were good news for me; is that I remembered seeing maps for sale in a petrol station, when John stopped for petrol once. The shop was good, because it had food. Of course I didn't have any money. I thought that food was more of a priority at that very moment, so I decided to stop at the shop first.

I thought I would go in and see what it sold, before I decided what to do. As I got to it, I saw that it had some baskets out the front. In one of them were some carrots, with cabbage in another and then other vegetables in the other two. They had been hidden from me by the steps as I approached. I climbed the steps and try the door. It did not open to my touch on the handle. Then I saw the sign on the window of the door, which said 'CLOSED'. I stepped down again and looked at the vegetables. The only ones I knew I could eat without cooking were the carrots. There was a bundle of brown paper bags in one of the baskets, so I took a couple and filled them both with carrots; as many as I could get in the two bags and get them closed.

I had still not seen a soul out walking. Another car passed me, going the same way as me and then another going in the other direction. Neither of the drivers gave me a second look, or at least I hoped they didn't. The car that passed me, going in my direction; pulled into the petrol station and stopped in front of the petrol pumps. The driver got out and looked around. By the time I got to the garage, there was still no one other than the driver visible. He gave me a quick glance, but then turned, as a man came out of the building.

He walked to the pumps and started to put petrol in the car. I walked up to the office bit and looked through the window. The man, who was putting the petrol in, looked over at me by the office. But then he concentrated on what he was doing again. I couldn't see any maps in there, so I turned away and walked towards the front of the garage. They had finished filling the car with petrol and they were now both walking towards the office, for the driver of the car to pay. I walked round the car and saw that he'd left the door wide open. What did I see in the door pocket? I saw a map book. I glanced quickly over my shoulder, but they were busy. Two seconds later I had the map book in my hands and then another second later, I had it stuffed up my jumper. I walked away quickly and out of their sight.

I was now on one of the side streets. I thought it unwise to stay on the main road, with my goodies on me. Behind me, I heard the car start its engine and drive away. It didn't come down the road I was on. I was hoping he hadn't missed his map book yet.

Chapter 18 Maps

I took the first right turn and then the next right again and soon I was back on the road I started on. I turned to the left and continued to walk along the pavement. What I really wanted to do; was find some cover and have something to eat. I also wanted to get well away before someone stopped me; to ask where I got the bags from and what that thing was, stuffed up my jumper. I passed an old lady, walking the other way, before I reached the end of the village. I then passed another thing that when I turned round, was a great help to me, at least I hoped it was going to be a great help. It was the name of the village I had just been through.

As I looked at the sign, I saw a couple of people walking towards me, but still a distance away. I could see they were looking at me and not just ahead of them. I turned and started walking away from the village. I resisted the temptation to look over my shoulder. I thought that would just attract more attention my way and I didn't need that, after I now had a map in my possession. There was a corner coming up and as soon as I was round it, I crossed the road and found a way through the hedge, into the field beyond. I went to my left, which meant I was actually making my way back towards the village again. Hopefully, I thought, that if they were following me, they would not be expecting me to do that. I followed the hedge back towards the town, stopping every few yards, to look through the hedge and listen. I had to walk quite a way, before I came across them. They had stopped to talk, on the pavement opposite. I couldn't hear what they were saying, but they didn't appear to be talking about me. How I knew that I don't know, but that was the feeling I had.

I stayed there for a couple of minutes, until one of them went through the gate next to them and walked up to the front door, while the other one turned round and walked back towards the centre of the village. I was reassured that they hadn't sounded the alarm and I didn't think they would, until later at least, if they learnt I was on the loose.

I walked away from the village again and went over a couple of walls, before I found a secure place for me to stop. I ate a couple of carrots from my bag, before opening up the map book. Marjorie and John did show me how they work. The one I had in my hands was more used than the one they had. It has been used a lot. I didn't know which page to turn to at first. Marjorie and John did and in their book it was on page 30, but I didn't recognise anywhere on page 30 of this map book. I remembered what they told me and I turned to the back of the book. It took me a while to read through the names of places, but I did eventually find the name of the place I had just been through. I turned to the page and scoured the page for this village. Again it took me quite a while, as I think I had missed something. Marjorie and John seemed to know which part of a page to look at straight away.

Having found that, I started to look at the other places close by. None of them were familiar to me. I spread my search further out and it was what I saw up in the top left corner that made my heart go bump. I saw the name of the place where Marjorie and John lived. What I had no idea then and I do now, is that different map books have different scales to them. I could see both villages, but had no idea how far in distance they were apart.

The next problem I had was to work out where I was in relation to the map. It was then that I remembered the crossroads in the village and I also remembered there was a signpost there. So that I didn't go off in the wrong direction, I needed to go back there and see what places were in which direction. I made my way back across the fields and got as close to the village as I could, before going through the hedge. I left my bags of carrots and the map book, hidden just on the other side of the hedge.

Ten minutes later I was back with good news for myself and some bad news. The bad news was that the man from the garage saw me and called out to me. When I didn't respond, he went inside and I saw him picking up the telephone. The good news was that I had already read the signposts. I had the information firmly in my head. I ran back to my things and grabbed them, before running alongside the hedge. This was the right direction I needed to go. That was just a matter of luck, but it seemed to be on my side.

On one hand I didn't want to go too far from the road, but on the other hand, I didn't want to be too close. If the man had indeed called the police about me, then they would be coming along here looking for me. So, I moved to the field one over and continued my journey along the hedge. I heard a car go along the road every now and then, so I knew I was still quite close to it.

I kept up a good pace and tried to stop as little as possible. I had two reasons for that. Firstly I wanted to get to Marjorie's house as soon as possible and secondly; the further away from the village I got; the harder it would be for them to track me down.

There came the point when I was so tired I just had to stop. I came across a natural place that had some cover and sat down for a rest. That was also the first opportunity I had taken to look at the information I got off the signpost and the map, with regard to distance. The town on the signpost, in the direction of Marjorie's house, had a number beside it. I knew it referred to a distance. I just didn't really understand what that distance meant. When I looked at the map, I saw the town from the signpost. It was about a third of the way from the village to Marjorie's house. The number on the signpost was a 10, so I'm guessing that makes the total to Marjorie's to be 30. But 30 what and how far that was and how long it would take, was something I didn't have the knowledge to know.

But anyway, my spirits had been lifted just by the knowledge I had gained from the map book and the signpost. That was enough to keep me going. I had a good rest and started out again. But I was tired and I knew I wouldn't be able to keep going for much longer. That was disappointing, but I was realistic enough to know that I had no choice. I kept a lookout for somewhere I could stop and also be safe and dry for the night. I came across a piece of woodland, just a bit over from my path. That was more to my experience. It didn't take me long to find a suitable place and I made the necessary additions I needed, to spend the rest of the day and the night in there. I intended to get some sleep and stay there until the morning and then set off as early as I could, at a reasonable pace.

It was mid-morning the next day that I came across the town from the signpost. I had quenched my thirst from a stream and I was down to one bag of carrots by then. Ideally I wouldn't have gone through the town to find my road on the other side, but I was worried that if I didn't, then I might lose my way. That thought, in the end, outweighed the negative side of walking through the town. Once again I brushed my clothes down and made my looks as tidy as I could.

Half an hour later, I was out the other side. I had been noticed by a few people. But then I was little and out on my own. But I was carrying my bag of carrots and the map book openly, so I was hoping people would think I had been sent out to get some things by my Mum. As soon as I could, I reverted to the fields and was on my way again. I noticed as I went through the town, that Marjorie's town was on the signpost, with the number 18 beside it.

I came across another stream early in the afternoon and got my fill, before moving on. I had now eaten half of the second bag of carrots. Thankfully I was feeling stronger that day and it was late in the afternoon before I felt that I had to stop again for the night. I had no idea how far I had travelled of the 18, but I was hopeful that this would be my last overnight stop outside and that the next day I would make it to Marjorie's.

Chapter 19 Marjorie's

I tried to stay awake as long as I could, until it got dark. I then managed to sleep through to first light the next day. I was up and off as soon as I was awake. I think it I was because I was excited at the prospect of seeing Marjorie, at the end of my day's trek. I had been lucky up to this point, in that the weather had been kind to me. I had felt the change when I woke up, as it was cooler than I'd expected and certainly not so bright. The clouds looked threatening and as if they might let the rain come down. I was not dressed for that, but I just had to see what happened.

I made my way, continuing as I had been for the latter part of the day before, quite close to the road, in fact in the field next to the road. There was some traffic on this road and I kept my ears open, in case one of the vehicles slowed down. I was always ready to dive down onto the ground and lie as low as I could. So far the rain had held off. The clouds had still got a heavy look to them. I finished the last of my carrots. I didn't want to see any more carrots for a while, but they had kept me fed, so I was grateful to them.

It was about an hour later, just after I'd stopped for a drink; that the rain started. It wasn't heavy, but I was getting wet all the same. I needed something to protect me, so I could keep going. A couple of fields on, I saw a scarecrow in the middle of the field. It was dressed in something. I made my way there and saw that the farmer had dressed it in an old coat. It was going to be far too big for me, but it would keep me warm and drier than I was at that moment.

I pulled the scarecrow to the ground and undressed it. Luckily for me, it was more of a jacket than a coat, but it was still too long for me. I found though, that if I tucked the sides into the pockets, rather than do the jacket up, that it took it all just off the ground. I then used the piece of rope from the trousers of the scarecrow, to tie round my middle, to keep the coat as close to me as possible. The hat was a little bit big for me too, but I took it anyway. I was much drier now, even though I must have looked a little odd.

I made my way back towards the roadside hedge and was almost there, when I heard a shout behind me. The farmer was running across the field towards me. He hadn't reached his stripped scarecrow yet, but he would soon. I ran a best as I could the last few feet to the hedge and found a way through. I then crossed the road and found a way through the hedge there. I ran along by the hedge to the end of that field, which wasn't far. I went through that and then ran further away from the road, up that side of the field. I went through that hedge and then turned left. I thought I was now safely out of his way. I found a place in the hedge between the two fields, where I could stop and rest up for a bit. I was tired from running and I was worried that if I continued then, I would not have enough energy to reach Marjorie's that day.

It was dry in the hedge and I waited there for quite a long time. I didn't hear anyone at all and was hopeful that the farmer had given up on chasing me. Suddenly I felt hungry again, but I had nothing. I was also thirsty, but I hadn't anything to drink either. Both would have to wait. I knew I should start up again. I didn't know how far I had still got to walk. I needed to get there in daylight, as I was not sure I could find her house in the dark. I wasn't sure I could find it in the daylight either, for that matter. I had only walked from her house to the shops before, when I lived there.

The rain got a bit harder as I left the shelter of the hedge. The jacket may have been old, but it was doing a good job of keeping me dry, as was the hat. My feet were another matter, but there was nothing I could do about that. The scarecrow didn't have feet and therefore no shoes. Even if it had, they would not have been anything like small enough for me to walk in. I tried to keep to the drier parts of the field by the hedge, but still my shoes were soaked. There was nothing for me to do, other than carry on.

I knew my progress was slower, as I was tired and the weight of the jacket was also slowing me down. Despite that, I reached the houses late in the afternoon. I ventured through the hedge onto the pavement. I was heartened by the sign that greeted my eyes. I was there in Marjorie's village.

I walked past the first houses. It wasn't long before I passed someone walking the other way. They gave me a funny look as we passed, but nothing more than that. I followed the road until I came to a crossroads. I didn't recognise it. I decided to stay on the road I was already on. I passed a few more people and again I got funny looks. I just smiled back from under my hat. The rain had started to relent a bit then, but it was still drizzling.

Then a voice behind me said something to me.

'Are you alright? You look a bit small to be out in this weather in those clothes.'

I quickly made up my mind to risk asking something.

'I'm lost. I'm looking for Marjorie's house.'

It was a woman I faced as I was saying these words.

'Marjorie who? What is her last name?'

'I am not sure, but she lives with John.'

'Marjorie and John. I don't think I know a Marjorie and John. Where do they live? Do you know the name of the road?'

'Sycamore Drive' I answered straight away.

'I know where Sycamore Drive is. What number do they live at?'

'34'

'Come on. We will walk there together and find Marjorie for you. What is your name?'

'Jay'

'I'm Mary.'

Mary took my hand and we walked along the pavement. We turned left at the next junction and then after a few more turns, I saw the shops that I had been to.

'I go to those shops when I stay with Marjorie' I said as I saw them.

'Do you stay with her often?'

'I did for a while, but then I stayed with other people for a time.'

'I see.'

I'm not sure that she did. I noticed she was keeping a good hold of my hand. It wasn't that she was holding my hand tightly, but I knew that if I tried to pull my hand away she would not allow it. I wasn't going to try though, as she was taking me to Marjorie's house. It was only a few minutes' walk and we were in Sycamore Drive. My instinct was to run forward and run up to Marjorie's front door, but Mary would stop me. I had to contain my excitement for a few moments more.

The car was in the drive and there was a light on in the front room. Mary stopped and pressed the doorbell. A few seconds later the door opened and Marjorie was standing there.

'Jay' she exclaimed as she saw me.

'I found Jay walking at the edge of the town. Jay was lost, but told me this is where you lived.'

'Come in come in. Where have you been? They told me that you had run off.'

'I'll tell you everything, but please may I have a drink and something to eat first.'

'I'll need to tell them that you are safe and well. You are alright aren't you?'

'I'm just tired and hungry and thirsty. Please don't let them send me back.'

'I do need to tell them you are here. But I will hear what you have to say, before I let them do anything. Is that alright?'

I smiled at her. She took my hat and jacket off me. When she saw what I was wearing underneath and that was wet too, she took me upstairs and dried me off, before giving me new warm and dry clothes. Mary had gone on her way, but not before I thanked her for bringing me to Marjorie's house.

Half an hour later, Marjorie had made a phone call, but had told whoever she was speaking to that I was staying with her that night and that they should not come here until the morning. I had also had a hot drink of tea and Marjorie made me something to eat. I polished off everything on my plate. Then Marjorie took me through to the sitting room and sat me down on one of the chairs. She asked me to tell her everything that had happened, that made me run away from school several days before. I missed out nothing at all, as I told her exactly what had been happening in my life, at the children's home and at the school too. When I'd finished telling her, she gave me another drink and a biscuit, before asking me to go through everything just one more time, in case she had missed anything. This time she wrote notes as I told her, asking me to stop from time to time, so she could make more notes.

With that done, she took me up to my room and put me to bed. It was lovely to be in a warm bed, where I was comfy and safe. I wished I could stay with Marjorie forever, but I knew even before I drifted off to sleep, that I was not going to be able to do that. The next thing I knew, the sunlight was streaming through the windows and Marjorie was there in front of my eyes when I woke up.

Chapter 20 At Marjorie's house

Marjorie told me that there would be some people coming that day to see me. But she also said that I should not be worried. She was extremely concerned about what had gone on since I left her care, particularly moving to another district and my treatment in the children's home, spilling over to the school. She would not allow them to just take me away.

I was of course worried about who would come and what they would say, but I also had faith that I had come to the right place and Marjorie would protect me.

The first person to arrive was my old social worker. I had to show her some of the bruises I still had under my clothes. She was shocked at what she saw. She should have seen them a few days earlier. They were much better now than they were then. She asked me to tell her my story. She listened without interrupting. Marjorie was sitting near me, but did not say anything, other than when I'd finished, she said that I'd said exactly the same story to her.

Next to arrive was the social worker from where I'd been living. With the other two listening, I told her my story again and showed her my injuries. I could see that she knew she had missed things.

The next person to arrive was one of the supervisors from the children's home. She interrupted me all the way through the story and kept telling me that I was lying. At the end, she just stood up and says that she didn't know why they were wasting her time with my lies. I could see that the other three did not like this woman. The two social workers walked outside with her. They were gone for quite a long time. They came back in together. The woman from the home was not with them.

The last person to come and see me that day was a policeman. He was a big man, but he had a nice face and a nice smile. He told me that a lot of people were very worried about me when I ran away. I could have got myself in a worse position. He told me that if it ever happened again, and he didn't think it would, but if it ever did; then the place I should run to was the police station. They would help sort things out for me. That would be much safer than walking alone in the countryside, with no food or water for several days.

I agreed that I would do that. It never occurred to me I could do that before. Anyway, I just wanted to get away from that place and those people.

I'd thought that maybe the teachers from the school would have come to see me, but they didn't. They had been informed that I had been found.

It was a school day, but Marjorie didn't take me to school. She said that there were things that had to be sorted out. She gave me some lessons at home that day and for the next few days. No one else came to see me in that time. The social worker came to see us a couple of days later. She was going to bring my things, but when she got to the home, she found that the other children had slashed everything and there was nothing left to bring. She said to us both that it just proved that I was right and had been telling the truth. I would not be going back there. She said she was trying to find a good family, who would take me in for the long term. Marjorie has said that until they find that family, then I am going nowhere. I am staying with her and John for the time being.

It was the best part of three months before they found this family. I was hoping they wouldn't, but in my heart I knew that Marjorie and John could not bring me up for the next ten years. They said they are too old to do that and they were planning to move away anyway. That saddened me, but for them I was pleased.

In the end it was Bella and Kevin who asked to meet me. They hadn't intended to foster a child, but they heard about what had happened to me. They lived in the same town as Marjorie. In fact they only lived about two minutes' walk away, in Maple Drive. Someone had talked about Marjorie and me and they had thought about it and then decided they would meet me and see.

Bella was in her forties. She worked in the library and was quite a serious woman. Kevin was a carpenter and he worked for a company in the next town. He was also in his forties. He had more fun about him and he had a nice smile, like the policeman.

They met me at the play park one sunny afternoon. I liked Kevin straight away. He started to push me on the swings and he also made the roundabout go faster for me. Bella watched on and chatted to Marjorie. I think she was asking more things about how I was, but I didn't know. They came back with us to Marjorie's house for tea. I showed them my room and my things.

The next day the social worker was there to see us when we got home from school. She asked me what I thought about Bella and Kevin. I told her they were nice. She told me that they had an older son. He was 18 and he'd gone away to University. He wouldn't be there much of the time, but he might come back during the holidays. I told her that it was their house, so of course he comes home. I would just be glad if they gave me a home.

The good thing as far as I was concerned, is that it meant that I could stay at the same school I have been going to, St Johns. I would also be close to Marjorie, but I was not to call round there, unless I was told it was alright for me to do so. I sort of understood why they were saying that. They wanted Bella and Kevin to be the ones who looked after me.

The next few weeks seemed to race by. Bella and Kevin had a room just for me. They asked me how I would like it decorated. Then Kevin did that one weekend. They were of course very different from Marjorie and John. I was learning that everyone was different and that you have to accept that. They were very kind and although Bella was serious, she was also really good with me. After school, I had to walk to the library on my own. They said from the beginning that they would trust me to do that. For my part, I knew I needed them, so I did as I was told, pretty much all of the time.

The library was a fantastic place. I had of course been reading books at school and in the evenings, Marjorie listened to me reading. But the library had so many books and on so many subjects. I soon become involved in reading these, while I waited for Bella to finish for the day. I think they were worried about this part of the day, but I was happy being there reading and I could see that this made them happy too.

The months fly by and everything was going well. The only thing that changed was that the time came when Marjorie and John came round one day, to say they were moving away. I had thought that they were just going to move to another town, somewhere else in the country. But they told me they were emigrating. They were going to Australia to live, to be near their daughter and son-in-law and their grand-children. It was going to be odd for me not to have them there, but I was happy where I lived in Maple Drive.

I noticed that Bella and Kevin made things even more special for me, after Marjorie and John emigrated. They didn't have to. I knew I had landed on my feet there. They had been very good to take me into their home. I knew they didn't have to.

The months continued to fly by and then the years too. I moved on from the primary school to the secondary school. I continued to keep my head down and work hard. Marjorie taught me that first, but Bella and Kevin also instilled that discipline in me. I was not the brightest person in the class, but I did well enough. Soon I was in my last year at school.

Chapter 21 Moving on

My world more or less changed at the same time. I finished school in the summer, after my exams. The plan was that I would start University in the autumn. At the same time, the local authority said they were going to stop paying for my care, as I had reached the end of education at school. I would have grants to pay my way through University. That was fair enough. Bella and Kevin had said that I could still stay with them, but I would need to get a part-time job, so that I had my own money and could pay for my keep. That was fair enough and I did that as soon as I finished school. I was working in a local business three days a week during the summer, covering for when people went off on holiday. Everything was running smoothly and life was enjoyable, with the world at my feet.

Then it all changed in an instant. Kevin and Bella had gone out to see some friends one evening. I was staying at home, because I had a friend coming round. Bella and Kevin went off for the evening, but they never came home.

I had waited up for them, after my friend had walked home. They had said that they thought they might be home about midnight, so I waited up for them. It wasn't unusual for them to stay out at these particular friends later than that, so when they still hadn't arrived home again by a quarter to one, I went to my bed.

I was woken by two things happening simultaneously. The phone downstairs started to ring at about half past one and then the doorbell rang. I thought at first that maybe they had forgotten to take their door key. That had happened before, if only rarely. Of course that didn't then give me an answer as to whom might be on the phone.

I ran downstairs, in my dressing gown, and made for the door. I couldn't see who it was, but I could see a blue flashing light through the door glass. I asked who it was. They said it was the police. I opened the door, still with the chain on, and there were two policemen there, well a man and a woman actually.

'Do you need to answer that phone? The policewoman asked.

I had a sinking feeling in my stomach, but that deepened even further when I answered the phone. It was Bella and Kevin's son. He asked if they were there. I said no, but the police have just come to the door. He said a friend had rung him and told him there had been a fatal crash on a road near there. His first thought was that his parent's used that road frequently at night and he too had had a horrible feeling in his stomach.

The police had stepped into the hall by now and closed the front door. I looked at them as I was speaking on the phone. The policeman asked me who was on the other end of the phone. I told them. He put out his hand to take the phone, while the policewoman took me into the sitting room. There she broke the news to me, that Bella and Kevin had been killed, in a head on crash with a drunk driver. The drunk driver was killed too.

So as I said, things changed in my life at that point. I stayed in the house for a couple of weeks, but to be honest I couldn't face things. It also became apparent to me that their son was not too keen on me staying in the house on my own. Not for my safety, but more because he didn't want me in their house, without them being there anymore. I guess he thought I might go through their things. Anyway, I knew I would have to be moving on soon enough.

I contacted the social worker and she put me in touch with the University I was going to. They managed to find me digs there, that I would also be able to move into now and be able to stay in during the holidays. I borrowed a big suitcase, which I was told I could keep and more or less got all of my belongings in it.

It was a sad day when I moved out of their house. I had written to Marjorie a couple of times over the years. At first she had replied, but I hadn't heard from her for over three years now. Maybe something had happened to her too. So although I wrote her a letter telling her what had transpired, I really didn't expect to get a reply from her. In the letter I gave her my new address.

So I had now got no one left in my life from my growing up years. I hadn't heard from my Dad since he was taken away by the police and I hadn't heard from my Mum since she hit me and they put me into care. Care has now all but finished. The social worker has said that she was there if I needed to ask anything, but in essence she was no longer officially in charge of me. I was an adult now.

The journey to my university digs was uneventful. My room was in one of the halls. Even though it was summer, there were other students there, as they hold summer courses. I managed to get a part time job. More than ever now, I was aware that I had to stand on my own two feet.

The summer ended and the new intake, the rest of the students coming to university for their first year, joined me.

I worked reasonably hard during my first year and made it to the summer, quite pleased with how I was coping with things. I stayed over in the digs and picked up some extra hours work to keep me busy and to keep me fed. The grant I had was insufficient to live on and I was by far the poorest of my close friends.

At the start of the second year, for some reason which I did not understand, someone started rumours about me and my behaviour. I think it might have started after I shunned someone, who to be quite honest I didn't like. They then started telling people I had done things that I hadn't done. It even spread to the lecturers in my classes. I strenuously denied it as lies, but even my close friends were taken in by it. Maybe they were afraid of having the same done to them if they sided with me; I don't know.

I lasted to Christmas, but by then it was becoming impossible for me to go anywhere without people staring at me, pointing at me, or even making comments to me that weren't nice at all. I went to the student's union, but they couldn't help. And when I complained officially to them, nor could the University. The person I had upset had good connections, or at least their parents had. They had done a good job of ruining my reputation and my life there. It was suggested that maybe I should consider moving to another university, but they said if I did so, I should make sure that I didn't tell anyone where I was going to.

I did approach another couple of universities, but they weren't keen for me to move there in the middle of my course.

Eventually I took the only course of action that I thought I had open for me to take. I packed my bags and moved away. I didn't tell anyone I was going. I waited until there was the big Christmas Ball and then quickly packed my stuff. I walked down from my digs to the nearest call box outside of the university grounds and called for a taxi, to take me to the station. I had been working hard since I got to university and had put by whatever money I hadn't spent on living costs. It wasn't much I'd saved, but it was enough for me to get to London and hopefully find somewhere to live and work. I had no idea how I was going to do that, but I was sure I would find a way when I got there.

The taxi dropped me off. Unfortunately I was too late to catch a train that evening, so I had no choice other than to spend the night in the waiting room and catch the first train in the morning. It was not ideal, but I had no choice.

I arrived in London about lunchtime the next day. I was a little tired, as I didn't get much sleep overnight. All I needed to do was to find somewhere to stay.

Chapter 22 London

I don't know how I did it. I suddenly realised just how out of my depth I was. Here I was at a railway station, in a place I had never been before. I had my case with me, of course, which wasn't making my task any easier. I looked around me, trying to grasp some inspiration from mid-air. I had thought about this moment on the journey down to there. But as I didn't know what I was going to find, I didn't get anywhere.

Something told me that I would have a better chance of finding a solution to my problem there in the station, rather than start wandering round the streets; streets that I didn't know.

'I've been watching you' a voice startles me out of where I was in my thoughts.

'I beg your pardon?'

'I said I've been watching you.'

In front of me was a man, maybe in his early thirties. He was well dressed and had a clean cut look to him. He was wearing a smart raincoat and I could see he was wearing a suit under that. He was carrying a briefcase in one hand and an umbrella in the other.

I'm not sure what he was meaning or wanting me to say. I think he could see the confusion on my face. He continued to talk to me.

'I recognise the look of someone arriving in London, when they have never been here before. I also think that you have nowhere planned to go.'

I felt my head nodding as he said this. He smiled at me, as he knew he had got this right.

'When I saw you standing there, looking round, it took me right back to the time I arrived here with a suitcase and nowhere to go. That was many years ago now. But on that day as I stood there, someone walked up to me and said what I have just said to you.'

'I see' is all I managed to reply.

'It seems a good idea when you set out on the journey here, but when you get here, you realise the vastness of the task you have set yourself. Anyway, I can't stop for long, as I have got a meeting in Piccadilly.'

'Oh ok.' I thought for a second he had just stopped to tell me his tale and then he was going to march away again. I was wrong.

'Back when I was in your position, the person who walked up to me helped me find somewhere to stay. If they hadn't done that, then I hate to think where I might have ended up on the day. I am going to try to do the same for you today.'

That comment perked me up. I grasped the opportunity with both hands.

'That's good of you. I really appreciate you taking the time to help me.'

'I'm sure that one day you'll do the same to someone else who arrives here. We need to go over to the telephone kiosks over there. What we need is a telephone directory.'

I looked over to where he was pointing and I could see a long line of telephone kiosks. I was happy enough to walk over there with him. When we got there, we stopped outside one and he went in, to look at the telephone directory in there. He couldn't bring it out to show me, as it was tied in there. He started to flick through the pages and then he stopped. He ran his finger down the column and then it came to a stop. He took a coin out of his pocket and put it in the telephone. He then dialled a number. He drummed his fingers on the directory while he waited for the call to be answered. Eventually it was and he asked if they had any room for me. The answer was a short no. He put the phone down again.

'They're full, but she said to try another two. I have their numbers here.'

The first one was also full, but with the next one we had some luck. He turned quickly and asked my name. I gave it to him. He asked another couple of questions and then he put the phone down. He opened up his briefcase and took out a notepad and pen. He quickly scribbled down some information and then tore the sheet off and handed it to me.

'I've really got to rush. I don't mean to be rude. I've written it all down here for you. I hope you can read my writing. My name is Robert. And you're Jay.'

I took the piece of paper he was handing to me.

'Thank you Robert. It is very kind of you to do this for me.'

'You're welcome. I must go now.'

At which he turned and walked very quickly away, towards the underground entrance. I watched him go, knowing it is most unlikely I would ever see him again. Once he had disappeared from my view, I looked down at the piece of paper in my hand. It hadn't got a lot written on it, but it was enough for what I needed.

'The House, 95 Denmark Hill, Camberwell. £5 + per week, including board and lodging. Mrs Downs.'

That was the sum of what information I had. I had no idea where Camberwell was, but I would be able to find out about that somehow. I heard him tell Mrs Downs my name and he said to her that I would be there that afternoon. I needed to find out how far it was I had to go. I saw the information desk in the middle of the concourse. There was a queue, but it didn't take long for my turn to come. The information I was given was that I needed take the northern line south, to Elephant and Castle. Then from there, I needed to catch a bus to Camberwell. The 35 or 45, she thought, were the ones I needed, but I best check when I got there.

It took me a while to get to grips with the underground system (the tube), but I got on the right train and soon I was at Elephant and Castle. I went outside and crossed over the road, to where I could see some bus stops. I asked someone who was waiting for a bus, if this was the place to catch one to Denmark Hill. It was, so I waited with them and when the bus arrived, I put my case in the luggage space and sat on the bench near the door, so I could still see it.

It is only a couple of miles to Camberwell and the start of Denmark Hill. I got off when the conductor told me we were there. As it turned out, I was at the bottom of Denmark Hill and I had a bit of a walk up to number 95. When I got there, I was surprised to see that it was a big house, probably Victorian. It looked as if it has seen better days, but I was not bothered about that. I would just be glad to have a room and a roof over my head.

As I walked up to the door, it was opened and a matronly woman came out and smiled at me. I assumed this was Mrs Downs. That was confirmed.

She welcomed me in and told me to leave my case in the hall, while she showed me around. On the ground floor, there was a huge television room. Next to that and facing the back garden was a games room, with a darts board and a table tennis table. Next to that was a study. There were also a couple of bedrooms on that floor. We went upstairs to the first landing. There was a big bathroom and six large bedrooms. Some rooms had two beds in, some three and some four. We went up another floor. There were just two bedrooms and a bathroom that she showed me up there. The rest of the rooms were her quarters. Both of the bedrooms on this floor had three beds in. She said that the room at the back was mine. I would be the only one in there for now, until more people came to stay.

She then took me all the way down to the basement. This was where the kitchen was and the dining area. She said that I would get breakfast every day and an evening meal. At weekends I would get lunch too. I got all this for the princely sum of £5.50p. She handed me the front door key.

We went upstairs again and I took my case up the stairs to my room. I took a minute or two deciding which bed I was going to have. With that done, I started to unpack my stuff into the wardrobe and chest of drawers by my bed.

Chapter 23 London

I had of course one major problem that I had to overcome. I needed to do something to earn some money. Of course I gave up the job I did have, when I decided to move there. George, who was my boss, had given me a written reference. He said that he would give me another reference, if prospective employers needed to contact him directly.

That was something I was going to have to leave until the next day. I was hoping Mrs Downs, or maybe some of the other residents, might be able to point me in the right direction.

I wandered down to the common room, but there was no one there, so I decided that I would take a walk outside and investigate the local area a bit, in the time I had before dinner.

I got back about an hour later, to find there were now a few people about. Introductions were made. There were about ten of us who went down, when it was time for dinner. There were five male and five female residents there. The others 6 or 7 who haven't come for dinner yet were all male. They tell me that it used to be an all-male hostel, but because of the pressures of keeping the place going and not being able to keep the hostel full enough to pay for its ongoing needs, they started taking women in a couple of years ago.

Most of us were about the same age, but there were two much older ones. They both worked in the hospitals that were close by. One of the others there; was a baker from Newcastle. There was also someone who worked for the customs office at Heathrow. The rest all worked in the city, in offices and shops. They all said they would ask if there were any jobs going, when they went in the next day. I have worked in an office with the employer I just left. I also did pretty much whatever needed doing in the business too. I thought I was flexible in my work skills.

After dinner, when we had all tidied up and Mrs Downs had gone up to her quarters, some of us went and sat in the common room. One of the older ones approached me and said he thought I should go round to the hospitals in the morning and try to find work there. He was an ambulance man. He said there are always vacancies for different sorts of jobs. It depended on what I wanted to do. I guessed what he was saying was, that if I needed any job, then I would probably be able to pick one up quite easily. But if on the other hand I was looking for a career, then it would take longer and of course it would depend on what experience I have in the respective areas.

He then told me that he would give me some advice. He thought that the advice was good, but he said obviously it was up to me if I took his advice. I listened, because I genuinely not only wanted a job, but wanted something I could depend on and progress with over the years. He said that what I should do; is make an appointment with the personnel department at the hospital. It would probably be quite quick, so I was not to worry if it took a day or two before they saw me. Then when I did go, I should tell them what department or type of job I was interested in, but also that I was willing to do any job, until such time as I could be considered for the job I wanted to get. He gave me the name of one of the women who worked in personnel. He told me to tell her that he knows me and I was staying here where he stayed.

I thanked him and he said he was going out to the pub for a pint, if I wanted to join him. I thanked him for the offer, but I had to refuse, as I needed to eek what money I had out, until I had an income again. He understood.

One or two others came home and joined us in the common room. They were a friendly bunch and it looked like I had landed on my feet there. By the time I went to bed, I felt as if I belonged there and almost as if I had been there for quite a long time.

The morning was very different again. Breakfast was available from 7 o'clock. By the time I got down there just after 8 o'clock, I was alone in the canteen. Also there was not much left, as it would appear I was the last one down. There was enough for me though and Mrs Downs came in just as I was finishing up. She confirmed I was the last one down. Everyone else had gone off to work. I gave her a hand to clear the things away. She asked what I had planned for the day. I told her that the others were asking around for me at their places of work and that Andy had suggested I go round to the hospitals and try there. She thought that was a good idea.

I paid her for my first two weeks lodgings, before I went back upstairs to get ready to go round to the hospital. Well the one that Andy worked for was the one I decided to try first. Mrs Downs had told me how to get there, something that Andy had assumed I already knew.

I put on my best clothes and made my way round to the hospital. I made my appointment, which was for the next day. I was pleased at that and with the fact that Andy had already been up there to speak to them about me too.

The time came around quickly on the next day. I wasn't sure which department I should go for, but she was very good. She asked me what jobs I have done and enjoyed, before then deciding what departments would be within my scope. She said it might take a day or two before she saw if there are any vacancies due to come up, but in the meantime she said there were always vacancies for porters. She rang down and after I had filled in a couple of forms, she sent me down to the porters department to work there. They were glad to see a new face, as they had been very understaffed for a couple of weeks. I was told where most patients go when a porter is involved. They sent me off to get my bearings and find out where the wards, A & E, x-ray and theatre were. Half an hour later I was back and they sent me on my first job. I was so excited at the prospect of working there. I was also pleased that I had some work and therefore I would have an income. I wouldn't have to worry about how I was going to keep the roof over my head.

I probably took a bit longer than the other porters would on that first day, but part of that was that everywhere I went, I had to introduce myself. It just took a little longer than it maybe should have done, but no one complained. In fact it was the opposite; they were pleased that I was there. I was really surprised when the finishing time came. The head porter told me that I had come to the end of my shift. He then asked me into the office, to have a chat me with him. He told me I had nothing to worry about. He was really pleased with how I had worked that day. He said he would like to keep me, but understood he might lose me to another department. Funnily enough I had really felt at home that day. He asked me if I would be alright to work every day for the next few days. He said they have been so short staffed, that no one had had a day off that week. There were three new porters starting the next day. If I was confident enough, he would get me to take them quickly round the hospital, to show them where the departments and wards were. I willingly agreed to do so.

When I got home, Andy asked how I had got along. He was really pleased for me. I told him I had really enjoyed it and I would almost feel a bit guilty if I then left them in the next week or so. He gave me another piece of advice. Again it was up to me whether I took it or not. Why didn't I go up to personnel and say that I would stay with the porters for a while, before going to another department.

That is what I did, which was received well. In fact I think it was received better than if I'd said I wanted to go to another department, as soon as a job became available. The head porter was pleased too and so that was where I spent my first year in London. Things only changed then because, as is the case in my life and most peoples; nothing lasts forever. The numbers staying at the house had not improved. They decided to close it.

Part 3
Chapter 24 David Petrich

My parents came to England at the start of the Second World War. My father was a pilot in the RAF. He used to do reconnaissance flying. My mother worked at the same airfield, as a cook in the canteen. They were ever so grateful to this country for taking them in and were determined to do their bit to defeat the aggressive forces that had invaded and overrun their country, Poland.

My sister was born at the end of the war. My parents had thought that is was not right to try to start a family while the war was going on and there was a chance that one or both parents might not survive the war. Or, of course, they could have been on the losing side and they didn't want to bring a child into that arena either.

Thankfully the war ended in 1945 and my mother finished straight away, but my father remained in the RAF for a further year, until he too was demobbed. There was hardly any discussion at all, so they told us as we grew up, as to whether they would stay in England, or go back to their native Poland. They said they could not face going back to the place where they lost so many family members and friends. They were welcomed here when they came and they are happy to stay and have their family here in England.

Where they lived was dictated, as is always the case, by where they could get work. My father was an engineer by trade and he soon found a job in an engineering factory that was starting up, near one of the big car plants. They were hoping to make components for the car industry. As such they were already living in the area, but had to move house. The house they had rented was needed back by the owner for his family. My mother then managed to get a job, working in the canteen at one of the local schools.

They spent the first few years getting on their feet. The engineering factory had many ups and downs during that period, which that industry quite often does anyway. Things were tight after the war and it took time for the country to return to a peaceful living. So it was as we turned into the 1950's, that my older sister was born. My mother continued to work at the school after Anna was born. Even though she wasn't a well-baby, they needed her wages. They had decided to buy their house, just before my Mother got pregnant with Anna. My father's income was a bit variable, as when things were tight they did not get full pay. It was that, or they might lose their jobs and it was thought to be better to take a wage cut to get through the sticky periods, than to not have a job at all.

Luckily there is a strong community feeling amongst the Polish families who had stayed in England after the war. They pulled together and looked after each other's children, so that the families could stay in work. My mother and father gave their share of this, by helping out at weekends for the families who helped my mother be able to keep working, even after having Anna.

They waited three years after Anna was born, before I was born in 1953. Even with two children under school age, my mother kept working at the school.

I am David Petrich. We were a happy family and we grew up together. Things were easier for my parents once we both went to school. Anna was always the more confident one. She would be out there, trying this and that. I was more for my own company. I used to stay at home, when I was not at school. I had some friends I would play with at school, but I didn't transfer that friendship to playing with those same friends out of school.

I would spend my time at home, playing with my metal construction Meccano set, or my dinky toys. I was also the one to help around the house. I would do all the chores that needed doing and could be found in the kitchen or around the house, helping my mother. Or outside in the garden helping my father with the vegetable plot, or cutting the grass or weeding the flower beds. I helped a bit more, I think, because Anna was always off somewhere with her friends. She made excuses for her not doing her chores around the house. My parents didn't mind, as they said they wanted her to do what she wanted to. I think they saw the fact that I was a home child by my actions, was an indication that I was achieving my happiness. I guess it is just that Anna and I had totally different characters. Would I say what I did made me happy, well I really don't know. I certainly wasn't unhappy, but I think I thought of it in the way that I had to pick up the slack that Anna left, by not being there to do things.

Dinner was always on the table when my father got in from work. My mother never seemed to stop working. If she wasn't at work, then she was working in the house, to keep us all going. They were strong on discipline too. Anna was her own worst enemy in that respect. Whatever they said or told her to do, she always chose her own actions and reaped the consequence of those actions. My mother was the stronger disciplinarian. Anna was on the end of her dishing out punishment all too often. I, on the other hand, very rarely felt the wrath of my mother's hand, or my father's, although he rarely dished out the punishment.

I was never top of the class at school, but I also wasn't anything like the worst in any of the lessons I took. Physically I wasn't the strongest, and when it came to sports and physical education, I definitely wasn't amongst the most talented individuals in the school, or my class. That of course was the absolute opposite of my sister, who not only was very good academically, but was also talented at any sport she chose to turn her hand to.

I didn't mind and still tried my best at whatever I attempted to do at school. I made my way through primary school and into secondary school. I had no idea what I was going to do when I finished school and even when I made my choices, I didn't have a clue as to what subjects I might need, to follow my career path. Anna, on the other hand, knew exactly what she wanted to do and was always going achieve everything she aimed at.

When I was half way through secondary school, Anna finished school and went off to University. Of course she chose to go to a University away from where we live. It was at that time I think I became even more trapped at home than I think I had ever imagined. I don't think my parents ever intended things to be that way, but events dealt their hand to make that happen.

Anna went away in the September and almost immediately my mother started to act differently. At first I just thought that she was missing Anna, but as the weeks went by, it became obvious that there was something else amiss. My father was going through a stage when things were really busy at work, so he was working all hours to get things done there. I was the one who was in the firing line for what was going on with my mother. I tried to tell my father that something was wrong, but he just said she was missing Anna and for me not to worry.

It was early in the December that my mother was sent home from work, not well. She went to see the doctor, but he could only send her for more tests. My father by now was on side that something was wrong, but his work needs were still very high. So he asked me to do more around the house, to help get the jobs done.

What I noticed straight away was that the more jobs I took on board, the less my mother did. She was still off work and there was little prospect of that situation changing. Even when Anna came back briefly over the Christmas holidays, my mother did not pick up at all. Anna being Anna, she kept to doing what she wanted and was rarely round the house anyway. She went back to university in the New Year and I was left there, with my mother in general decline. By early spring she was sometimes not getting out of bed some days.

Chapter 25 David Petrich

By the time I was finishing school, my mother was more or less housebound. She had been to countless appointments at the hospital, but they had not been able to come up with any firm diagnosis. She had lost her job a while back, having been off work for over a year, before they had to let her go. My father was frustrated about the situation too. Work for him had been going really well and that had put even more pressure on me in the house at home. With his work requiring him to now go away at times, it meant I was the only person there to look after my mother. That situation wasn't helped by the fact that she had alienated virtually all of their friends, who had originally come at times to look after her.

Anna came home less and less as the situation deteriorated. She was well and truly getting on with her life. I suppose I could have pushed that I had a right to get on with my life too, but I didn't. I did have, at one time, ambition to follow her course of action and go to University. But when the subject came up at home, my father said he thought I would be better following him into engineering. What he meant by that was that he wanted me to take an apprenticeship and start at the bottom. Basically all I would ever be is a manual worker, whereas he was a technical engineer, deeply involved in design.

I did put up a protest, but it wasn't a strong enough one. So as soon as I finished school, I took up an apprenticeship at the same engineering firm he worked for. He arranged for me to have extra breaks, so that I could go home twice a day to look after my mother.

This arrangement continued right into my thirties, when my father retired. To be honest he did not want to, but the situation was forced on him. There had been a takeover at the engineering company and he had a fall out with the new management. Things escalated and either they made it really awkward for him, by changing the team and the department he worked for, or maybe it was that he made things hard for himself. Either way, it resulted in him taking early retirement. It wasn't that much early, maybe a couple of years or so at most.

It hit him hard and he took to the bottle in the evenings. He also came to realise what hard work it was looking after my mother and keeping the house going. That was something that had come my way more each year. Anna hadn't been home in a few years, as she couldn't cope with how they were at home. She was off here, there and everywhere with her job and her friends. She didn't marry and she never mentioned anyone else being in her life. She talked of friends and the like, but not of anyone close who might share her life.

For the first time in my working life, I managed to put in a full working day like any other worker. It didn't help my prospects any at all, as I had already been shelved on the same job for years. I was a bit surprised that they kept me on when my father retired, but then I don't think I am the same sort of contentious person that he was at work. I am a steady worker. I get what I have to get done at a good pace and I believe the quality of my work is the same, or maybe even better than most. I get on well with my work colleagues. In fact I think they talk to me more now that my father doesn't work there anymore.

The first year after his retirement was probably the hardest in the house. I think he got really annoyed at my mother for being the way she was all the time. When she did get out of bed, all she would do is sit in a chair in the living room and stare at the television screen. She took her medication and ate what little food she needed to keep her going. She had become remarkably fussy about what foods she would eat. I had been dealing with that for years, but my father did not understand her. We did what we have done for years and that is to make her a meal and then we would have something different.

I very rarely went out socially. I certainly never had a relationship with a woman. I never got the opportunity to go out to find one. I don't think I would even know how to. The only times I did go out, were when the works had a do, which they did every Christmas. Occasionally one of my colleagues would have a special do as well and we would all go out to a pub somewhere. But that was not a common occurrence.

About five years after my father had retired, we found my mother dead in her bed one morning. They had slept in separate rooms for the past twenty years at least, ever since she became ill. Of course we had the police come round. A post mortem was done, but it was ruled that she had died of natural causes. The funeral was a quiet affair, as had been her wish. Anna came home for the funeral and beside my father, her and me; there were only maybe a dozen others who attended. She had specifically requested that there were only a maximum of twenty people attend.

After that my father came a bit more to life. I would get home in the evening, quite often to find that he was not at home. I tried asking him where he was going, but he didn't tell me. He was always a bit evasive. I did wonder if he was visiting a woman somewhere and that he was embarrassed to say so. Anyway that stopped some months later as suddenly as it had started, which also led me to believe I had been right.

He busied himself in the garden after that. He made the vegetable plot bigger and even got rid of the flower beds, so he could grow more. He would spend hours out there, digging and weeding. If he wasn't doing that, then he was busying himself with seeds and whatever, in the greenhouse. He appeared to be quite content. But he also became quite withdrawn. At first one or two of his old work colleagues would come round once a week to play cards, but that stopped after a while. I have no idea why, as I kept out of the way when he had his friends round. All I know is that at first there were more who would come round and then they dropped off, one by one. Then one day, no one came round. He was there ready and waiting, but no one came and no one came ever again.

He had rarely gone out before that, but now the only time he would go out, was when he needed to get something for the garden. I was the one who did the food shopping.

After mother died, Anna did come back home a couple of times, but she soon tired of that and she soon went back to her own life and came maybe once a year.

One day I was at work and father had decided that he was going to spend the day in the garden. There was nothing new in that, but for some reason he decided that he was going to dig up part of the lawn and add that area to his vegetable plot. The ground was very hard and he must have overdone it. All I knew was that I got a telephone call at work, from one of my neighbours, to say that she had seen him lying on the ground. When she went to see if he was alright, she found that he had had a heart attack. He had been taken to hospital.

He was in there for a few weeks before he came home again. At first the district nurse would call in daily to see him, but he didn't like that. So it wasn't long before he was left to his own devices again. He had been told to take it easy, but that didn't stop him, several months later, going out into the garden again and having another go at converting the lawn to vegetable plot. He had another heart attack and this one was much more serious. He spent many months in hospital before coming home. I cut my working day down again and somehow I managed to keep him at home and looked after. He wasn't in any state to go out to work in the garden anymore.

Chapter 26 David Petrich

Things went on like that for two or three years. Really he should have had more carers, but he was quite an awkward person. He should have had someone there all the time, but he was totally resistant to that. He would not even hear of having someone else coming in to do jobs in the house. That of course meant that I had to do everything. Ideally he would have liked for me to give up working, but I didn't, for several reasons. Mainly, for my sanity, I needed to get away from the house and him. I couldn't bear to be trapped in there with him, day after day. It was bad enough at the weekends when I wasn't working. I did the food shopping and any other shopping that needed to be done on Saturdays.

Although he couldn't do his beloved garden any more, that did not stop him insisting that it still be looked after properly. He would sit by the window, looking out on it for hours on end. I didn't mind doing the garden for him, as it kept me busy and stopped him moaning at me.

Moaning was something that he had become really good at. From dawn to dusk and beyond, he would moan about something. It became quite wearing at times. Anna, as I said, came a few times after his second heart attack, but he as good as drove her away, by his comments to her when she did come.

She apologised to me each time she came and said she would try to come more often, to support me in his care. I don't think she did try that hard, because if anything the visits became scarcer. She would ring me occasionally, but when I asked him if he wanted to speak to Anna, he always said no. Anna did say on more than one occasion that she would make it up to me. I didn't know what she meant by that.

Once or twice he became so unwell that I had no other choice but to call the ambulance. He resisted their attempts to take him back to the hospital though. There was little they could do if he wouldn't go. Sometimes I think he just wanted to die, but he never said as much.

Then inevitably one day he had another heart attack. As circumstances would have it, I was at work when it must have happened. I found him slumped in his chair, by the window overlooking the garden. It was easy to see that he was past help. I had to phone the police anyway and the ambulance. They confirmed what I already knew, that he had died from another heart attack. In many ways it was a blessing for us all. I don't believe he suffered, at least at the end it must have been pretty swift.

He must have suffered mentally prior to that, frustrated that he could not do the things he loved to do.

For my part, I was released from caring duties for the first time in nearly forty years. Anna came home as soon as she heard and she helped me clear his things. We had cleared most of my mother's things after she had died. I cleared out just about everything there was. Those few bits that I decided to keep, I put in the cupboard in the living room. Anna said that she didn't want any of it at all. There wasn't much that was worth having. They weren't ones for ornaments or anything like that.

The numbers were again limited when it came to the time for the funeral. This time it was more that the people who had known him were no longer around, either having died or moved away. A couple of my colleagues came from work, out of respect to me and Anna, more than to him.

When that was all done and dusted, we went through the legal process of sorting out his assets.

Anna said that although he had left everything equally between us; that that wasn't fair, as I have stayed at home all my life to look after them. She insisted on signing over the house to me, which was very kind. We then split his money, after all the bills were paid. I offered her a bigger share of that, but she wouldn't have it. In fact she said she didn't need any of it really, as she has done quite well for herself over the years. I am still not sure what she does. I did insist though that she have half of the money. Mother and father had not been frivolous with their money over the years. In fact they had always been very careful with their money. When we divided what was left after probate, we had in the region of £100,000 each. I too have been careful and other than the car I run, I have not had much to spend my money on over the years, so I have savings too.

Things never stay the same for long in my family. I had tried to get increased hours again at work, but they said there was no money to do that at present. I spent my time putting the garden back to its original state, with lawns and flowerbeds and just a small vegetable plot. I started to feel quite alone, but when I did try to do something about that and go to some groups for singles, I didn't have any luck in finding anyone who was interested in having any sort of relationship with me. I did ask why and one very blunt lady told me that I was boring. I think it must be true, as when I asked others if I was; one or two of them did say that I had very limited conversation. It was only a matter of time before I stopped going to these places and resigned myself that I would always be living alone.

There was little for Anna to visit for any more and the most I ever got from her was a card on my birthday and a card at Christmas. We had long ago stopped giving each other presents. I did try ringing her every few weeks, when she hadn't rung me, but she was never in on the number she gave me. I would leave a message on the answerphone, but she wouldn't ring back very often.

Maybe three years after our father died, the police turned up on my doorstep one evening. Anna had been found dead in her flat. She had been there for a few days before anyone found her. They said that she had died of a drug overdose. I never even knew that she took drugs. She had never said or indicated that she had. It was only at that time, that I realised how little I knew about my sister Anna.

When I went to her flat, I was surprised by how nice it was and so tidy. Her papers were all stored neatly in a desk, in the corner of her living room. She must have had a pretty good job and been well paid. She worked for an insurance company. I never knew that before.

She had indicated which funeral director should be used in the event of her death. That was the one close to where she lived. The service was short and one of her work colleagues spoke about her. I did not know what to say anyway and it seemed appropriate that someone who knew her better than I did; spoke. What surprised me was the numbers who turned up for the funeral. She must have been a really popular person. The other thing that surprised me; was that no one was aware she took drugs.

Anna left everything to me. She had not had a relationship and she had not had any children. Her friends said she was a fun loving person, but that she never let anyone get anywhere close to her, emotionally. That surprised me some about her.

The probate was dealt with by her firm's solicitors. They sold her flat, but only after asking if I wanted to keep it. They gathered in all her assets and paid the tax due. She had also got a life policy with the firm she worked for. By the time all the assets were gathered and the tax paid, I was sent a cheque which made my eyes open really wide. It ran into seven figures, which I never expected. The cheque I received was to the value of just under £1,500,000. It is just a shame I have no one to share my life with and share my money with.

Chapter 27 David Petrich

I made an effort to smarten up the house. I could well afford it. I was tempted initially to give up work, but as it was my only real valuable contact with other people, I decided that I couldn't afford to. It is only at work that I actually have any conversations with anyone. If I give that up, then I will really be totally alone.

I spent quite a long time going round the furniture stores before I bought anything. I then got someone in to redecorate the entire house. Someone at work recommended the decorator and he was very good. He was a quick worker and tidy too. I arranged through him to clear the furniture I didn't want any more, before my new furniture arrived. I then realised that the kitchen and bathroom looked shabby compared to the rest of the house, so he then replaced them with more modern things, in my opinion. It probably wouldn't have been to everyone's taste, but I liked it and that was all that mattered to me.

I replaced my car with a nice model and booked a coach holiday. I had thought about going abroad on a package holiday, but the thought of being abroad and on my own didn't appeal to me. I enjoyed the coach holiday, even though it was only a week long and the weather could have been kinder to us. But the Lochs and Glens tour was a wonderful experience, going through some beautiful countryside. Most of the people were friendly, but again although they were polite to me, I couldn't say that I made new friends on the trip.

When I came home, I knew I needed to do something, to keep me interested in living. I was also hoping that if I did something, it might make me a more interesting person to others. I suppose I still haven't totally given up on myself.

It took me a little while to find what I was looking for to do. Of course when I did find it, I also realised that it would have been so much easier at least to start with, if my parents had still been alive. I have decided to try to research my family history. What little I do have left of my parents things are in the cupboard in the living room. I am sure that I didn't throw away any papers that might be useful to me now. I also can't remember seeing many, if any, papers about our family history when I put them in there. I don't even have my sister left alive to ask.

I realise before I start that this might be quite a tough ask. I do remember that when we were young, that neither my mother nor my father talked about Poland. They didn't talk about the circumstances that made them come to England and I can never remember them talking about their childhoods. It wasn't that we didn't ask, but rather that they didn't want to talk about it.

I was quite excited as I emptied the entire contents of the cupboard onto the living room carpet. I found a few things, but not a lot. Their birth certificates were not there. I knew that already, as I had tried to find them before. What I did find was more about my father than my mother. There were a few things relating to his time in the RAF. The most interesting being his log book, with his flying hours. I spent some time reading through it, not that it helped me in my quest for family information about him.

There was precious little about my mother, other than the one main piece of paperwork that joined them together, their marriage certificate. But that was all it was. As far as giving me information to track down, there was zero.

I made a note of what paperwork there was, before packing it all away in the cupboard again. Most of the paperwork concerned their time in England. What I had wanted; was paperwork that would lead me to their life in Poland. I have to admit being a bit lost at this stage, as to how I progress a bit from where I currently am. The answer was obvious when it was given to me, but it took someone online to give me the clue before I ever thought it.

I found that there were genealogy websites in Poland, but the information I have to hand is not enough, in my opinion, to get started on that yet. But that wasn't what I was told by this person online. It was much simpler than that. My father had been in the RAF and it was suggested to me; that that should be my starting place for information about him. I really should have thought of that myself.

The first problem I encountered was that the airfield that my father and mother had been stationed at was no longer a working airfield, well not for the RAF anyway. It is still used by a flying club. Anyway I was pointed by them in the right direction. It took time for me to actually speak to the right person, but that was down to me. If I had been a bit cleverer, I would have got there sooner.

There was little information about my mother. Technically she hadn't been in the RAF, but employed to work in the kitchen, as a civilian. But as far as my father was concerned, they at least had some information that I hadn't got.

They had a record of where he had been born and where in Poland he had lived. They had note of his engineering qualifications and of his flight training. But what they didn't have; was information about his family. There was no information about who his parents were, but I did have an address in Poland, where my parents used to live.

I still didn't feel I had enough information to go on a genealogy site, but I tried anyway. It is not helped by the fact that I am not very proficient at searching online. It is not something that comes naturally to me and I really do struggle. I don't think there is anyone I can ask to help me with this.

So what I end up doing, is taking a trip to Poland. It is one that has been organised by Polish families in England. For the first time I am actually talking to other people who are trying to track down what happened to their families, when they have precious little information. I have to say though that most of them are further ahead than I am with their search. Also I am the only person who is travelling alone. But the really good thing about this trip, is that the organisers have arranged that when we get to Warsaw, that we will be allocated a researcher, to help us find as much as we can about our family history.

The trip was a successful one and when I returned home, I had made huge strides in finding more about my parent's history. I also have the resources of the researcher I used when I was there. There will be a cost to this, but that doesn't bother me. I need the help to be honest and I am not short of money.

Over the ensuing months I make quite a lot of progress with my family history. I feel I have achieved quite a lot and the more I find out about it, the more I get the urge inside of me that I might actually like to live in Poland. As the months go by this feeling grows. I talk about it to my colleagues at work. In fact I become quite consumed by the idea.

Then one day I become ill at work. It is nothing that they can diagnose straight away, but over a period of just a few months, I find it increasingly hard to do my work and as a result, I have to take more and more time off sick. This puts paid to any plans I may have of moving, for the time being. The doctors are hopeful that I might get better, but I then take another turn for the worse. I spend a couple of weeks in hospital, before I am well enough to come home again. My doctor comes to visit me a few days later, along with a health worker. It is the health worker who asks me something I should have thought about before, but to be honest I have done nothing about, up to now. Do I have a will? The answer is that I do not. My parents had a will and Anna had a will, but I do not. They all had someone they wanted to leave their possessions to; I do not. It is suggested that it would be a good thing if I make one, otherwise I will end up intestate. It is better that what I leave when I die goes to where I want it to, rather than the state, if they can't find any living relatives. Unfortunately that is the one fact that my genealogy search has thrown up so far. I do not have any living relatives. There probably are some very distant ones, but we haven't uncovered them yet, if they are there to be discovered.

So I make my will with a local solicitor, leaving my possessions to some different charities. The solicitor says he will send my copy of the will through the post to me.

Chapter 28 David Petrich and Jay

I don't receive anything for well over a week, but I am not too bothered. I am managing by myself at home, but I know that there will be areas where I am going to need some help. For example, I don't feel well enough to go out and do my shopping and actually walk around the supermarket. Thankfully the people in the local corner shop have been quite good and have delivered the basics for me, when I have rung them up. But that is not going to be a long term solution.

I have to admit that I find it most frustrating that at the very point in my life when I am free of all the constraints that have shackled me throughout my life, I am now unable, health wise, to be able to take full advantage. I am interrupted in my thoughts by the doorbell sounding. I lift myself slowly and for some reason today, painfully, out of my chair. The doorbell sounds again before I am even in the hall. But it has taken me the best part of a minute to get that far. I call out that I am on my way. I can't see who is out there, as it is dark outside. When I switch on the outside light, or at least when I try to; I remember that the bulb has blown. I haven't felt the energy to get round to replacing it.

'Who is it?' I ask through the closed door.

'My name is Jay' the reply is instant.

I don't know a Jay, but then I don't know many people. I hope this person isn't going to try to sell me something. It isn't late as such; it is just the time of year that has made it dark at this time, just gone 6 o'clock.

I open the door. The light from the hall floods out of the front door and onto the person standing there.

They are about 5 feet 9 inches tall. I say that, because that is about two inches shorter than me. I would guess that they are about 10 or fifteen years younger than me, but it is not something I would say I am much good at; guessing at people's ages. What I can say is that they are good looking. They are dressed well; very smart. The hair is well cut and shortish. The face has a nice smile on it. It is not a sight that sends any concerns to me. The person is holding a large letter in their hand.

I can see that they are going to say something, but before they can do so, I get a sudden pain in my side. It causes me to reach for the wall to support me and I bend over some, in pain. I don't bend over too far, but it is far enough to concern my visitor.

'Are you alright?'

I can hear the tone of genuine concern in their voice. It takes me a few seconds to answer them.

'I think so. I have been ill and in hospital. I don't things are quite right yet.'

'I'm sorry I disturbed you, making you come to the door.'

'You weren't to know.'

'I think you should go back through and sit down. Do you want a hand? I only came to drop this letter off to you. It has been delivered to me by mistake. I live in Moss Drive and you are Moss Avenue. You'd think they'd know the difference, but I guess they sort them at quite a speed.'

I need to sit down, so I don't even think about what I am doing in front of this stranger I have never met before. I turn away from the door and start back along the hall towards the living room. Then I hear the voice from my visitor.

'Shall I just put this letter on the hall table? Or would you like a hand getting back to the living room?'

I have to admit to not feeling very well. Maybe it is better that I have someone with me at this very moment. It could have happened as I got up to make myself a cup of tea when I was alone. No, I am glad I have someone with me, in case I need more help.

'Yes please' I reply, realising as I say it that I am not being specific about which question I am answering.

My visitor appears to understand what I mean anyway. I hear them step into the hall and shut the front door behind them. I am almost by the living room now. I hear them approach me from behind. I then feel an arm steady me, just as I am feeling really unwell again. The hand supports me as I go through the doorway into the living room. In the room they move beside me and lead me to my chair. It is obvious which chair is mine, as all my things are around it. They sit me down gently and then stand back, while I adjust myself to get more comfortable. I already feel a bit better, just for being sat down.

'Shall I make you a cup of tea?'

'I don't want to be any bother.'

'It isn't a bother. I would just hope that someone would do the same for me, if the circumstances were reversed.'

That comment makes me smile. All of my life I have been the carer and now my life is changing. I now too need someone to care for me.

'A cup of tea would be lovely. Make one for yourself too, if you have the time to stay and drink it.'

'Yes, I will. I am not in a rush. I've had the letter a couple of days now, but it has been too late to bring it round. I didn't want to have to bend it, to get it through the door. It is quite stiff and wont fold easily. My letter box is big enough for this to go through easily, but yours is a small one. I know, as I came round the first night, but there were no lights on.'

'It won't be anything urgent, so don't worry. You could have just put it back in the post and they would probably have got it delivered correctly second time around.'

'I did think about that, but well it isn't too far away, so I just decided to pop it round here personally.'

Chapter 29 Jay (I am now Jay) and David Petrich

Jay knows full well that the easier option would have been to just put it back in the post again, but Jay didn't want to do that. Jay has a reason for bringing it round personally. Jay wanted to see the person the letter was for. Jay wanted to see if the person lived alone too. Jay wanted to try to find out why this person has done something which is quite unusual. The reason all of this has come up is quite simple. Jay had arrived home from work one evening several days ago. There had been several pieces of mail waiting on the mat. At the time it never occurred to Jay that any of that mail might not have Jay's name and address on it. One by one the mail had been opened. Thankfully Jay opens letters carefully and tidily. It is just something that Jay has always done. Leaving the largest piece of mail to last was a habit that Jay had always done. The large letters were normally junk mail.

As it happened, the glue along the flap was quite easy to pull back. Jay had pulled the contents out; fully expecting it to be just another marketing mail shot, but Jay was wrong. Now what Jay should have done, was put it straight back in the envelope again and press the flap closed again. But Jay did not do that. Jay looked at the address on the front of the envelope for the first time. "David Petrich, 46 Moss Avenue, Middleton". That is all Jay needs to read. Jay then turns back to the contents and starts to read them. It doesn't take long, as the will is not a long and complicated one. But the puzzling thing; is why is this David Petrich leaving everything to charities? There isn't another person mentioned in there. There isn't even a note, saying why someone hasn't been left anything. No, it just names two or three charities that will get the proceeds of his estate.

Having read the will a couple of times, Jay then has a mug of coffee to drink, while sitting thinking about this letter than has been wrongly delivered. Something has come into Jay's mind. And the idea grows from there. From that moment the letter was never going to be put back into the post. No, Jay decided that this letter should be given to the rightful addressee in person. Then hopefully Jay might be able to engineer a way in, to investigate why the will has been written this way. Now by sheer chance Jay has delivered the letter and been invited in. It is obvious that no one else is here or expected to be here. David Petrich is not a well person either, which is probably why the will has been written. Excellent!

I make David a cup of tea. I make myself one too. When I come back into the living room his eyes are closed. I make sure that I don't walk too quietly as I approach him. I don't want to startle him. He might forget that I am in here, if he wakes up too suddenly.

He hears me coming and opens his eyes. There is a little bit of colour returning to his cheeks. I place the tea down, on the mat on the table beside him.

I then hand him the letter I have brought round. Luckily for me, he doesn't appear to notice that the glue on the flap isn't particularly strong. If it was, I think he might have struggled to open it. He pulls out the will and quickly flips through it. He doesn't bother putting it back in the envelope, but lays it on the table beside his cup of tea. I wait a few moments, before talking to him again.

'So are you on the mend now?' I deem to be a good opener.

'Well, I was well enough to come home and the health worker isn't coming anymore, so I reckon that at the moment I am probably not getting any worse.'

'What did they say was wrong with you?'

'There wasn't a conclusive diagnosis. That sort of situation runs in the family. My mother eventually died, after many years of an illness no one could peg down.'

'Is your father dead too?'

'Yes he died later than my mother. Then my sister died.'

'That's terrible. So have you got any family?'

'That's what I have been trying to find out. I have been tracing my family's history. My parents came from Poland and I have been across there, to try to trace my family. I even had the help of a professional researcher, but we couldn't find anyone who survived the occupation in the Second World War.'

I want to be quite careful how I go forward from this. I am already getting information that I thought would be much harder to access. I already believe that his sister was single. He hasn't mentioned anyone else. I believe he has no other siblings too. I'm assuming, but don't know, that he has had no children of his own either.

'That sounds awful, if you know what I mean?'

'I wasn't really surprised. My parents were the only ones of their family to get out and come across here.'

We have a brief pause, while we both have a sip of our respective drinks. I have a look around the room.

There are no ornaments. The furniture looks pretty new and the room has been decorated recently. I noticed the same in the kitchen, that everything is quite new. I also noted while rooting around for the tea bags, sugar and milk, that there isn't a huge store of food things in the house. I decide that I will proceed with our conversation, in that direction.

'I noticed that you are getting low on provisions in the kitchen. I think there is enough milk for a couple of cups of tea. You'll need tea bags too fairly soon. How do you manage to get your shopping in, if you are not well?'

I think that is a fair question and not too prying. I'm hoping he won't think I am too nosey. If I am going to try to get the rest of the information I want to get, then I need to keep his guard down and wanting to talk to me. I am not trying to get everything I want to know today, but I have to find a way of striking a chord with him, so he wants me to come back.

'I've not been home that long really. I am living on what was in the cupboards before I went to hospital. I haven't tried driving since I got home. Well to be honest, I haven't been up to shopping yet. So, for the everyday essentials, I have been ringing the corner shop and they have dropped some things round to me.'

'Shall I pop round there and get you some things now. Your milk won't last and I didn't come across any bread, when I was looking for the teabags.'

I can see his face light up at my offer.

'That would be asking too much of you. After all you have been kind enough to bring this letter round. I can't expect you to do shopping for me too.'

'It isn't a problem. I wouldn't have offered if I wasn't willing to do it. Now what do you want me to get this evening?'

'Well, if you really don't mind, that would be good. I meant to ring the corner shop earlier, but I dropped off to sleep and then forgot.'

Five minutes later I am off, with a short list of essentials and the necessary cash to pay for it all. I am back within fifteen minutes and quickly put things away. I then go back in to see him. He thanks me again, profusely.

'Look, I need to be going now. I have got some things to sort this evening.'

I then stop, as if something has just come to me. It hasn't, because I have thought of offering this all along. I only hope I am giving it a good show that this has just occurred to me.

'I tell you what. I'm going to do my weekly shop at the supermarket tomorrow evening. If you write out a list between now and then, I'll do your weekly shop when I do mine. I'll pop in after work to pick up the list and then come back after I have done the shopping.'

The offer is received well. In fact it couldn't be better. His face lights up and I know straight away he is going to accept the offer. I don't get any protests either, which is good.

I return 24 hours later and pick up the list. Then an hour or so later I am back with his shopping. I already have my next plan ready to implement. I could have suggested it earlier, but I thought he wouldn't go for it then. Again it has to look as if I have just thought of it.

I drop the bags in the kitchen and then go back into the living room.

'Would you like a cup of tea?'

'That would be very good of you.'

I then have my moment of inspiration, put on for his benefit.

'Have you eaten?'

'No, I haven't; not yet. I was going to do something in a bit, after you had brought the shopping back.'

'Do you like pasta?'

'It is pretty much my staple diet.'

Of course I knew that from the shopping list he had given me and the shopping I have just done.

'Why don't I do us both something to eat? It will only take as long as it takes me to put the shopping away. It then saves us both some time and we can eat with some company. I guess you eat alone most of the time and well, so do I.'

'That sounds like a plan. You really are being very kind to me.'

I think that I am too, but I have an ulterior motive, which you have no idea of yet. I go back to the kitchen and put the pasta and other bits on, while I put the shopping away. I don't rush things and by the time I have finished with the shopping, the meal is ready. I pop into the living room, to ask where he wants to eat, but as I get there I see he has readied the small table in there, with cutlery.

It was a nice change to sit at a table and have my dinner, being able to chat to someone. After we had finished, I made another cup of tea while I was doing the dishes. I am happy with how things are going so far. I could just wait until next week to do his shopping again, but I don't want to wait that long. I don't want him to die on me, is the real reason for trying to push on quickly.

Chapter 30 Jay and David Petrich

I make an excuse to visit David just two days later. I really wanted to visit him on the Sunday, but that would have been pushing it just too far. I have to be careful, because I don't want him talking about me to other people, not that I think there are any other people about. I don't know why no one appears to visit him, but just the fact he has to ring the corner shop for day to day provisions, is enough to tell me he hasn't got anyone visiting him. He has me now.

I make sure again that I visit him in the evening. I don't want any nosey neighbour taking note that I am becoming a regular visitor. Even when I had done his shopping for him, I had parked my car outside his house to unload it and then I moved it, round to my house. I walked back in different clothes. I also kept a good eye out, as best I could, to try to see if anyone was taking any notice. I am glad to say that I couldn't see anyone at all.

I had picked up a few bits and pieces on the way home, from a different store. Again I didn't want them to get too familiar with me. I then stopped off for a takeaway. I manufactured my story, to give me the excuse to call in again. I rang David, and told him I was going to have a takeaway with a friend, but just as I collected it, they had called off. If David hasn't already eaten, then I have some extra takeaway going begging. Luckily for me, he fell for the ruse and invited me round. By the time I got there, he had left the door on the catch for me to get in. Once again, he also had the table set ready.

We eat our dinner and chat a little. I am finding it awkward to turn the subject round to where I want it to be. I can't afford to push it though, because if he thinks

I am getting too interested in his finances, then he might start getting concerned about my motives. He would be right of course, but I don't want to pre-warn him unnecessarily. After I tidy up we sit down in the living room, to drink our hot drinks. I notice that the envelope I had brought round on the first day is still there. In fact it is more than still there, it is sitting out in the open. I mean by that that, the will is sitting on top of the envelope.

'Do you mind if I ask you something?'

I can hardly contain my excitement. I just know he is going to talk about his will. He picks it up and turns the page and reads to himself for a few seconds.

'Fire away' I answer, in the calmest voice I can muster.

'Well that letter you brought round to me; is my will. I was advised to do one when I came home from hospital. I know you'll probably say it should have been done before I went into hospital, but to be honest I had never thought about it. And that is odd, because my parents had wills. They ensured that when my mother died everything went to my father and when he died that everything went to my sister and me. When Anna died, her will left everything to me. I guess the reason I didn't do a will up until now, is that I don't have any family to leave it to. But they said it might just end up going to the state and I suppose I didn't want that. What do you think I should do with it?'

I note that he isn't telling me what is in his will. He isn't telling me that he has already decided to leave it all to charity. I, of course, already know that, but for the moment I am glad he has not told me that part. It is time for my first question back, rather than give an opinion.

'I suppose it depends how much you think you might just be giving away to the state, if you haven't got a will.'

'What do you mean?'

'Well, I suppose that; say you had a few thousand pounds. You wouldn't be as bothered as if you had say five hundred thousand pounds. If you had that amount of money, then you would want to have a say in where it goes when you die.'

He smiles at me. It is a funny smile. I can't quite place it, but I am thinking that I might have hit the mark, or somewhere like it, with the higher figure. This is getting interesting.

'That was exactly the reason why I decided, in the end, that I should do a will. The problem then, was who do I leave it to?'

He has thrown the question back at me.

'So there are no relatives that you know of?'

He shakes his head as an answer.

'So do you have any friends that have been close to you all of your life.'

I was as careful as I could be, phrasing that question.

I get another shake of the head to my second question. I take a few minutes in silence. But let him know, by my look, that I am concentrating on trying to come up with a good alternative.

'People do leave legacies to Cancer Research and other charities like the RSPCA. I suppose it depends what they feel close to. I can't think of any other area you could leave it to.'

I sit back in my chair. I am not expecting this conversation to go much further, if any further at all. I pick up my mug of coffee and take a long sip of it. David does the same with his tea. I can't tell if he is thinking something, or just that the conversation might be finished, because I have confirmed that what he has done is the right and obvious thing to do. Which charities you would choose is as I have said. It depends on what ones you favour. I know the ones he has chosen, but that is neither here nor there to me.

'I've got more than that.'

I am taken from my thoughts by his voice saying this quite quietly, but definitely loud enough that I am meant to hear.

'You don't have to say anything to me about how much you have.'

'I know, but it is much more than that. My sister left me everything she had and it was more than what you said.'

'I was just pulling figures from the air, as an example.'

'I know you were. I'm just letting you know you were right. It is definitely the sort of sum that should be left to something specific.'

'You need to put that will somewhere safe now. You don't want to be leaving that lying around, for anyone who comes in to see.'

'There won't be anyone coming in, unless of course I have to call in the doctor.'

'Well, you should still put it somewhere safe. Have you got somewhere that you keep your important papers, your things like your passport and birth certificate and things like that.'

'Oh yes, it is all in the one place. I have an A to Z file in the cupboard in my bedroom. All my financial and personal papers are in there.'

'That's good. It means that if something did happen to you, then whoever is going to sort your estate will have everything they need in the one place.'

I can't believe I have been given such a valuable piece of information, without having to force a question to get him to tell me. Of course I will still need to know exactly what he has his money in, before I do anything about it. One thing I am certain of; is that the money he has will not be going to a charity when he dies. The fact he has said there is more than the five hundred thousand pounds that I mentioned, is a big bonus to me. Five hundred thousand pounds would be good enough, but more is just great. I am thinking that I have really landed on my feet here.

'I have always done that.'

'Well' I said getting to my feet 'I need to be getting on. I have work in the morning and I need to prepare something, before I go to bed.'

'Thank you for coming round with the takeaway and thank you for helping me with my will.'

'I didn't do anything, other than, I gather, I have probably confirmed that whatever you are doing is the right thing.'

'You have indeed.'

I take my leave, but not before saying I will call round later in the week, to pick up his shopping list. I will ring him to let him know when that will be, but it will probably be on Friday. I have to say that David has improved a lot in just the few days I have known him. I will have to set my plan in motion relatively quickly. At first I didn't want him to die too soon on me, but now I am thinking that I don't want him to be getting too well either. It is not as if I have anything specific planned, as I haven't, but whatever I do, it will be easier if he is not well, rather than fitter.

Chapter 31 Jay & David Petrich

When I ring to say when I am going to pick up the shopping list, he tells me something that sets alarm bells ringing in me. He says he has been dying to tell someone what he has decided to do, but he didn't want to disturb me, by ringing me and telling me. He says he has decided that he wants to go back to Poland. He tells me that now he is starting to feel a bit better, he thinks that he needs to do it while he is well. Who knows if he might become ill again and not be able to move? He wants to go back to the country his parents were born in. He says he feels Polish and he has decided that he wants to die there, when the time comes. I tell him that I think it is a good thing that he doesn't just stay where he is and that he needs to do something that he wants to do. I arrange that I will call in on my way home on Friday evening, to pick up the list. He asks if I want to pick up a takeaway, if I am free and have the time to spare. Then he will tell me all about what he is planning to do.

I put the phone down. My first feeling is that I am going to be robbed of my opportunity, of doing what I need to do. I eat my dinner and think about what he has just told me. Then I decide that, depending on exactly what he has planned; then this might not be such a bad thing after all. That is because I have thought of another way of executing my plan. I have one or two things I may need to suggest to him, over our meal on Friday.

The day can't go quick enough, as I am keen to find out what he has planned and if anything, what he might have put in motion. I just get the feeling that he is not sitting on this idea, but that he is going to implement it very quickly. Depending on exactly what he has done and what he has planned, then I will move accordingly. I have too much to lose to let this slip through my fingers, now I know about it.

I have been wondering since, how many other people out there have no one to leave their money and assets to. I have also been wondering, just how one might get to that information. I haven't been able to come up with a solution to this problem as yet, but then it was just a thought that has crossed my mind. What all this has done, is to remind me that out there somewhere I still have a mother and father, unless of course they have died. It is not that I think for a minute that they would have anything to leave; it is just that talking with David about his parents, has reminded me that I have parents too. When all this is over, I might well try to dig around and see if I can come up with what might have happened to them. I very much doubt either of them has a will, or anything to leave, other than debt.

I pick up the takeaway and drop in at David's just after 7 o'clock. My car, as usual, is outside my house and I make it to his door without being spotted. I have a long dark coat on and a hat. I haven't worn either of them on a visit here before. As before, the table is set ready for us to have our dinner. I note on my way through the living room, that the will is no longer lying out in the open.

He can hardly wait to tell me his plans. As I had feared, but yet expected, he has already set his plan in motion. He isn't going to hang around. But as I thought earlier, that may well play into my hands, rather than make it harder.

He tells me that he has already spoken to the estate agent and that they are sending someone round on Monday afternoon, to get the particulars done. He says that it isn't long since he had the entire place decorated from top to bottom, so the house is ready to go. He says that he has already been looking online, at places he might get in Poland, but he doesn't really know where he wants to live. On one hand it would be good to live where his parents lived. But then maybe he shouldn't live where he knows so many of his relatives were taken and killed by the occupying forces. It is time I stepped in with a word or two of advice. Of course it is advice that is good for me really, but some of it is good for him anyway.

'What I have always been told is, that if you are moving to an area that you don't know, or that you don't know particularly well, then they say that maybe you should rent somewhere before you buy. Doing that, you get to know the area that you are in before committing yourself to buying a property.'

'That's interesting' he replies 'I would never have thought of doing that, but that is quite a good idea.'

'That way too, you could actually go there before this place is sold.'

'Of course, I don't need this place to sell before I buy there.'

I guessed as much, but I still don't want him doing that.

'But then you don't know how long this place will take to sell' I throw in, trying to change the tack back in my favour.

'That's true, but actually I like the idea of what you have suggested. Renting somewhere first before I buy, makes a lot of sense. I think I will do that.'

I am not going to let the conversation on his move stop now. I need to put some more things in place. I have given this a little bit of thought. I need to get my part done before the house is sold and before he disappears off to Poland. I have never been to Poland

and I would stand out there, whereas I find it quite easy to blend in here.

'You'll have to get in touch with your solicitor.'

'I was thinking of that, but surely I can do that when I have a buyer.'

'I was thinking that if you did that sooner rather than later, then if you did decide to go early to Poland, then they could complete the sale and forward the money to your account.'

'But wouldn't I have to wait to sign the sale papers and everything that needs doing when you sell a house. I have been looking it up online and there seem to be lots of forms to fill in when you sell.'

'Well, if you go to a solicitor now, then you can ask them about all that. I am just thinking about you and the fact you have been ill so recently. You have decided all this since I was here earlier in the week, so you might as well get as much of the preparation done now, in case you decide you don't want to wait for the sale to be completed.'

'Yes, I see where you are coming from. I think I will do that. It wouldn't do any harm to be all ready. As you say, I might decide that I want to just up and go.'

Those words send shivers through me, but I know what he means. After all, I have just put that idea in his head. I need to control this situation if I can, but as this week has proved to me, David is capable of deciding things very quickly and then implementing them. I need to watch that I don't lose this opportunity.

'They also need to go through money laundering checks these days. I think you will find the estate agents and the solicitors both have to do it.'

'The estate agent told me about that when I spoke to him. I will ring the solicitor on Monday. Now you've said that about moving early, I am finding that quite an attractive thought.'

We finish up and I leave. I think my window of opportunity is quite small. I have lots of things I need to plan. I have said I will go round on Monday evening, to see how he has got on.

Chapter 32 Jay and David Petrich

Monday arrives soon enough and it is a bit later than normal, when I arrive on his doorstep. I was half expecting to see the 'for sale' sign out the front already, but that is not there, yet. The door is on the catch ready for me. I have already rung to say I will be a bit later than normal. David wasn't in, so I had left the message on his answerphone.

I have had a bit of a dilemma over the weekend, trying to decide how to proceed and what to do with David; literally. I still have not come up with a definite solution, partly because this is all new territory for me. What I do know, is that I am going to have to think of something pretty quickly, or this opportunity has a very good chance of slipping away through my fingers. In my head, I am quite determined this is not going to happen. I am hoping that when it comes to the crunch, I am going to have the strength of mind to go through with it.

As usual, the table is set and we get down to eating our food. We get stuck in before I broach the subject of how far he has got.

'Well the day hasn't gone totally to plan' he opens with. 'I got a call from the estate agent first thing, to say that they are a man down today. Someone has called in sick. They haven't actually given me a new day and time, but they say it will definitely be soon. So I got onto the solicitor and as luck would have it, he had a space before lunch. I've told him what I am thinking of doing and he said that is fine. I have done all the money laundering things too. He says that all I need to do, wherever I am, is to email him with the information when the house is sold and he will do the conveyancing. He will even send me the paperwork and I can sign it and return it to him in the post, even if I am in Poland. Or I can fill in the forms now and sign them and I've given him the power to sign the sale documents. I have chosen that route.'

'That sounds like you have had a productive day. It's a shame the estate agent let you down.'

'These things happen. If you think that is productive' he is sounding animated. I can feel a pit coming in my stomach. He continues 'then you need to know what else I have been up to. I have contacted a couple of letting agents in Poland. I have looked at a few properties that I could rent for six months, before buying something. I asked them what they need before I can rent and they have told me. I think all I really need to do is to stay in a hotel for a week or so, while the paperwork gets sorted out. What I have decided to do; is go as soon as the property is on the market. I don't want to hang around any longer.'

I am taken aback at the swiftness of his progress since I saw him last. He is revitalised and full of energy. Not only that, but he is about to leave, well it is imminent, rather than weeks or months.

'What about all your things. What will you do with them, if you are going to stay in a hotel for a time?'

'I've decided I'm not going to take anything other than some clothes and my personal bits. I don't have many of those, so probably a couple of cases will be all

I need to take. I'll either leave all the furniture in the house for the next people, or arrange to get someone in to clear what I don't take, after I have left.' What do you think of that?'

I am in a bit of a state of shock, but I try not to leave a gap before I answer.

'You certainly don't hang about. I am pleased for you that you appreciate that time is of the essence. It is just a shame for you that the estate agent let you down.'

'Yes it is, as I have been looking at flights too. It will probably take me to the end of the week to sort through my clothes and other bits, trying to decide what I need to take. I have been so excited since I started thinking this on Saturday; that I had to take my sleeping tablets last night, so I could get some sleep. I haven't used them in ages. I slept like a log. Once I have taken them and get to sleep; then nothing wakes me up.'

Sleeping tablets, he takes sleeping tablets. A little light comes on in my head, accompanied by a little bell ringing, just to make sure I have taken note of this. I most certainly have.

We continue to eat our food. At the end of our meal and once we have tidied up, I sit and have a cup of coffee with him. I know I don't have long. I probably only have until the end of the week to get something in place, or this will be lost to me. I say that I will come round the next evening and see if there is anything I can do to help. My offer is accepted willingly.

24 hours later I am on his doorstep again and letting myself in. David had said he will prepare something for us to eat. He is in an even happier mood when I enter.

'The estate agent came today. He's done the pictures and everything. I've signed all the papers and so it is ready to go. All I have to do is to approve the particulars. He says he will email them to me tomorrow. I've told him I will be off next week, but I won't book the flights until I am sure I have sorted what I want to take with me. He says he knows someone who will come and clear the rest of the house for me. He doesn't think it a good idea to sell it with everything still in.'

The good news is that I know I have until the weekend and probably early next week. The bad news is that I still don't know what to do with David yet and that is important. But as far as everything else is concerned, David is making the rest of it really easy for me. The question is how long will it take for me to get everything ready that I need to? The problem with that is; that I don't know what I need to do. Then the first bit of inspiration comes to me. I have some holiday coming. I will see if I can arrange to have some time off, at short notice. I think that is what I need to do. The problem is that I doubt it will happen this week. But I will try to get it if I can.

I walk with him round the house, to see what he has done and how far he has got with his tidy up. In the living room he has moved some things into a pile by the cupboard door.

'It was worse than this when the estate agent turned up. You couldn't even see there was a cupboard there when he came, but then that was his fault. He didn't ring me first. I don't think he even noticed there was a cupboard behind this lot' he says laughing. 'It isn't important, as they will see it when they do viewings. It is only a small cupboard after all.'

And then I know what I am going to do.

We move around the house, which to be honest is in a bit of a mess. I tell him that I think he needs a van, to get rid of the rest of his clothes and things like that. He can just take them to the tip. He says that he doesn't think he is well enough to do that. That is quite funny, as he has been well enough to do all this in the house. I say that I will rent one for him and come on Saturday and do some clearing out for him. He jumps at that suggestion and he books it online there and then. He says that he will put everything that has to go, in one of the rooms, so that we don't have to sort it when I bring the van; just load and go. I do add in that it might be a good thing for him to wait until we have that done before he books his plane ticket, just in case something crops up, or he is not ready with everything. He says he will be, but he wasn't going to book the ticket until then anyway.

Chapter 33 Jay & David Petrich

I wear clothes I have never worn before when I collect the van and take it round to David's. I am also wearing glasses and have got a baseball cap on. I have a pair of heavy boots on too, just to complete my outfit. I reverse up the drive, so I have as little distance from the house to the back of the van as possible.

When David answers the door, he doesn't recognise me at first. I am pleased about that, because it means I have achieved what I intended to. Not necessarily for him, but for anyone else who might see me there. I just tell him that I have these things on, as I am going to the tip. He doesn't make anything of it.

I apologise for being a bit later than I had said I would be there. But I took the advantage of having the van, to go to the builder's merchant and pick up some materials for a job I need to do. It saves getting my car messy is my excuse. Ideally I don't want to unload it onto the drive while we clear the house, but if I have to then I will.

We go in and have a cup of coffee, before we start to unload my things and load the van with his. True to his word he has indeed been busy and has sorted pretty much everything. The living room is piled with things to be dumped. He says some of it could go to a charity shop, but I am not so sure about that. It depends how much time it will take. He then shows me the garage. There is a small pile of stuff in there, but no car. He tells me he has sold that this week. The garage he bought it from has bought it back from him.

I ask if I can put my building materials in the garage, until the end of the day, to which he willingly agrees. I then put his stuff from the garage in the van first and then load other stuff from the living room that has to go to the tip.

When the van is full, David comes with me, to help me unload the van when we get there. He is so much better than he was last week. The thought of a new life has certainly revitalised him. That though, is going to make my job harder. But then, even though I couldn't get any time off this week, I have got the next two weeks off. That will give me plenty of time to get done what I need to.

The second run we make is to a charity shop. He rings them first, to ask if they want the nearly van load of things; they do.

With that done, there is another full load to go to the tip and then we are just about finished. We have taken a few of the smaller bits of furniture to the recycling area beside the tip, as they sell pieces of furniture and other things there.

It is late in the afternoon when we return from the last trip. I back the van up to the garage, but don't reload my things into it as yet. I don't really want to, as it will mean double work.

Before we order the takeaway, we take a walk round the house, just to make sure there isn't anything else that needs to be taken away in the van. The house is looking bare. There are a couple of suitcases in his bedroom; one of which is packed and locked, while the other one is lying open and is half full. Apart from them there is only the bed, a chest of drawers and a wardrobe. The bedside cabinet has gone to the tip. The small stack of medicines that was on it is now on the floor, except for one box, which is in my pocket. Well it got in there just before we left the room.

The other rooms are all equally bare, as is the cupboard in the living room and all the kitchen cabinets. Just the basics are all that remains there; the things he needs for his last few days in there. Kettle, mugs, plates, cutlery and then the makings for tea and coffee is just about the extent of it.

There is nothing else to go to the tip. We order the takeaway and I go off in the van to collect it, about twenty minutes later. We then sit down on the settee to eat it. The chairs and table have gone earlier.

Today I have made sure that I have not had the same meal that David has ordered. I have my own reasons for that. We eat slowly and he tells me of his plans when he gets to Poland. He still hasn't booked anything. Not the flight, hotel, or any viewings for apartments he might want to see. The estate agent has completed the details and they have already had enquiries about the house, but no viewings have been booked yet. David has said he will drop a key in when he leaves, so they can show people round. Up until then they will ring him, if there is someone who wants to view the house.

As we are nearing the end of our food, David starts to yawn. It is hard not to notice it.

'You've probably done too much' I say 'even though you are feeling better, you need to take time to build up your strength more. I'll make you a cup of coffee and after that I will tidy the dishes. Then when we have had our coffees, I'll load the van with my stuff and get off, so that you can get off to bed. You look really tired.'

'I feel really tired.' He says, putting his fork down.

I get up to make his coffee. I have a cup of tea this time. Again I have my reasons for having a different drink than he has. He is still awake, just, when I return to the living room with our drinks.

'I'm sorry about this' he offers his apology 'I think you are right; I have just done too much. I don't feel as if I have any energy left. I think I am going to fall asleep here.'

'Shall I go and get you a blanket, so that you can keep warm if you sleep in the chair? Or do you want me to help you upstairs to bed?'

'No, I'm alright. It won't be the first time I've fallen asleep in front of the television, but a blanket would be good, as it does get a bit chilly sometimes overnight.'

I go upstairs to get a blanket off his bed. That is the only place there are any. By the time I make it back downstairs to the living room, he is fast asleep. He hasn't just fallen into a light sleep; he is fully gone. But then that is really no surprise to me, considering what I have put in his dinner and then for good measure in his coffee. The coffee is only half drunk, but he has had more than enough to put him out, as I can see in front of me.

I go over to him and feel for a pulse. There is one, but it is quite light. I go and put the catch down on the front door. The curtains are already drawn, as it is dark outside. I walk up the stairs and into his bedroom. I pick up a pillow and go downstairs and put it on the chair by him. I don't do anything with it.

I go out of the back door and into the garage, through the walking door at the back. I bring in some of the things I bought earlier. Then I decide that I might as well bring it all in. I put it in the kitchen for now, as I need to put a protective sheet on the carpet in the living room, before I take it in there. I then decide to risk taking the van back. He isn't going to be waking up anytime soon, with the dose of sleeping pills he has taken in his food and drink.

With the van back at the hire centre and my car now parked back by my house, I walk round to David's and let myself in, with one of his keys. He is still fast asleep in his chair. He hasn't moved a muscle in the time I have been away. I check his pulse once more and it is still very weak, but definitely there. I thought it probably would be.

I take a deep breath. I put on my surgical gloves and pick up the pillow. I step over him and then press the pillow down over his face. I hold it there firmly for several minutes, before I move it away. He hasn't struggled in the least. He was too far down to even know what was happening to him. I put the pillow in a black rubbish sack. I check his pulse, but there isn't one any more. David isn't going to be going to Poland after all. But this is just the start of it. I now have to make sure that he isn't missed or found anytime soon.

Chapter 34 David hides away

The sooner I get this sorted the better. My plan is to have the job complete by the end of the weekend, just in case someone wants to come for a viewing next week. I need to move David before rigor mortis sets in; otherwise he will go all stiff and I won't be able to get done what I need to for a couple of days. That would take me into the early part of the week and the longer he is not hidden away, the greater the risk of being discovered, and me being caught. And that just isn't going to be allowed to happen.

I lay out the protective sheet on the living room floor and then put another one on top of that. I check his pulse again, but it is still absent. It is a bit disconcerting as his body is still warm, but I do know he is dead. I know I have only a limited time window to achieve what I need to, but to be honest, just lying him on the floor in position will achieve what I need, so I can proceed. In fact I think it might be easier with rigor mortis fully set in. But then I really don't want to have to wait around for that, with his body lying on the floor. That would not be good if someone happened to find us like this.

With a little bit of difficulty, I manage to move him from the chair to the floor and onto the cover. It was much easier in my head when I thought of this. Thank goodness I hadn't taken him upstairs to bed. That would have been a nightmare to move him down again. He is a dead weight, literally, and it is way more awkward than I had ever imagined. I start wrapping him tightly with the rolls of cling film I have brought along with me. Originally I was going to use foil, but I am glad I didn't. I think it would have ripped too easily. It is hard enough with the cling film. I start at his feet and move on up his body. I think that is better, because by the time I get to his waist I already have a good tight wrap round him, which helps me lift him to get the roll under. I wrap him several times, doing all of the body and the legs, before moving onto the head. It is an odd feeling and thought that I have briefly, that I might be burying him alive, just before I put the first wrap round his head. He is dead. There is no doubt about that and by the time I have finished wrapping his head several times and then the entire body a couple of more times, there is no way he is ever coming back from the dead.

With that job done, I swiftly move on to the cupboard. I remove the shelves that are there and then remove the shelf supports. I measure the depth of his body and cut the supports to that length before refitting them. I attach my strong string to the one side, ready to hold him in place when I put him in there. But first I have to put him in the strong plastic sacks that I have made up. I do that next and then move him, with even greater difficulty this time, into the cupboard. It would have probably been quite funny to watch how I struggled to get him upright and then hold him, while I edged him forward into the cupboard. But I do get there, even though it has made me sweat some. I tie him in as tight as I can to the back of the cupboard. He hasn't taken up as much space as I feared he might.

I have bought 50mm thick blocks, so they take up less of the precious cupboard space. I bring in my mixing bucket and mix up my first mix. An hour later I have the wall in front of him up to his waist. I have made a good seal round each block. I then fill what gap there is on each side of David with the rubble I have brought with me, well they are bags of stones. I then mix up my ready concrete and fill that in. I had thought about waiting for the blocks to set properly, but I am impatient to get this part done. I have piled my other blocks in front of the others to hold them in place. It appears to be holding. The last thing I need is for the wall I have just built to come down.

I am very conscious that it is evening and that I can't start sawing at this time of night. I am not sure I should be making that kind of noise at any time, day or night. I don't want people remembering the noise of work going on. But again my impatience gets the better of me and I start to measure and then saw the shelves, ready to put them in the piece of cupboard that will be left. I saw slowly so there is hardly any noise, but then the progress is slower too.

By the time I have the shelves cut, it is getting late. The last thing I do before I leave for the night, is to build the wall up to one block away from the ceiling. That is leaving room for me to fill it with rubble and concrete in the morning. I have no wish to spend the night here with him, so I switch off the lights and leave the house as discreetly as I can. I don't believe anyone sees me go.

It is weird the next morning, letting myself into his house. I get there early and again I am dressed in the same clothes as the day before. I half expect to be met by David, asking why I had played a trick on him the night before. But the house is silent as I enter it.

There is no one there to greet me and there is only a dead David in the back of the cupboard. The wall has set quite well. I have used quick drying mortar, to help speed things along a bit. I keep the curtains closed for a while, as I finish filling the top of his tomb with stones and then concrete. I don't have to do the very top bit, as his head is already covered below that. I fill in the gap at the top and then set about putting the plaster board in place, followed by a quick skim of plaster. It isn't the best of plastering but it will suffice. After that is done and I have tidied up, I then fix the shelf supports in the cupboard and then the shelves. A quick coat of paint onto the still damp plaster follows and then I step back and admire my finished project. I shut the cupboard door and then open it again. I am pleased with what I have achieved. The fact it is still a cupboard is a good thing. Someone might wonder about the depth of it at one stage, but hopefully they will just open the door and see the shelves and stack them with things. I don't think they will think too much about the depth. On that thought rests my freedom, probably.

I have used virtually all of the materials I had brought with me. There are two blocks left and a bit of concrete and half a bag of plaster. I put it all in the garage ready for me to take away and dump.

The next thing on my agenda is to locate where David has put his personal papers. They obviously weren't in the cupboard. They are probably in one of the cases and that turns out to be the case that is open still. I don't spend anytime actually inspecting them. I just make sure I have every one of his papers that I am going to need. I have his birth certificate and his passport. I have his bank and building society books. I have the file the solicitor has given him and the information from the estate agent. As he had said, he used to keep it all together and he has done that ready for his move too. That is the move he is now not going to make. I empty out both cases, to make sure there is nothing else in there I am going to need, to get access to his assets. There isn't, so I shut them both up and take them down to the garage. I put the bag with his papers in in there too. I am actually ready to leave now, but I think it is a good idea if I wait until it gets dark. That gives me a few hours I am going to have to wait. In the meantime, I ring the estate agent and the solicitor. Neither of them is there of course, because it is a Sunday. But I leave them a message, in my best David voice; that I have managed to get a lift with someone who is driving to Poland and that I will be available to contact by email for the time being, until I get myself sorted in a new place in Poland.

Chapter 35 Jay

I leave in the evening when it gets dark. I then collect my car and take it round to David's. I load the cases into the boot and fit the other bits in around them. I then lock up the garage and go in to check on the house. I check on the cupboard in the living room. Because I had used the same old shelves, but just made them smaller, they look as if they have been in there for many years, which they have. I close the cupboard door for the last time, hoping things will stay the way they are for many a year. The rest of the house is tidy and so I lock up and leave, for the last time. I put all of the keys in an envelope I have brought with me. I have already printed the note that says what the keys are for and confirming I (David) has left for Poland.

Using David's email address, which I made sure I had before he died, I keep in regular contact with the estate agent. I don't have to wait too long before I get an offer on the house and then the solicitor does the conveyancing on the sale. Once that is done, the balance of the sale price is transferred into David's bank account. Something that I had done that was quite risky was to do forwarding at the post office for three months, while I changed the addresses on his various accounts to mine. Nobody questioned it too much and it ensured there was no mail piling up at the house, which the new owner might have questioned.

I have in the meantime been moving money across to accounts that I have opened in his name. I was going to move it into my accounts, but because of the sheer size of the amounts of money I was moving, I decided to just take over his identity for the time being. I will find a way of moving it, over time. I have created a company for this purpose and managed to open a business bank account. I just don't feel I can just move all of his money there in one go. Most of his money is in his bank account, so I am moving it into other accounts in his name, bit by bit. I am of course enjoying the new financial status that I have too. I have moved out of my house in Moss Drive and moved to another town, many miles away. I gave up my job because to be frank, with David's money, I don't really need it.

I eventually got it into place at my investment company and then into my control in my own accounts in my name. I then wound up the company and moved again to another new town, again a long way from both the other places.

It is funny how things just come to you when you are not looking for them. With David the letter had turned up at my address and I read it and took it round to him. Then what happened from there brought me here today.

I was doing some food shopping at the supermarket and just loading my shopping into my car, when an older lady walked past me, holding two or three carrier bags. Just as she was passing me, the bags gave way. Her shopping went down on the ground and she almost went with them, as she tried lucklessly to stop them falling from her grasp. I turned to help her as she got down to gather the things up. Two of the bags were beyond saving. I think she had just put too much in two of the bags and the handles just weren't strong enough for the weight they were holding.

I emptied my shopping out of three bags and offered them to her. She accepted thankfully. I then asked if she was going far, thinking that she was only going a few yards back to her car. I was going to offer to carry them there for her. But no, I found out she hasn't got a car. She is walking home and it is about a mile away, maybe a fraction less. She admitted that she hadn't realised just how much she had bought and that it was too much for her to carry, but she had done it now.

I offered to take her home. That was another offer that she accepted straight away. When we got to her house, I helped her in with her things. She offered me a cup of tea, which I accepted. Over that tea she told me about herself. She told me that her husband had died a few years ago and that she has never driven. They didn't have any children, because she couldn't. She owns the house and has plenty of money in the bank, but that she is not happy. She is lonely. She has a sister in Much Wenlock. She tells me that Much Wenlock is in Shropshire, somewhere I haven't been to before. Her sister is always on at her that she should move closer. She has thought about it, but has never done anything about it. I say to her that maybe she should think seriously about it. It would be good for her to be near her family. She says that is what her friends, the few that she has, tell her too.

I finish up my tea and take my leave, but not before saying I will take her shopping next week, if she wants a lift. She willingly accepts my offer. I of course have my own reasons for offering to take her shopping.

She gives me her telephone number. I am quite careful not to give her mine. In fairness, she doesn't ask for it. I turn up at the time I had arranged with her and we set off for the supermarket. She is quite chatty as we make the short journey there. When we are in, we separate to do our own shopping, agreeing that we will meet up in the café when we have finished. I am there first and have already loaded my shopping into the boot of my car. Mary wheels her trolley in. She parks it up while I go and order our drinks.

It is while we are sitting there sipping our overly hot cups of tea, that she tells me what has been going on her life over the past week. She has been giving it a lot of thought, about at least going up to where her sister lives. She has never been there. I wonder why, but don't ask the question. Then she says that she has heard from her sister too, that she has been taken ill. She has had to go into hospital. Mary thinks that maybe she should go and visit her sister. She has told her where she keeps the door key, so that she can stay in her house.

Mary then says that with her sister being ill, she has decided that being near to family is what she should do. She hasn't told her sister yet, but she has been to the solicitor to see him and she has contacted an estate agent, to put her house on the market. She says that she will probably move sooner than later, even before her house sells. She knows her sister has room for her there. I can't believe I have this situation presenting itself to me again. It is just like David and it is ready and waiting for me to do something about it, I think. And just like David, the window of opportunity is going to be quite small. I think that it is worth pursuing, even though I know even less about her than I did about David.

The easiest way for me to improve my knowledge of her and the way she keeps her things, is for me to offer to drive her to Much Wenlock. She can't believe that I am offering to do that for her. I tell her I have nothing on for a few days at least and that it is no problem. I also offer to come round to her house and help her sort some things to take, just in case she decides to stay there. She says that she thinks she will be back before she moves permanently away. I am sure what she is thinking is what she thinks she will do. But I have my own reasons for helping her get some things ready. I need to know where everything is that I will need, if I am going to plunder her assets. I haven't even begun to think how I am going to achieve what I need to. I just know that another opportunity has presented itself to me and I am certainly going to pursue it.

Chapter 36 Jay and Mary

Mary makes it so easy for me. I can hardly believe how open she has been with me. Of course I phrase my questions in such a way that it comes across I am asking her these things in her best interests, if she decides to move to Much Wenlock. Like David's important papers had been kept in the one place, so are Mary's. She says that she has just carried on with things, in the way her husband had when he was alive. By the end of the afternoon, I know what I need to know, should the opportunity arise for me to get control of her things. The only real difference between Mary and David; is that David had access to the internet and Mary has not. Mary has never embraced the technological age. That is the only thing that is different. But as Mary appears to have set things up to happen in her absence; I think that, in the end, it will work very similarly as before.

I go home and get myself prepared as much as I can, for something I know nothing about. What I do, is pack some basic tools in the car. I have no idea how this is going to pan out, or what will be involved this time. What I do know is that Mary and I are going to leave for Much Wenlock after lunch tomorrow. It is only because Mary has an appointment in the morning, that we aren't leaving any earlier.

I arrive at Mary's house with my case packed. I have a varied wardrobe with me, so that I can change my appearance as much as I can. I have read up a bit about Much Wenlock. It is just a small country town, with a small population of maybe around three thousand people in the Parish. Small towns can be completely different from large towns. In large towns it can be quite easy to remain anonymous, but in a small town that task is much harder. This is not going to be ideal. I will have to assess the risk when I get there.

Mary, to my surprise, has packed a couple of large suitcases. There isn't enough room in the boot for them both, due to my bag being there, along with my tools. One of them has to go in the back of the car. Mary doesn't question this, but then why should she? She doesn't even know what I do every day.

I make sure she has locked up her house securely. She has a spare key on the hooks in the hall, which I pick up as I follow her out of the house. She is unaware that I have done that.

The house, when we arrive in Much Wenlock, is in a side street. It took a minute or two to locate it, as the address is a bit confusing. The road changes name half way up, but if you turn right at that point, the road you were on continues. We park up near to the front door. There is no pavement here, but it is not a road that many people use. It goes nowhere other than to service these properties. There are a couple of people walking towards us as we park, but they don't pay us any heed. Mary gets out of the car and walks towards the front door. But she stops short of that, at a pot that hangs from a hook by the front room window. She lifts the pot out of its holder and feels inside the space it has left. She comes up with a key.

'This is just to let me in. There are spare keys in the house' she says.

I have not told Mary that I have no intention of going home today. She thinks that I am driving her here, unpacking her things, and then making the journey back again today. I haven't said that I am going to do that, but when she has been talking, what she says makes it clear that she thinks that is what I am going to do. I will let her know at some point that I am not doing that, but not until I have had a chance to see how the land lies here.

She walks along to the door and opens it and goes in. I follow her, a couple of steps behind. I close the door behind me. The house is quite dated. That is the first impression I have. The house is cold too and I shiver as we walk through the living room to the kitchen. Mary knows what she is looking for. She opens a drawer and takes out a key, which she goes and tries in the front door. She then goes outside and puts the other key back in its safe place.

We then continue our investigation of the house. We go upstairs, to a very dated set of bedrooms and a bathroom. Mary has been told she can use the far one on the front. It has a window to the side that overlooks the car park. She stays there, while I go down and bring her cases in. I take them upstairs to her room. She leaves them as they are and we go downstairs to the kitchen. There is a back door that leads outside. We find the key for that and unlock the door. Outside there is a concrete section under a flimsy roof. There is a solid looking door on the right, which I think must open up onto the car park; interesting. Straight ahead is a brick built outside toilet as was, but it is now accessible under this flimsy roof. To the left, there is a rubble floor where the concrete stops and then a window that looks out onto a path. There is a door on that side too. We unlock that door and go out into the garden. There is a path running down one side. At first look the garden is enclosed. There is no vehicular access to it. There is a four foot high wall between this garden and the next one. There is a higher wall between this garden and the car park. We go back inside. Mary gets through the door and stops. She has a good look around. The building is not in a good condition in this part. The floor is worse than that; it is literally just rubble.

'She has said for a long time that she needs to do something about the state of this area. But she never seems to get round to it. Either that or she hasn't got the money to do it. Judging from the state of repair of the rest of the house, I suspect she hasn't got the money to do it. What do you think it would take to improve this?'

I am surprised she is asking me the question. Why would she think I have any idea what it would take? Anyway does she mean what would it take physically to improve it, or does she mean how much will it cost? Both answers really depend on the degree of work that you want to do. I take a good look round.

In my opinion it would be best if you took the entire thing down and started again, but I don't think that is what Mary wants to hear. I think it is quite important that I give a practical answer, rather than one that is the ideal solution. I keep looking around and prod the rubble floor with my foot. It is not even very compacted. The units under the window are only just serviceable. They aren't standing level, but that is probably because of the floor. I make up my mind what I am going to say. To be fair to Mary, she has given me time to think about my answer. She is still looking around.

'I think the roof will be alright. I am not saying it is ideal, but I don't think it would be wise to meddle with it. You might have to spend a lot to change that. What I would do is dig out that floor and concrete it. Then I would change those units under the window, as they aren't very good. You could probably pick up something at IKEA, or the likes, quite cheaply to replace them. Overall it shouldn't cost more than a few hundred pounds I should think.'

'Is that all?' she asks.

'I am only guessing at that, but I shouldn't think it would be more than that, or not much more.'

'Well I think I will do that for her, while she is in hospital' she announces.

It is at that moment I get my inspiration. I knew it would come from somewhere.

Chapter 37 Jay & Mary

I jump in there while the iron is hot.

'I can do that for you. If you tell me what you want in there I'll do that for you. I've done stuff like that before. I do a lot of my own DIY.'

'I can't expect you to do that. I thought you were going back home this evening.'

'I've got a friend in Telford' I lie 'I was thinking of dropping in on them for a few days. Anyway I thought you might need a lift, to take you to the hospital every day, to visit your sister.'

'You must let me pay you then' the resistance is short lived, as she sees the chance to get the job done quickly.

'Let's go and have a look. I don't think we need to do more than replace the floor units and concrete that bit of floor.'

'I think you are right. Where will you get the materials from?'

'Well the units from IKEA, as they won't be expensive from there. I am sure there is a builder's merchant somewhere round here. I'm just thinking though, that it might be a good idea to get a small skip. We can use it to put these old units in and for the rubble we dig out of here. There is quite an area. It shouldn't be too much, maybe £80 or so. Anyway I will let you pay for materials, but not for labour. I'm doing it for you and anyway, I'm sure I'll feel great satisfaction when it is done.'

I have my own reason for saying that, as you know. I then continue.

'We'll get onto it in the morning. I'll check on the internet tonight about skips and the furniture. Do you want to go to see your sister this evening?'

'No, I'll just go out for a bite to eat and then probably have an early night. Are you sure your friend will be there?'

'Yes, I'll give them a call on the way there. I think this is all rather exciting.'

'It is certainly not what I thought would happen when we got here. Thank you for today. I'll ask around about the builder's merchant if you like?'

'No, it's alright, as I can easily get the information I need.'

I leave her to it. She comes to the door to see me off. I drive out of the town and stop. I need to find where I am going to stay. I know there will be hotels in Telford, but I need to locate one. I settle on a Holiday Inn near the town centre. I find it quickly and check in, for three nights to start with. They say it won't be a problem if I need to extend my stay, as they have plenty of room at the moment.

The next morning I start to get things organised. I have been on the IKEA website and I know what units we need to buy. I have gone for nearly the cheapest ones. I order the skip and it should be with us today or tomorrow. I asked if they thought it would be alright to drop it on the car park, but they said they couldn't. The council would object to that. It has to go outside the house, if I can make sure there is a space for it. I said I will try, but we have to go out at times. Mary is going to pay them cash when they drop the skip off, if we are there. At that I am given a time. Funny what temptation cash is to some businesses?

In the meantime I go out the back and measure the floor area. I'm trying to calculate how much of the different materials I am going to need. I need to dig out quite a lot and then allow for what is going back into the hole and the depth of concrete that I am going to put in there. I do the calculations and then walk up with Mary to Travis Perkins, to order what I will need. I am surprised that a town of this size has a builder's merchants. They will deliver the goods in the morning, probably earlier than later. I ask them if they can deliver to the side gate in the car park; that is not a problem.

We walk back down Queen Street towards the town again. Mary wants to take a look at the town in daylight. It had been dark when she went for a meal the night before. She had chosen The Talbot in High

Street. We come out of Queen Street at Bull Ring and turn right. The church is an impressive one, on our left, with the Guildhall on the left after that, before we reach the square. The High Street is off to our right. Mary had been up there the evening before. To be honest, I am not so keen on walking round the town openly. I have my reasons for saying that of course. But Mary is insisting that we stop somewhere for a coffee and maybe something to eat, before we have to get back for the skip delivery.

There is quite an interesting array of shops in the High Street, for such a small town that is. We walk up as far as a building that says it is the Bank, before we turn round and walk back down the street. We pass a pharmacy and The Talbot where she ate yesterday. We also pass a couple of book shops, a deli, an estate agent, a sweet shop, a craft shop, a butcher, a tea shop, a Chinese takeaway, an art shop, another pub, a Spar and a couple of clothes shops before we reach the bottom. In the square there is another clothes shop, a hairdresser, another art shop, a smoothie café and a gift shop. On the other side of the road there is an Ecclesiastical outfitter (I haven't come across one of them before), a baker, a small superstore, another estate agent and two more tearooms. We choose the one facing the square, Tea on the Square.

A while later we arrive back at her sister's house, just in time for the skip being delivered. With that done we make our way to the hospital, so that Mary can visit her sister. We park up and while she finds the right ward, I go to the café and get myself a cup of tea to drink, while she sees her sister. I am surprised that only forty five minutes later, she finds me in the café. She doesn't look too happy, but I wait for her to tell me what is wrong. She sits with me and has a cup of tea before we go back home. It is only on the drive home that she tells me; that her sister hasn't been very nice to her. I say that maybe she isn't well and that it is the pain talking. Mary says that she doesn't think that is the case. She will be in there for another week or so, before she is allowed home, but she isn't in any pain.

The next day when we visit, the mood isn't any better. Mary is even more disgruntled when she joins me in the café. The journey home is done in virtual silence.

I have already started digging out the hole in the outside area, in the morning. The cabinets had all but fallen apart when I tried to dismantle them. The annoying part is that I had to walk them round to the skip. I didn't want to take them through the house, partly as the route through is a bit awkward. I see a couple of people on my journeys round there. In particular I see a man who lives a few doors along, coming out of his house and then later, on his way back there. I know he has noticed me. He is probably wondering what we are doing in Mary's sister's house. Luckily he wasn't close enough to talk and I didn't stop and wait for him to reach me. I just kept my head down as much as I could, as if I was hard at work.

The removal of the rubble that I was taking to the skip took longer. I could only carry only so much at a time. I noticed that the neighbour was out in his garden a few times, looking over. I decided to get Mary to go along and see him, to tell him what she is doing for her sister. That is what she did and he stopped taking so much notice of us, thankfully. By the end of this day, I have the area dug out and ready to be filled. I have a pile of rubble on the concrete, ready to pack into the hole. I also have a pile of bags which the builder's merchant has delivered.

Chapter 38 Jay & Mary

I don't do anything out there the next morning, but we go to IKEA instead, to buy the units. We take the opportunity to have a breakfast there, as it is such good value. It is a long time since I've been round an IKEA and I don't think Mary has ever been to one at all. It doesn't take long to order the units and the worktop. It is going to be tight getting it in the car, but we will get it in, even if Mary has to sit behind me, rather than in the front seat. Mary doesn't pick up anything on our way round the store, but I pick up a few things. Then we go through the checkouts and along to the collection area. We only have to wait a few minutes before our goods are wheeled out to us.

Back home at her sister's house, I unload through the side gate and park up in the lane, by the front of the house. Ideally I would have preferred to park a bit further away, where people wouldn't necessarily be able to associate the car with her and this address. But that isn't an option, without Mary asking some awkward questions. I start to assemble the units, even though that is going to leave me a bit short of space to work in. Mary questions why I am doing that and I say that I am letting the ground settle after digging it out and I will fill it in tomorrow; it is the way I have been taught, is how I put it to her.

By the time we are ready to go off to visit her sister, I have the units assembled and I have even, to satisfy Mary, put some of the rubble back in the hole in the ground. As usual I go to the café while she visits her sister. It is only half an hour before a very red-faced Mary joins me in the café. She declines the offer of a coffee. She is too angry to sit down. I can see that she needs to let off steam, so I leave the rest of my coffee and we walk quickly back to my car.

We only just get the car doors closed, when she starts to tell me why she is so angry. She had only just got into the side ward where her sister has been moved to, when she started on Mary. She told her that she is too stuck up and that she has never liked her. She doesn't know what possessed her to say that she should move nearer the family. There is no way she wants Mary to be living near her. Why do you think she has lived so far away from her for most of their lives? Mary then said she carried on with her tirade, accusing Mary of doing things earlier in their lives and blaming Mary for the way she has had to live since. Mary said that she was lost for words, but did manage to say to her sister that she wasn't going to live here after this outburst. She couldn't tolerate her having this attitude and she would be going home tomorrow. Then of course she thought about the work that I am doing and realised that wouldn't be possible. So she told her sister about the work she was having done, to which she got a grudging thank you, but then her sister started again. So Mary told her that we would have the work done in two days and she would then be gone. She said she didn't expect to see or hear from her again and she would make no attempt at contacting her. On that note they parted, or rather Mary left.

On listening to what she has been saying, my first reaction was to start to feel panic. Here I have it all set up and then she and her sister have fallen out. She will be going home to her own house and she will cancel the sale and I will lose my opportunity. But then as we started to drive home, the thought strikes me that in fact the situation isn't anything to panic about; it is in fact almost unbelievable good luck. If things hadn't changed, then there would always have been the question from her sister Rose, wondering what had happened to her. But now her sister knows that Mary is leaving and going back home. She knows about the new units and the concrete floor. She isn't expecting to see, or even talk to her sister, ever again. Where Mary's house is, no one there is expecting to see her come back. They think she has moved away so, if Mary doesn't come back, there is no one who will be concerned about her whereabouts. There may be one or two people who might have expected to hear from her with a new address, but it is doubtful they will come looking for her.

So by the time we get back to the house, I know that I have to do what I am going to do this evening. I only have a couple of days to get clear of the house. There is always the risk that her sister will get someone in her family to call round. They haven't so far, so hopefully they will continue to stay away.

Mary has asked me if I could possibly start to get the concrete started tonight. The sooner we get out of this place the better as far as she is concerned, but she isn't going to go before we have completed the work outside. I tell her I will, but when we get back I will make us a cup of tea or coffee first. Then I will drink that, get changed and get started. That pleases her a lot.

Mary has a coffee and I make myself a cup of tea. I am purposely not having the same drink as Mary. Of course as you know, I have my reasons for that. I have put a good dose in her coffee. I only hope she doesn't complain about the taste. She is still incensed though about her sister's attitude and doesn't appear to notice her coffee isn't quite all it should be. She keeps sipping at it, in between berating the sister, the house and anything else she can think of. Then all of a sudden she stops and gives out a long yawn, followed quickly by another. She is obviously puzzled by this and she looks across at me. I sit forward in my chair and try to look concerned.

'Is something wrong Mary?'

'I'm not sure. I just suddenly feel quite strange. I am feeling so sleepy all of a sudden. You are sure it was coffee you have given me?'

'Of course it was coffee. Just rest for a bit and hopefully you'll feel a bit better in a minute.'

I don't get an answer from her when I look across. Her eyes are closed.

'Mary, are you alright?'

I don't get an answer, but then I am not really expecting one. I get up and go over to her. She is still breathing, but it is very light. I feel for a pulse and I can feel it there alright. I need to get on with the job. I run up the stairs and fetch a pillow from her bed. When I get back into the living room, I close the curtains and then check her breathing and her pulse once again. I place the pillow over her face and press down firmly. There is a moment when I think that somehow she is going to struggle against me, but that is very short lived. I hold the pillow there for far longer than is necessary, before removing it and checking her vital signs. There are none. I don't waste any time and go out to the car and bring in some of the other things I will need. Then I move the car into Racecourse Lane, to park it there for the night.

Wrapped and ready, I drag Mary from the living room into the kitchen. I have switched the lights off before going in and dragging her along the floor. It is dark outside, but there is a bit of light coming from a streetlight in the distance. I can see enough to do what I need to. I open the kitchen door and drag her through and over to the hole in the ground. It is a bit awkward to drag her into it, but I manage ok in the end. I press her down. Thankfully there is enough room for her to lie down and it is deep enough even with the rubble I put in earlier.

Chapter 39 Bye-Bye Mary

The need for speed is with me, but I also want to make sure I don't make any noise. The last thing I need is to attract any attention. So I keep the lights off. I have the kitchen door open, but have the living room light on. I am getting just enough light to see what I am doing. To use tools to move the rubble into the hole would probably be too noisy, so I use my gloved hands to scoop the rubble in. I put in as much as there is there. I do that for two reasons. Firstly I think it might look odd to anyone who might see me taking the surplus out to the skip, even in daylight. Secondly I am giving myself less to do with mixing the concrete.

I trample the rubble down, until I have it all firm. Mary is well concealed under it now, so even if someone did pop in, then there would be nothing for them to see. I mix up my first batch of concrete, in the kitchen. I then carry the mixing bucket through to the hole and pour that in. I do that several times, until I have the hole filled to within an inch or so of the surface.

With that done I go upstairs and change out of my clothes. I tidy the house and then leave for my hotel. I was thinking at first that I would stay here, but then I need to check out of my hotel in the morning anyway. Also, I just think it would be a good idea for me not to be in the house without Mary, just in case a relative did call in.

In the morning I check out of my hotel early and am back in Wenlock, as the locals call it, just after 8 o'clock. The house is as I hoped to find it. The quick setting concrete is hard, so I change my clothes and set about applying the top layer of concrete and smooth it over. I go upstairs and pack her things into her cases. I don't bring them downstairs as yet. I take the unused bags of concrete and put them by the side gate, ready to load into my car. I ring the skip people and say the skip is ready for collection. They say they will collect it in the next day or so. I am not going to hang around to make sure they do. I have asked them to collect it and I am sure they will.

I am feeling a bit peckish and the concrete top layer is not quite set yet, so I walk along towards the square and into the baker, to buy something to eat. They do a good meal deal, so I get a large bap made up and have a drink and a cake to go with it.

After eating it and putting the rubbish in the skip, I then go round the house, making sure it is as we found it. As far as I can, I wipe down anywhere that I might have touched, though to be honest I am not expecting Mary to be found anytime soon. I then bring her cases downstairs into the living room.

It is after lunchtime that I think the concrete is hard enough to take the weight of the units. The last thing I need is it to start to sink. The units go over where Mary is under the concrete. I fix them to the wall at the back and then fit the worktop to the units. It has taken a bit longer than I thought it would, but I need it to look right. I think Mary would have liked it, but I guess she would never have had it done if she had known how her sister was going to be when she saw her. The concrete is fully set and the floor looks good. You would never know to look at it, what lies underneath. The units are smart and it has generally improved this area no end.

I retrieve the front door key from Mary's bag and put it back in the kitchen drawer, but only after getting the one from the pot out the front. I move the cases through to the back by the gate and then check that area and the rest of the downstairs one more time. I appear to be getting a bit paranoid, but it is what it is.

I fetch the car and drive round to the car park and park as near as I can to the gate. It only takes me five minutes to get everything into the car. As far as I am aware no one sees me packing the car, although of course I can't be 100% sure. I go back in and lock the gate, check the outside area one last time. I then go into the kitchen and lock that door. One more quick check to make sure nothing of Mary's has been left behind and I am out of the house and have put the key back in its hidey hole. A minute later I am in the car and off out of the car park. I have started my journey home and Mary is tucked up under the concrete in Wenlock.

When I get back home, I unpack Mary's things into my garage. I drive the car in there to do this, as I don't want my neighbours to see me unpacking two big suitcases. Over the next couple of days, I sort out the things of hers that I need to keep and those that I don't. The clothes are a bit of an issue. I would have taken them to a charity shop, but I am concerned that someone who knew her might recognize some of her clothes. But then if I take them to the tip, then that would look suspicious, if someone opens the bag and sees her clothes in there.

It may have been a bit over the top, but I drove 100 miles away and then bit by bit offloaded her clothes and personal bits and pieces in various charity shops. When it came to her jewellery, I have hung onto that for now. I was going to take it into a jeweller and cash it in, but what I have decided to do is sell it online instead. It is highly unlikely that anyone local will buy it, or recognise it for that matter. The suitcases were given to two different charity shops on my travels round.

I then set up an email account in Mary's name and email the estate agent, so that he can contact me in this manner. I make the reason for this, that a younger relative has introduced me to modern technology. I wait a day or so before sending similar information to the solicitor. But with him I write the letter, well I mean type it and print it. I give him my email address for Mary and then sign it for her. I have a few examples of her signature to copy and it is quite an easy one. No doubt an expert would spot the difference, but I doubt it will be scrutinised that closely. I omit to give them a postal address other than her home address, stating that as soon as I have a permanent address I will forward it to them. I have an idea what I will do about that when the time comes, but there is no need to get that just yet.

The estate agent acknowledges my email and says they will let me know when there is a viewing. I get an acknowledgement in the mail a few days later from the solicitor. His letter of course goes to Mary's home address. I have been round there a few times to check what is there and to retrieve her mail. I have managed to sneak in there unnoticed. Of course when the time comes and the house has to be cleared, then the neighbours are going to notice. But when that time comes, I will get someone to do a house clearance and so they should come round in a marked van and shouldn't draw too much attention. But that is in the future. Before that happens, I have to sell the house.

All the time I am waiting for that to happen, there is always the chance that her sister might try to make contact, to patch over the break-up they had. I have the telephone disconnected, so they can't get frustrated by that not being answered, should they try. As far as I know they don't.

While I am waiting for the house to sell, I make myself useful and start moving her other assets around. Again she has her assets in a few places and it takes a few strategic moves, before I manage to take total control of it in my own account.

Chapter 40 Jay

Eventually her house gets an offer, which I accept for her. I advise the solicitor and he then starts the conveyancing. I make contact with a house clearance specialist and once we have exchanged contracts, I get them to come to clear the house. I then get a cleaning company in, to make sure the house is clean and tidy for the new owners. I know Mary would have liked the place to be presentable for them.

The money comes through into Mary's bank account and the final papers are sent to her address, where they are forwarded to me. I know it is now time for me to be moving on. I just need to get all the money across to my accounts before I do so.

That is done over the next few weeks and I am ready to restart my life somewhere else. I am happy with my life, although for the first time I do actually think it would be nice if I had someone to share this with me. It would be so much more enjoyable to share the places I'd like to go to. I think part of me was looking at what happened to Mary, when her sister Rose was so rude to her and shunned her. Mary at least did have a husband, until he died. I have not had a partner. And from out of nowhere and for the first time in I don't know how long, I take my thoughts back to my parents. I never saw my father after he left the house and I haven't seen my mother since she hit me that day. I try to put it out of my mind over the next few weeks, as I settle in to my new home. I have moved to Kent this time and have rented a house in Southborough. It is nothing grand, but is pleasant enough and in a good street. I am not planning to stay here for anything more than a year. I want to move on and do something with my life. I have all the money I need and will never have to work again.

I do settle down and get involved in some local groups. The thoughts about my parents slip away and I don't think about them again for many years. They literally don't enter my thoughts. My first thought that I will only stay there for a year changes and for more than just the one reason. I have got involved, as I say, in several local interest groups. I take up learning a language at night school and I meet a good group of people there. I find there are a lot of people who are single like me. I also get involved in helping out with good causes.

For reasons of my own, I decide not to be known as Jay when I am out and about. I arrange for my mail to be delivered to a PO Box. Nobody has any reason to question me about my name. Why would you? Who questions someone they meet about their name? You just take it that what they tell you is it.

Another reason I stay there far longer than I had ever planned to, was that the person who owned the house I was renting, died. Their relatives approached me and said that they were going to have to sell the house, as they needed to split the assets between quite a few people. They did though give me first refusal on buying the house. When the estate agent came to value the house, he said he was doing it for probate. I asked what that meant, compared to a usual valuation. He replied that normally the valuation would be lower for probate and the family had asked him for it to be specifically as low as he could reasonably make it. I asked him what the true value was and then after a couple of weeks I approached the family and made them an offer half way between the two valuations. They almost bit my hand off with the speed they accepted my offer at.

It was years later that things changed in my life again. That was prompted by something that I had never imagined happening. I thought that I had been quite successful in not leaving a trail behind me whenever I moved. I really thought that I could not be found easily, not that I was trying to hide my identity from anyone other than the people I socialise with here in Kent.

I was just sitting in my living room one afternoon, browsing the internet and half listening to the music coming over the radio, when the doorbell sounded. When I answered the door, I found a smartly dressed man there. He had stepped back a pace or two, after pressing the doorbell.

'Jay Stott?' Those were the first words he uttered.

I have to admit my heart jumped into my mouth. Was this a policeman who has come to arrest me, for one or maybe even two murders? I do think about those occasionally. But then I didn't think he looked like a policeman. He has a clipboard in his hand and a briefcase too. I hope my face hasn't collapsed, with a look of total guilty shock. If it has, he doesn't let it show.

'I am' I reply, in a slightly guarded tone.

'I'm from a company of private detectives. I am looking for a Jay Stott.'

He hands me his card and waits while I read it. I look back up at him when I have read it.

'Do you think I can come in and go through a few things? I need to establish that you are the right Jay Stott. It is not a common name though, but I do need to go through some information.'

I invite him in and offer him a hot drink, which he accepts. Over the next half hour, I give him more than enough proof of exactly who I am. I am of course the Jay Stott that he is looking for and before he leaves, he gets me to sign some papers. It would appear that my father has died and he had some assets. He had no will as such, but there was something that he wrote down before he died, that he wanted his assets split between my mother and myself. My mother they had managed to find quite easily, but I had been more of a challenge to find.

What I have found out of course; is that my mother is still alive. I haven't thought about her for a very long time, probably not since I moved in here to be honest. And of course, I now know that my father has died. I don't feel anything at that. I don't know if I am surprised by that or not.

I did ask if he could tell me where my mother is living, but he said he couldn't do that without her permission. He did though say I could write her a note and he would make sure that it got to her. I quickly scribble my name and address on a piece of paper and a very short note. I also include my phone number. I put that in an envelope and hand it to him.

I am not sure how long it will be before I hear from her, if I will at all. I certainly don't in the few weeks that follow. In fact I have received the inheritance that my father left me and still I haven't heard a word from her. I have been slightly unsettled by this episode. I was surprised to find out that the sum I received was just over £100,000. I assume that my mother received the same. I wonder how he managed to accrue that amount of money. They certainly weren't in that league when I was living with them. And he obviously didn't have anyone else to leave his money to.

It was quite a bit after that, when I found out that my father had been in an accident and had a pay-out from an insurance company. The sum he'd received was considerably more than he had left when he died. He had spent a lot of money in his last couple of years. By that, I mean as much as he had left us and a bit more than that.

Then out of the blue, I got a phone call. It was maybe nine o'clock one evening, when my phone rang. I answered and initially there was no sound from the caller. The number was an unknown one. I guessed straight away who it was and said into my phone:

'Is that you Mum?'

'Jay' she replied and I recognised the voice, after all these years.

Chapter 41 Jay

The phone is put down and I haven't got the number to return the call. But I do know it was my mother on the other end of the phone. I expected she might try again in a few minutes, but it was actually a couple of days later that she rang again. Once more we went through the question from me and the one word answer from her. The telephone was put down again. The next time she rang, later that day, I tried a different tack.

'Do you want to meet up?' is what I said as I answered the telephone.

'Yes' she replied.

'Where do you want to meet?'

'Where do you live?'

I know she knows the answer to that one. She has my telephone number and she has my address too.

'Kent' I say, as relaxed as I can be.

'That's a long way.'

'I will come to you. Where are you?'

'I'm still in the same place, but at a different address.'

I wait a second or two, to see if she is going to give me the address. But there is nothing but silence coming through the phone line.

'Shall we meet out somewhere then?'

'That would be best.'

'Have you anywhere in mind?'

Again I am met with silence. I haven't been there for who knows how many years. I don't know what the place is like. I don't have much of a memory of the centre. I don't know where we can meet.

'There's a tea room just off the square. It's called The Parlour. I'll meet you there.'

'When do you want to meet?'

'What about tomorrow? Say about 10 o'clock?'

I don't even think about the logistics of that; I just agree to the meeting. I have an odd feeling about this all. There is a reason why she wants to meet me and it is not purely to see me.

'I'll be there.'

The phone goes dead in my hand. She hasn't given me any way to contact her, either by phone or her address.

I start to wonder what the real reason is for her wanting to meet me again, after all these years. The only thing I can think of; is that it is something to do with my Dad dying. I then try to work out how long it is going to take me to get there. I look it up on Google.

I could do it if I left early, but I would have to go round London and that could be very busy and also make me late. I can't afford to do that, as I have no way of contacting her, to let her know. Also I would like to know a little bit about my surroundings, before I meet up with her. I want to see how the place has changed. I want to see if it is anything like the little I remember.

So, I decide that I will drive up this afternoon and stay in a hotel for the night, maybe two. I don't want to stay there, but I don't want to be too far away either. I again use the internet, to find somewhere in the vicinity. I find somewhere about ten miles away. That is ideal. I book it online for two nights.

I park up when I get there, to the town and not the hotel, I mean. I have parked in a small car park, in a back street close to the centre. I wander round to the centre. I find the square she is talking about, easily enough. I don't remember this at all. I find the tea room too. That looks alright. It is not the best, but it is quite busy. It is more a café than a tea room. I make a tour of the rest of the centre. There isn't much to see. It is typical of so many towns these days. There are quite a few empty premises. It has its share of charity shops and a couple of smarter tea rooms. I think I would have chosen one of those, but no matter.

I take a walk a bit further out. I don't recognise anyone or anywhere. I am almost certain that no one will recognize me after all of this time. I do find the playing fields and the park and I wander over to the woods, but I don't bother going in, as I am certain my den will not have existed for years. I don't feel anything for the place. I have moved on from all this long ago.

I walk slowly back into the centre. I'm guessing it is going to be highly unlikely that my mother will be out and about. It wasn't something she used to do way back then, so I hardly think that will have changed.

I don't think there is anything else for me to do, so I make my way back to the car and then drive the ten miles to my hotel for the night.

I don't sleep particularly well. I don't know why that is precisely, but it is likely because of the impending meeting. I don't know what to expect. But I do know that I am an adult now. I am also quite able to look after myself. My mother will be an older woman, probably an old woman. There will be no physical issues this time. Not that I think that is what this meeting is about.

I have a shower and a light breakfast and leave the hotel just after 9 o'clock. I park the car in the same place as I did yesterday and then, still with twenty minutes to go until we meet, I find a place as far away from the Parlour I can get, where I can see the entrance. I have no idea which direction she will come from. I also then have a thought, that I will maybe not even recognise her. That is a distinct possibility, in fact almost a probability.

I try not to be too obvious and by the time my watch winds its way round to 10 o'clock, I have not seen one person either enter or leave the tearoom. In fact there has been a distinct lack of people out and about. I leave my position and amble across to the tea room. When I get there, I have a look through the window before I try the door. There are no customers in there and I can't see any staff either, but it is open.

I step inside and look around. I don't know why I do that, because the place is empty. A young girl appears from out the back.

'Good morning'

I say good morning back and make my way to a table in the farthest corner, away from where the girl appeared from. I sit down and order a coffee. I am hoping this is not going to be like the telephone calls, in that it is going to take several attempts to make contact.

I am almost finished my coffee and haven't been joined by her or anyone else for that matter. I look at my watch and see that it is now between quarter and twenty past. I debate whether to have another coffee, or just call it a day. I decide on the former and order it. Just as the girl is bringing it over to me, another customer comes in. I look up to see if it is her. Immediately I am almost sure it is not. This lady is not much older than me. She does look over at me, but there is no recognition, as she takes a seat over the other side of the tearoom.

Then the door opens again and an old lady walks slowly in. She is obviously having trouble walking. I can see that her clothes aren't totally clean and they are old like she is. She does not look at the lady who has just come in before her. She looks straight at me. I get to my feet. I can't say that I recognise her from memory, but there is no doubt in my head that this woman is my mother.

'Jay' she says, but without a smile.

'Hello Mum' I reply.

'It was your fault you know' are the next words that come out of her mouth, in a very accusing tone of voice. 'I blame you for it all.'

I am temporarily lost for words, but I gather myself and answer her.

'Is that what this meeting is about?'

'Not exactly' she softens her tone a smidgen. 'I just want you to know that I blame you. And your Dad definitely blamed you.'

Chapter 42 Jay and her Mum

We stop for a few seconds while she orders a coffee. The girl goes off to get it and my Mum continues to speak.

'He never came back you know.'

'You can't blame that on me, because you hit me too and I was taken away from you. So it is nothing to do with me, that you two didn't get back together.'

'Hmmmph' is all she says back at that comment.

I know there is a reason why she is saying this, trying to blame me. I am probably going to find out what that is soon enough. It is quiet for a minute or so. The girl brings her coffee over and Mum puts two sugars in it and then stirs it for well over a minute. I keep quiet while she does this. I am not expecting to get asked how was my upbringing after I was taken from her, which is just as well as she has no intention of asking me, I am sure.

She picks up her cup and sips at it, but it is way too hot. It is at that moment I smell the drink on her. It was as she opened her mouth when the first sip was too hot. It is not overpoweringly strong, but it is there all the same. I take the time while it is quiet to look her over. The clothes are really old and well-worn, as well as not being overly clean. I look at her hands and they are a bit grubby too. Her face shows the signs of a hard life. Not a life of hard work, but a hard life, if you know what I mean.

'When he left, I was left with nothing. He was the one who brought the money in. I had nothing to live on at all.'

I listen to her and know I could say some things, like even when they were together, there was little spent on food, clothes and things on the home. I could say that they rarely fed me properly, or cared for me. But there is no point, in my eyes, reflecting back on that period with her.

I just look at her while she is talking to me.

'They moved us away and gave us a little money, but it was nothing like what your Dad used to earn. I was never able to work, so that was all I had to live on. Then you left and they took some of that money away from me each week. I had even less then. I didn't know what to do and I suppose I just shut myself away. In the end they moved me out of there, as I wasn't paying my bills. They also said that I needed to get a job, but I have never worked. I did resort to other methods for a bit of extra money; I had to, so that I could survive.'

I dread to think what she is referring to and I am definitely not going to ask that question. I don't want to know about that period of her life. I also hope that she doesn't enlighten me as to what came after and how she got to today, other than the final reason of course, for this meeting. I drink my coffee. She isn't expecting me to talk at the moment. She probably thinks I am just her small child and will accept being talked at.

'He had an accident you know?'

I shake my head in response.

'That is how he got the money. I only knew about it at the time, because it was in the paper. Someone dropped a copy of it through my letterbox. I don't buy papers. The bit in the paper was telling about his pay-out. It was well over half a million pounds, but then he was badly injured.'

She looks at me for a reaction, but she isn't going to get one from me. So she drains her cup and then continues:

'It gave the place where he lived, but not his address. I tried to find him, but I couldn't. I haven't got experience in finding people. I am not that clever. I did try though, as I believe he owed it to me to share it. I always expected him to come home to me after his sentence was served, but he never came back. So in my eyes, we were still together. We hadn't separated as such, so we are still together. What I am saying is that what is his is mine. So he has this big pay-out for his accident, but I should have been benefitting from his injury pay-out.'

I get an idea come into my head at this moment that I think I know where this conversation is heading. I think the moment is virtually upon us, to have the reveal.

'I wrote a letter to the newspaper and asked them to forward it to him. They must have done, because I got a reply a week later. It was short and sharp. It said the money was his. He said that it was your fault that he was put in prison and it was my fault that he wouldn't come home. He said some really nasty things about me and you. He said he could never come back if you were there. I wrote back via the newspaper, as he hadn't given me the address, saying that you weren't with me and that I would never have you back ever. I said that you were the cause of all our problems and that it was best you had been taken away.'

Am I really hearing this from her? Firstly it is not a true version of events and secondly, all she was trying to do was to get to his money.

'I said that you had always been trouble and a nasty child. I said sorry to him that I had you and that you had turned out to be so revolting and bad, evil even. You see, I let him get me pregnant. I should never have had you.'

I've had enough. This is a nasty bitter old woman I have in front of me. She is not talking like a mother should to her child; a child that other people have had to bring up, because she couldn't, or maybe as I am hearing now, wouldn't.

'So what did you want to see me for then?'

'I want my money of course. I know they gave you half of what he left. But he has spent more than half, so there is only less than my half left.'

'What do you mean; your half? The only half you are entitled to is the half he left to you and me. You are not entitled to half of what he was awarded for his accident.'

'I am, as we should have been together. If it wasn't for you, our little scumbag, I would have had that money when he got paid out. As it is, I only have been given half of what he left. What was given to you is mine and I want it; I want it back.'

'It is not yours.'

'It is' she replies, raising her voice. 'That money is mine. If you hadn't caused all that trouble and got him arrested and put in prison, then we would have been together. He would have left me all that money when he died. I don't know why he left you half now, to be honest.'

'Well he has. Why don't we go back to your house and try to settle this in private?'

'I'm not taking you there. My money is there.'

'What do you mean by your money is there?'

'I mean just that! My money is in my house. I am not going to trust those banks to keep it. Look at what they have done; how can you trust them? I withdrew it.'

She sits back with a smug smile on her face, as if I am not smart enough to have done the same with the money I received. She opens her bag and takes out a quarter bottle of vodka and takes a slug of it, before putting the bottle away in her bag again.

'Well I am not going to sit here to discuss it in public.'

'You can come to my house when you bring me my money' she challenges me with her offer.

But I have a reason for the answer I give her, I'm sure you will understand why I am offering this. That is because I have seen an opportunity for me and anyway she has been so nasty about me.

'I'll have to go and get it. Obviously I don't have it on me.'

'Will it be in cash?' an excited reply and she even smiles at me. I'd rather she hadn't, as her teeth are awful.

'I don't have cash and I won't be able to get that sort of money in cash quickly.'

'No, you're right. They only let me take out a bit at a time in cash. But you will bring it as a cheque or something like that?'

'Yes I will' I reply willingly.

'How long will it take you?' her eagerness is becoming more prevalent, at the thought of her getting my half of the money.

'I'll have to go home and go to the bank to get it transferred, so that I can write a cheque. I guess if I get there today, then it will be done straight away and so I could give it to you tomorrow. If you give me your address, I will bring it round.'

'I'll ring you in the morning and give it to you then, when you have the cheque with you. I don't want people to see you giving me my money back.'

That is about as good as I can expect.

'Alright, I should be ready by 11 or 12 tomorrow.'

'Pay the bill and you then leave first. I don't want you to follow me.'

I have no intention of doing that. I don't need to, if she is going to give me the address tomorrow. The other customer and the girl haven't been paying us any attention. There is no need to force the issue, for the sake of twenty four hours.

I get up and pay the bill. She watches me leave and I walk away. I don't look back even once. When I get to my car I get in, start it up and then drive off, back towards my hotel. It is a good job I booked for two nights.

Chapter 43 Jay & her Mum

I don't go straight to my hotel. Instead I make for a supermarket and purchase a couple of bottles of vodka. I also buy some mixers to go with them. I then go to another supermarket, a smaller one this time and buy a further two bottles of vodka. I have paid cash for all of them. They are not for me you understand; I have a reason for buying them, but I am sure you know that already.

I don't have a precise plan. In fact I haven't actually got a plan at all. I have an idea, out of which I hope a method will arise, probably as the time approaches. I know what I could do with, as the method has been very successful previously. But I don't have that to hand. But then there may be something else I can use. I will look it up when I get back to the hotel. There may well be something I can buy over the counter that will serve my purpose just as well.

I have a drive around the area, before eventually arriving back at the hotel mid-afternoon. I go straight to my room and start to look up alternatives. I find out something I have to admit I didn't know, but have never had the cause to. There are some apparently very effective sleep aids. I decide on the one I want to buy; Nytol. It isn't going to do the same job by any means, but it should be useful in addition to what else I have got.

I look at my watch and think about going out now, but decide against it. I will drive somewhere further away in the morning, to get my supply. One box will be more than sufficient for my purposes. I watch a bit of television and then go down to the restaurant for my meal. In the morning, I check out of the hotel after breakfast and then drive about twenty five miles, in the opposite direction to Mum's house. I decide to buy them from a supermarket pharmacy, rather than an independent pharmacy. I am sure loads of people buy this product all of the time, but I want to try not be memorable. Like before, I am hopeful that there will not be a price to pay.

I wonder what time she will ring me. She has not been the most reliable in this up to now. But then this time she has an incentive to ring me. She thinks I am going to give her over £100,000. I know that is not going to happen, but she doesn't; she thinks I have folded to her demands.

I have finished my purchase and am back in my car, when my phone rings.

'Jay. It's Mum. Have you got it?

'No, I haven't got it in the way I think you mean.'

'Have you got the cash? Remember I know exactly how much there should be, because I have had the same amount already.'

'We have already been through this. It is not going to be in cash. I told you that I can't get that amount of cash. You said even you had to draw it out in cash, bit by bit.'

She is quiet at the other end for a minute. I don't say any more; I wait for her to answer.

'So I am not going to get the money. You've gone back on what you've said.'

She sounds a bit groggy to me. It is probably the after effect of over celebration on her part last night.

'Yes I am arranging the money to be available as we speak. But it won't be in cash. You know that. I have to wait for them to ring me when they have the funds available. Then I have to go down to transfer it into my account.'

'When will you be here?'

'I don't know exactly. It depends when they ring me. I expect it will be very soon. Give me your address and telephone number and I will come as soon as I have the cheque to give you.'

The phone goes down on me. She is a really hard and awkward person to try to have a conversation with on the telephone, or in person for that matter. That is even with the incentive she has, of this huge sum of money coming her way.

I'm not going to get worked up about this. I know she will ring back, because she is desperate to get this money from me. I go and find a place where I can get something to eat. I get something to take away, as I want to be free to speak with her privately when she rings back.

It is nearly two hours later that she calls me. I know it is her, as the number is still showing as unknown. I let it ring for nearly a minute before I pick it up.

'Have you got my money yet?' she says quite aggressively over the phone.

'I have just finished arranging it. I will start back, if you give me the address. It is going to take me a while to get there, as I will meet lots of traffic at the time of day I'm going round the M25.'

'I really wanted to meet you at the tea room again.'

'We agreed I would come to your house. I'm not handing this money over in a public place. I don't want people to see us doing this. I'm sure you don't either.'

I'm giving the impression that she is going to get cash. I am not going to go through the problems of getting that amount of cash, if that is what she thinks I am going to bring.

'But I don't want you there. You will know where I live then and I don't want that.'

It is time to fight fire with fire.

'Look Mum. I don't really want to give you this money, but I have agreed to. I have wasted all morning trying to organise it and then here you are again, demanding this and that. Well it is not going to happen that way, if you want the money. It will be dark by the time I get there. The tea room will be closed probably and I'm not handing the money over in public. I promise I won't keep a note of your address and I won't ever see you again, if you like. But if you want the money, you have to give me the address and I will come to you.'

The phone is cut off once more. She really is a very tiresome person. She certainly hasn't improved with age. I move my car to another place, where I will sit for a while.

I am only just there when my phone rings again.

'I'll meet you in the square.'

'I'll give you one last chance. Give me the address and I'll bring the money to you, or I just keep it. Trust me; I have a legal right to do that. I can use the money just as much as you can. Do I make myself clear?'

I cut the call this time. I sit there for a good half hour, waiting for her to ring. I'm thinking she is not going to ring me again. But I should know better than that. The driving force here is the money and she isn't going to let go of that. My phone rings again.

'Meet me tomorrow at 10 o'clock in the tea room.'

I cut the call without speaking a word. I start the car and move off. About two minutes later the phone rings, but I don't stop to answer it. I am tired of her games. I'm going to make her sweat on this. As I drive for about half an hour, to book in to another hotel, the phone rings about six times. Each and every time I ignore the ringing. It stops after a couple of minutes each time.

By the time I've found another hotel, checked in for the night and gone to my room, the phone has rung at least another four times. I have turned the phone on silent the minute I was leaving the privacy of my car. I don't want people to remember me and my ringing phone, which I wasn't going to answer.

I make a cup of coffee and sit down to drink it. I'm watching a bit of afternoon TV. My phone is still switched to silent. I keep an eye on it. It lights up every time she tries to ring me. I'm hoping what I am doing will make her desperate.

I am not sure if that is what has happened, or she has just made a mistake, but my phone rings and shows the number of the caller. It isn't a number I know. It could be her or anyone. I decide to answer it.

'Hello.'

'Jay.'

It is my Mum and she is ringing from a landline.

'I'll give you my number, but you'll have to come tomorrow now.'

'No, I will come today, or not at all. I have things booked that I need to do tomorrow. It is either this evening or not at all.'

For a change she doesn't put the phone down on me. She blurts out her address and then before I get a chance to respond or check it with her, she puts the phone down. I write it down, before I forget any of it. I then sit back and have a good smile.

Chapter 44 Jay & her Mum

I'm not going to make it too late, but I am not going to make it suspiciously early. She only has herself to blame. Mind you if she had any idea what I have planned to do, then she would never have given me the address, or even met me anywhere that she could be followed home from. But then her only concern has been that I might not give her the money.

I almost wish that I hadn't booked into the hotel now. I haven't brought my bag in yet and I have already paid and you can do check out easily from the room. I will have to think how to play this. I make another coffee when I have finished the first one and then watch some television for a while. She doesn't ring me back. In her eyes I'd like to think that she is assuming I am on my way.

I notice the darkness come in and I wait in my room. It isn't going to take me too long to get to her, but I'm certainly not going yet. I want to make her wait, until I am ready to go.

It is about nine o'clock that I leave my room. I make sure there is nothing in there. I see that the person on the front desk has changed. I am hoping that they will change again, before I am planning on coming back.

I did think that she might have rung me by now again, maybe starting to panic that I wasn't coming with her precious money. I arrive in her town a while after and park in the car park near the square. There are a few cars in there still and mine doesn't stand out too much. I take my shopping out of the boot and make sure I have the box of tablets in my pocket.

I have looked up the address on a street map and know which way I have to go. I do not know what sort of house I am looking for. There aren't many people about and even less I have to walk past. I have my long coat on and my hat. I keep my head down. The streets aren't that well-lit, so I don't think I will be remembered.

I make a few turns and know I am getting close. I have to say I had not really thought about the type of house she might live in. I turn into her road. There is no one walking here and all of the curtains are drawn, in the houses I pass. They are small terraces of bungalows. I guess they are retirement homes, probably only one bedroom. I think that makes sense. Where we had been moved to all those years ago had at least two bedrooms; it might even have had three.

The numbers are easy enough to see from the footpath. Hers is one of the houses past the place where those who have cars, park them. I don't look around me, to see if I am being watched. I really don't think I am. I step up to her door. Her house is an end of terrace. I decide not to ring the bell, but try the door first. I am expecting it to be locked at this time of night, but it is not. I open the door and step in. The hallway is lit. I call out. I am not intending to frighten her, by just walking into the room. I have the thought that I wouldn't be surprised if she has gone to bed. The time is approaching ten o'clock after all.

'Mum, I'm here' I say it in a normal voice. I don't know how sound will carry in these houses and if the person next door will be able to hear things.

'I'm in here' the voice comes from behind the first door.

I am wary as I open the door. I don't know why I am, but then maybe I am still uncertain about her and her potential volatility. She could bonk me on the head as I go through the door, or maybe she could have someone with her. That would be a total disaster. That would change the whole dynamics of this visit and the money too. I don't dwell on that horrendous thought. I push the door open; as far back as it will go. There is no way there could be anyone behind it.

Mum is sitting, slouched on a big armchair. She has a bottle on the table by her chair and a glass in her hand. She looks me up and down as I take off my coat and hat, but not my gloves. I take out one of the bottles of vodka I have brought and put it on the table. I then put the rest on the floor in front of her.

'I've brought these for you. I noticed the other day that you had the smell of drink on your breath, when we were in the tea room.'

'That's better than the stuff I normally drink. I've been drinking beer recently, but now I'm getting the rest of my money, I have been celebrating with this.'

She holds up her glass and points to the bottle on the table.

'Do you want one of these' I ask her.

'Don't mind if I do. I've had enough of this, waiting for you to arrive. I didn't think you would be this late. I'm normally in bed by now; or asleep in my chair if I've had too much.'

'Do you want it in the same glass or a clean one?'

'There is a clean one in the kitchen, but before that you can give me my money.'

It is hard not to notice the greedy glint in her eyes, as she watches me take her cheque out of my pocket.

'That's not cash' she says, as soon as she can see what I've brought out.

'It's as good as' I reply 'this is what they call a Banker's draft.'

It isn't of course, but I'm banking on the fact that she won't know what that is and that she has never seen one before. I have used a very fine print to write the cheque.

'At least you brought my money.' She reaches out a shaky hand, for me to give her the cheque. 'That's a bit more than I got' she says with a slight slur when she inspects it. She isn't challenging me about it not being a Banker's Draft.

'I got them to round it up. They said it was easier for them to do that so I did it.

I'm hoping she'll think I'm stupid for doing that. I can see her thinking that now, as she looks at it and me.

'You need to make sure you don't lose it. It is just like cash. You should put it safely away with the rest of your money, until you can get it to your bank.'

She starts to try to get up out of her chair. Then she looks at me.

'You can go into the kitchen and get me a clean glass, while I go and put this away.'

I wait for her to get to her feet, before I move off towards the kitchen. She goes into the hallway and then turns left. I turn round and follow her. I peep round the doorframe, in time to see her go into the next room. I move quietly along and peep round that doorway. She is down on the floor by the bed, lifting up the covers. She slides the divan drawer open and puts the cheque in there. I back off quickly and make my way, as fast as I can, to the kitchen. I open the cupboard doors and lift out a glass. It is supposed to be clean, but I can see that it isn't. But it probably is to her.

I wait a few seconds and then make my way back into her living room, but not before crushing a couple of my tablets in the bottom of the glass. I make it to the bottle on the table, before she comes back into the room. I fill the glass at least a third full of spirit. She comes in and sits back down on her chair. She picks up the glass I have just filled and downs it in one. I know she didn't even look at it. I put my hand out and she gives it to me. I fill it again and hand it back. It goes the same way as the first one. I fill it up again, before saying I am off to the kitchen to get a glass for me to have a drink too.

'I suppose you can stay for the one' she slurs at me, while necking down this one. I have to turn back and refill hers, before I go to the kitchen for my glass. In there I take another glass from the cupboard and crush two more tablets in it. This glass is also for her and not for me. I have no intention of drinking out of any of her glasses.

Chapter 45 Jay & her Mum

By the time I make it back to the living room, she is more than ready for another top up. Her voice may well have been slurred, but her eyes are steady as she watches me walk into the room.

'Pour one for both of us and we'll drink it together.'

Now that is going to be a problem for me, as I have already told you I have crushed some tablets in the bottom of the glass. I can see from the look in her eyes; that she is going to insist. I hold my glass up quickly and then make a tut-tut noise.

'It's dirty' I say, as I quickly turn back towards the kitchen.

'The alcohol will do for that' she says to my departing back.

It may well do, but it won't for the powder I have put in there too. I wash the powder down the sink and then wipe the glass on my clothes. I don't fancy wiping it on the cloth hanging on the rail. I walk back through to her.

'It will have to be a small one, as I am driving. I don't want to get done for drink-driving.'

'It wouldn't be a bad thing if you were' she retorts 'at least then it would make it harder for you to come and see me.'

The smile she gives me at that comment is not a nice one. She is not a nice woman.

I pour us both a drink. Her glass is filled to the brim, literally. My glass has an inch of liquor, but I have no intention of having anything more than a sip of it. She holds out her glass for me to tap it with mine. Reluctantly I do so and hers is back to her mouth, before I can even think of taking a sip of mine. While she is engaged drinking hers, I slop a bit of mine over the arm of the chair, on purpose. It will look as if I have had some, to her eyes. I hope.

She doesn't quite finish her drink this time. She stops and holds the glass in both hands, while staring across at me.

'I don't know where we went wrong with you. You could have turned out so well.'

I really don't know what to make of that. I also don't know what to make of the fact that her voice was not slurred as she spoke. Suddenly she gets up and sprints, relatively, across the room and out of the door. A few seconds later, I hear her retching in the bathroom, followed a few seconds later by the toilet being flushed. She appears back in the living room, quite buoyant.

'Always happens when I change the brand I drink.'

She throws the rest of the drink that was left in her glass onto the carpet in front of her and reaches for her own bottle. She slops a generous measure in her glass and starts the drinking session again. She isn't bothered whether I am drinking or not. What concerns me; is the question of when she is going to ask me to leave. I can see that coming any minute and she is far from passing out, from either the drink or the powder.

She has three large drinks on the spin, without a breath between them. When she finishes the last of these, she slams the glass down on the arm of the chair. It spins out of her grasp and drops to the floor. She looks across at me, as if that is my fault too. She starts to mouth something, maybe she is starting to say something, but it doesn't come out. Then she suddenly smiles and flops back in her chair. It takes me a bit by surprise. The question is; is she faking it, or has she passed out.

I give her a minute or two. In the meantime I take my glass back to the kitchen and wipe down anything I may have touched, although I have been extra careful. When I go back through to the living room, I find that she hasn't moved a muscle. I don't sit down, but go over to her side. She has a strange look on her face. It is a bit like she has had a shock. This puzzles me, as I didn't expect her to stop like this and so suddenly.

I then notice she has a strange colour to her too. I reach for her hand, expecting her to open her eyes and make a grab for me, or even strike out at me. That doesn't happen. I take her hand in mine and then feel for her pulse in her wrist. I can't feel anything. I quickly feel for the one in her neck, but that isn't there either. I give her a shake, but she doesn't respond.

My mind starts to race. My first instinct is to run through to the bedroom and gather up the cash and then make my escape and let whoever might be next through the door find her like this. In fact I get as far as doing that, in so far as I get all the cash and my cheque out of the divan draw and into the bag I have brought with me to carry it away. It is one of these shopping bags that fit in a pouch. I only just get all there is in the drawer in there. I am just on the verge of leaving the house forever, when the thought comes to me. They will have seen us together in the tearoom, and someone may just have seen me walk along the path. I think she has died from something other than the powder I put in her first glass of vodka from me. If I were to guess, I would say she has had a heart attack, or something similar. What I am thinking is that she has died from natural causes; or the drink at worst.

I make a decision and action it immediately. I take the bag and go into her bedroom. I wrap it up in one of her jumpers and put it back in the divan drawer. I then check on her once more and then ring for an ambulance. I then sit nervously and wait for the emergency services to arrive.

It is a close call, but the ambulance makes it there first by a squeak. They come into the house and it takes them no time at all to establish what I had. She has died and she is beyond help. At that moment the police arrive too.

Of course I am asked what transpired. I tell the story as it is, except I miss out the part about the powders. I also miss out the part about the cheque I have brought. That is back in my possession. I am taking no chances that it would legally come back my way. Anyway there is nothing to say I was going to give it to her. I very much doubt she will have publicised the fact that she was about to receive more money. People may have noticed she was flusher with money, but I doubt she told them about how much she had inherited.

The ambulance crew are fairly certain that she has had a heart attack. One of them goes through to the bedroom and the bathroom. They reappear a few minutes later with some pills. They confirm that she did have a heart problem.

There is no question that I have anything to do with this. They eventually leave, having taken my details of course. The police have contacted her doctor, who must have been overjoyed that he was called that late in the evening. But he confirmed she had a heart problem and had been advised to stop drinking. He was not surprised to hear she had dropped down dead. Apparently she had seen a specialist just two days ago and he told her she was at serious risk too. I was asked if I wanted a post mortem doing, as if I did not, they didn't have a problem with me contacting an undertaker.

The undertaker arrived about an hour later and about ten minutes after that, I took my leave of her house for the last time. I had scouted round her papers, but there was nothing of consequence. All she had was the money my father left her and I have that. I have the numbers I need to contact for the housing association and I have her door key. I will pay someone to clear the place. There is nothing in there that I want. I will settle up with the undertaker and I expect I will attend her very low key funeral.

Two weeks later the funeral was attended by a dozen people. They were mostly her neighbours. We had an afternoon tea in the common room of the centre, at the end of the road. I had settled up with the undertaker, after I went to register her death. I took him the certificate he needed. He gave me the number of someone who would clear her house and by the time the funeral came round, they were already working on her place to get it ready for the next occupant.

Part 4
Chapter 46 BACK IN WENLOCK

As you can imagine, I wasn't the first in the queue to move to Much Wenlock. It certainly had never been my intention. But a lot of water has gone under the bridge since I was last here. A lot has changed. I have changed. In many ways I am not the person who was here at one time in the past. And when my partner became so keen to make the move, I was rather swept along with it all.

I reasoned with myself that it is just another place, except I have a little bit of history here. But it was a while ago. I was hardly in the place. I kept to the house for the vast majority of the time. There were very few people I came into contact with when I was here. Yes, there were very few people indeed that I came into contact with. After all, that was something I tried to be most careful about at the time.

And as I said, I am a different person now. Inside I am the same, but I have had a bit of work done on my features. Not a great deal, but enough to satisfy changing a part of me that I wasn't very struck on. And while I was doing that, I took the opportunity to restyle myself. I changed my hairstyle to something much more modern and I changed the way I dress. But then I only wore working clothes when I visited Much Wenlock before. I didn't wear anything like the clothes I wear now.

So when my partner and I went on a tour of the Midlands, as well as a journey into Wales, I had no idea where we might finish up at the end of each day. We really hadn't planned anything. We stayed in Bridgnorth and for our evening meal we found a place in Whitburn Street. As you do, we got chatting to the people at the next table. They were giving us advice on some of the things that they thought we should consider visiting, in the local area. Ironbridge of course came up, with the bridge being the top attraction recommended. They said that, depending on our interests, the other museums there are good to see too. Then they talked about other places and the next one they mentioned was Much Wenlock, the home of the modern Olympics.

I know I must have reacted in some way, as my partner asked me if I was alright. I managed to cover over the shock I had felt at the mention of Much Wenlock. My partner continued to talk to the people at the next table and I looked on, only realising as the conversation progressed, that we were less than 10 miles away from the place. I hadn't realised that we were that close.

The next morning we drove over to Ironbridge and took in one or two of the sites. After a pub lunch, we drove the short distance to Much Wenlock. The direction we came in from was less familiar to me. I know I have been in this way before, but I didn't really take notice of things then. I was on a quest at the time.

I did recognize the car park, as my partner drove into the St Marys car park. We take turns at the driving. Today it is their turn. It gives the other an opportunity to take in the countryside sights, as we drive through it.

I was a little nervous as went over to the meter, to buy the parking ticket. I quickly felt better, as I convinced myself that no one would recognise me from the last time. Why would they? I'm very much hoping that there is no reason to need to remember me. I'm very much hoping that she is still under the concrete, in the house I can see as I walk back to the car with the ticket.

We walk through the Mutton Shutt, down the side of the George & Dragon. We emerge onto the High Street and turn left. For such a small town, there is a good variety of retail establishments. By the time we reach what appears to be the end of the shops, we have passed a couple of clothes shops, a couple of book shops, a deli, a butcher, a sweet shop, a takeaway, a pharmacy and a tea room. That list doesn't include the craft shop, charity shop, the Chinese takeaway, another pub and an Indian Restaurant or the estate agent.

We turned round when we got to the end of the shops and walked down the other side of the street, looking in all of the windows as we did so. My partner took special interest in the properties being advertised by the estate agent.

'They look quite nice' was the only comment offered though.

We have been talking about moving from where we live and finding a new house for the both of us, somewhere new in the country. I just wasn't expecting that house to be in one of the few places I have some history. But of course, my partner knows nothing of that. They know nothing of the old me.

We move on down the High Street and into the square. There are more shops there, with three more eateries in that area; a Spar, museum, another clothes shop, a baker, a hairdresser, a superstore, a couple of gift shops, an art gallery, antique shop and yet another estate agent. That one attracted more of our time again, with more local properties to tempt my partner.

We go into Tea on the Square for afternoon tea and cake; very enjoyable it is too. After that we wander over to the Museum and Tourist Information office and have a look around there too. We pick up some leaflets and then retreat to the car, to decide what we are going to do next. I know my partner is keen to spend some more time here and I do not want to make a fuss, about something I would not and could not explain to them. After a brief chat, we walk back into the town again and are guided towards the Raven, as a possible place we could stay. We note they have a shop attached, but at the time we are now at, it is past its closing time.

With a room secured for the night and a table in the bar for our food in the evening, we take to the streets, to take a wider tour of the town. We wander down to the Bull Ring and take a right, down towards the Priory. It too is closed when we get there, but a mental note is taken, as a place to visit the next day. We get the idea that it would be hard to get lost for long in the town, so we walk round some of the streets, looking at the styles of houses. The further we walk round, the more I get the feeling that my partner has fallen in love with the place.

Somehow, about an hour or so later, we end up at the Broseley end of town, coming out onto Barrow Street. Even then I am sure we haven't seen all there is to see, but we have seen a good variety of styles of property as we walked round. Something else we note; is how friendly people are as we walk round. We don't pass countless numbers of people, but the ones we do pass do speak to us. And it isn't the sort of look you sometimes get in these places of "who are you and what are you doing here?"

I have to say the meal in the evening is excellent and the service is ever so good. The chef in the kitchen is extremely talented. I know that it is the sort of place we would use regularly, if we did ever move here. That is something I am hoping won't happen, but by the minute I have been seeing that battle is going to be lost, not that we have battled about anything yet.

I half expect that in the morning we will be trooping down to the estate agents, to not only pick up some particulars, but also to arrange viewings too. But that does not happen. We have a quick walk around the town, before we depart around mid-morning. We don't do the Priory, or the walks we had found out about. They are to be for another time.

Chapter 47 Jay tours

We spend a few more weeks travelling around, moving further west as we go. My partner doesn't mention Wenlock once, after we have left that morning. In fact I am actually at the point of hoping that the whim has passed, so to speak.

There are so many beautiful places that we stay in over that period and my partner is, in my opinion, nearly as enthusiastic about some of these places, as in Wenlock. We even visit estate agents in some of these places and pick up some particulars. On reflection, I should have noted the difference, in that we did not engage in the walk around the residential parts of these places.

Although our tour has no real time boundaries as such, there was always a time that we have to be home for. We both have a number of appointments that we had purposely made well into the future, at the time. So with about four days to go until we have to be home, we decide we will make a leisurely return to base. Admittedly it isn't going to be as leisurely as the outward journey, but it isn't going to be a one day dash.

Although technically it is not their turn, my partner decides that they will drive the first leg. We haven't discussed which route we are going to take home, or where we will stop. I guess I assumed that we would be taking a route that we haven't covered so far; wrong!

I am not sure why we don't have a discussion, or more to the point why my partner does not discuss it with me. I think, also in retrospect, it was because they had a suspicion that I would have said no at the time, to come this way. I think I just know when we join the A5; that we will be going close to Wenlock. It is when we get to Shrewsbury and they just swing our car onto the A458, that I feel the pit in my stomach.

'Guess where I have just thought of stopping'

My thoughts immediately doubt that this is just a thought that came as we neared Shrewsbury. My cynical mind very much doubts that this is anything, but a definitely pre-planned excursion to visit Wenlock on our way home. But, I am not that much against it that I am going to challenge them, well not now at least. It will be remembered and as I fear we will be moving here sometime in the future, I really don't want there to be anything major for them to make a connection from. I try to put on my best smile. I am trying to give the look that I have been expecting this and it is a treat that we are doing this.

What I don't know until we get into Wenlock; is that my partner has been busier than I thought over the matter. Not only does it come out that they have been looking on Rightmove and a couple of other similar sites while we have been touring. But they have also gone one step further and been in contact with the estate agents of three properties. Further to that, and I am starting to get seriously pissed off by the secrecy that is being revealed to me, three appointments have been made for today for us to view properties.

I find it really hard to keep my composure. I thought we had a relationship, where we are honest with each other. Just to make that statement clear, I do mean about our life together. There are things we don't know about each other's past, but we have been clear about our relationship being a fresh start, where we don't have to justify our previous lives. Now, for the first time that I am aware of, we have a situation where one of us has done something, which kind of breaks the magic, in my eyes. I know we aren't actually committed to anything, but it was unnecessary not to talk about what was being planned and arranged.

In the nicest way I can muster, I do register my dissatisfaction with the way this morning has been approached. I say it, holding back my urge to explode. If there is one thing that I really struggle with, something that I find really hard to deal with, something that I know I react to badly; and that is surprises. I really, really do not like surprises and my partner knows that, but on this occasion they have chosen to ignore that. The question I really want to ask is; why? But I don't think at this particular moment in time, I will get an honest and precise answer, so I don't ask it. I just make it plain that I am not happy and am now not in a good mood.

I know they realise that they have done this the wrong way, but it does not dampen their enthusiasm for what they have arranged. I try to put the annoyance behind me and we keep the three appointments. The cynical side of me comes to the fore once more, as we do the viewings. My partner, I believe, should know what kind of property I would like to live in. Saying that, what we have here is nothing like what we live in at the present, so maybe I am being a bit harsh here. But then even saying that, it is obvious to me that the first two properties are not going to satisfy our needs. They are new houses and as such the rooms are quite small. I don't see myself in either of these houses. I like a bit of space and the first two just don't provide that.

The third house is much older, but there is something about it. I find it cold. I can't explain fully what I mean by that, but there is just something characterless about it. The problem I have; is that I think because of the way things have been handled today, my partner is expecting me to not like any of them, because of that. So the fact that I don't like it now as I see it; is a bit awkward. I can see that my partner does not like the first two, so that is alright, but he hasn't dismissed the third one out of hand and that is going to be a problem, if this is the extent of the houses to view.

The agent who is showing us around is very keen on us for some reason. Maybe that is just his way, but I think he spots a potential sale and he is directing his efforts onto my partner. I guess I would do the same in his position.

We finish the viewing and the agent says he will be in touch, in a couple of days, if he doesn't hear from us first. What I find is interesting, is that we haven't discussed finances. When we got together, my partner and I obviously had separate residences. Probably as I am more insistent that the past is gone and I don't want any connection with it in my new life. So when we decided we would live together, it was me who gave up where I was living. As it so happened I was renting at the time, but my partner knows I have my own money and I don't depend on work, or a pension, to live. But they have no idea, or at least I believe they don't know what I am worth, if you know what I mean. So I also do not know what my partner is worth, but I do know they own the house we live in. That has been mentioned in conversation. I could have looked it up on Zoopla to see what it is worth, but I am not bothered, as that is their business.

But my point is; that they have arranged to see these houses without us discussing where the money is coming from to buy it. Maybe I am doing them an injustice and they are going to buy the house solely from their own funds.

We stay in town and grab a bite to eat in the Copper Kettle, before resuming our journey a bit further towards home, before we stop for the night. I think my partner had been thinking of staying over at the Raven again, but saw that was maybe a step too far for today. I do get an apology after we leave town and as we don't talk about the property again that day, things more or less return to normal. Normal being, that we get on very well and our chat is light hearted and loving.

Chapter 48 A House in Wenlock

Much as I'd thought would happen, my partner embarks on a charm offensive. They can be very persuasive when they do that. Part of how they get away with it, is because generally they know how to get round me and what I like. They also know that I love having their attention focused on me.

We give ourselves a couple of weeks at home, catching up on the things we need to from our absence. We then take a week-long trip to East Anglia. Naturally while we are there, we also take the opportunity to look at houses. We not only look at particulars, but we also do one viewing. It was going to be more than that, but after just the one we both agree that there is nothing wrong with the house. It is the area that is wrong for us. We just don't want to live in that part of the country.

We spend several separate weeks over the next three months, travelling and staying in different parts of the country, but each time we come up short. There is just nowhere we come across that is even close to how we both feel about our first trip, to the Midlands and Wales. And to be even more specific than that, there is nowhere we like better than Shropshire. To go one step further than that, Much Wenlock is head and shoulders above the rest.

I have on more than one occasion gone to the local library. My intention is not only to change my books, but also to use the internet there. Yes, I do have internet on my phone and yes, I do have the internet at home. But what I want to look up, I do not want there to be history on either of those, just in case.

I have been keeping track for a while and even more so since we visited Much Wenlock and stayed there. But there is absolutely nothing that has surfaced, literally, about my history previously with the town. Nor for that matter has there been anything I could find about the one before that, for a long time, but it did eventually come out. But the story seemed to drift into insignificance in the news value and I didn't get to see what and how any investigation might be going. I am fairly sure, as I am about the one in Much Wenlock, that there isn't a trail for them to follow and certainly not one that will lead back to me. I stop looking at that one after a while. I still keep an eye on Much Wenlock.

Well, they say a lot of things in life are about timing. Sometimes timing can work in your favour and some people would call that luck, probably good luck. And then sometimes there is the type of timing that just comes at the wrong time. That is the type of timing I experienced and the bad timing, as you may well have guessed, comes from Much Wenlock.

We have just committed to buying the house there. I have given in, well in my head I have, outwardly I am enthusiastic. Then I pick it up, in a piece in the Shropshire Star, about a body being found, under the concrete in an extension in Much Wenlock. It didn't say exactly where, in the article I read, but it didn't have to. I admit to having a private bout of nerves and I was no doubt a bit edgy for the next couple of weeks. But then I pull myself together. I am extremely confident that no one knows me and that there is no trail to follow.

The day comes for our move and we travel to Much Wenlock. I take to buying the local papers, to keep in touch with what is going on in our new neighbourhood. It is pretty much the only contact we have with the town initially, as we take the time to get the house to our liking. In the meantime, there is little in the press about the discovery. As far as I am aware they never even make the connection between the owner of the property and the body they found. They might have done, but none of that information reached the print stories I found.

When we are ready, we start to make forays out into the town on a regular basis. I am a bit nervous at first, but of course there is no one around to point a finger at me; or so I think at the time.

We have read about the Monday walking group. We have seen them on occasion, while we were doing up the house, well my partner has and they have reported back to me. We are at the stage when we are ready to get involved in the community. We decide that a good way to make a start; is to go on the Monday walk. As it happens, the first morning we do so; there are three other couples who have made a similar decision. All of us are relative newbies to the town.

There is a good crowd before the walk and there are more than one walking group available, depending on ability. We choose the one that most people choose. The four couples stick together and generally we have a good time. After we get back, it is suggested that we go to one of the tea rooms and have a cup of coffee. It is only when we come to pay, that one of the people does something that is very odd. It certainly shows her and her partner up, to a lesser degree, on their true nature. My thought is that she isn't a nice person and that she tries to act above her station. She certainly thinks she is better than she is in reality. And for sure she is tighter than a gnats arse (excuse my language). To be fair, I think he is embarrassed by her, but it is easy to see this is not the first time.

Over the next few weeks, we keep going on the Monday walk and then going for a cup of coffee afterwards. They make their excuses each time and to be honest none of us miss them.

I am not sure which week it is that I first notice something. At first I am really not sure at all, but once my awareness is raised, I take a closer look. I take my mind back, to try to find out when it first might have happened. I'm actually thinking it could well have been the first week we went on the walk. I didn't think anything of it at the time, but on reflection I do remember a man looking over in our direction. As I say I didn't think anything of it at the time, but it is when I notice him standing in the telephone box while we are in the tea room, when it comes to me that he is watching us. Of course in my head, I come to the conclusion that he is watching me, of course. Why would he be doing that? The answer does not come to me for a while. In fact it is a while later that I think I get the reason. And that is only after I happened to have walked down the town for some shopping.

My intention had been to go to the butcher for some meat, get a few things from the Spar and some bread from the baker. I complete the first part of my task and have just gone into the Spar. I turn left once inside and walk past the fruit and veg, on my way to pick up the milk I need. I stop as soon as I see him. I could have carried on and it might have been interesting to see what he would have done, but that is not the path I choose to follow. I abandon my idea of picking up a few bits and pieces and embark on a different quest. I start to follow him. I keep back and more or less out of sight, in case he comes back my way, but he doesn't. He walks round the top end of the shop and goes to the tills that way. I am now at the top end of the shop, looking at beer. Once I see him pay and leave, I walk to the front of the shop, to follow him. Hopefully he will be going home, wherever that is.

By the time I am at the front of the shop, he is already across the road and in the square. I hesitate before leaving, to see where he is going. That turns out to be the bakery.

Chapter 49 Wenlock

I make a quick U-turn and go to look at a display, where I can also keep an eye on the front of the bakery. I know I can't stay too long, as I will make the staff suspicious of me, potentially. I decide to leave and look at the notice board by the museum instead. I can see enough out of the corner of my eye as I stand there. I don't have long to wait. He comes out of the bakery carrying his bread, and crosses the road. I don't want to turn round yet, just in case he glances across my way. He walks across the square towards the arch between the Smoothie and the gallery. I already have an idea he would be making in that direction. I also know that going this way will make it harder for me to follow him, at any distance.

As soon as he is out of sight, I start to follow. I am guessing that he won't stop now and I only hope he won't turn round in the first section, because there is nowhere for me to hide. And obviously I can't dart out of view, or quickly turn round either, so I am quite exposed. Thankfully that does not occur. By the time I am through the arch and have done a right and a left, the next time I see him he is almost at the first house on the right in St Marys Lane. It is at this point I feel the sinking feeling in my stomach. I slow down and keep my head down as much as possible. He walks past the first door and the second door and then the third one. My spirits are about to rise again, when he disappears from view. He has gone down the side beyond the last of the terrace.

The pit is well and truly in my stomach. This is exactly what I had feared. This must be the neighbour who we saw, when we were working out the back of the house, on the floor of the extension. But I am puzzled. I know I have changed my looks and I am certainly dressed differently, but evidently he has spotted something familiar about me. I don't know exactly what that is, but he has.

I turn round and go back to the shops, to pick up the rest of my bits and pieces. My mind is racing fifteen to the dozen. I then make my way home and make an effort to put on my best calm face when I get there. Thankfully my partner does not appear to pick up on anything. If they could see inside my head, they would see a completely different picture.

Giving myself some time to reflect on things, my thinking is that if the man I'd followed had any concrete suspicions, he would have gone to the police. And if he had done that, then I am certain I would have received a visit from them at the least, the moment he had reported anything.

On the Monday we congregate for the usual walk. The weather is fine and there is a great turnout. As is now the norm, the eight of us walk more or less as a group, although it is more like two groups of four, one men and the other women. All goes well, until we return to the square afterwards. While six of us file off towards the customary cup of coffee and chat afterwards, Martin and Maggie walk away, either to go shopping, or to go home. Possibly they might be making for the pub, as it has become clear over the weeks that they like a drink, Martin particularly.

We are just going through the door of Tea on the Square, when I turn round. Something made me do it and I am glad I did, but that is not how it makes me feel at that moment. The man I had followed the other day; has stopped them and is talking to them. Maybe they know each other. I have no way of knowing whether that is true or not. I position myself so that I am in a seat facing the window, but not in a direct line to them. I would judge that from his body language in particular, that he doesn't know them, but that is just a guess or wishful thinking.

We order our coffees and we have started to drink them by the time the trio break up outside in the square. The man goes through the arch and Martin and Maggie glance across at us, before walking off towards the High Street.

I try to not be too distracted by what has just occurred in front of my eyes, but it is hard. What springs into my head, is that he was asking questions about me, possibly. Maybe I am becoming paranoid about this. But then I have good reason to be. If everything is about to fall apart just because I have come back to Wenlock and someone has remembered me being at the other house doing the floor; the floor which had a body buried in it.

I am probably a bit quieter than I normally am, but the others scarcely notice, as they chat merrily away about this and that. We resist the temptation to have a second coffee and we leave. I need to go to the pharmacy, so I go that way and my partner goes home. The others go off in their respective homeward directions.

I have been to the pharmacy and stopped off to look at a book in the bookshop. I am just coming out of there, when Martin and Maggie come out of the alley beside it. That is the alley that is part of the Talbot. I can smell the beer on him, even with him standing a few feet away. Maggie has a glow too, that shows she has had a couple of drinks. I don't think she is the hardened drinker he is, but she likes a drink nevertheless. They spot me, which would be hard not to, and Martin speaks to me.

'Funny we should meet you just now. I don't know if you saw when we parted, but a man stopped us and was asking about you two. It was quite odd really. He was asking if we knew you well and how long you have lived here. We don't know for sure, but told him we thought it was recently, like us. I have no idea why he was asking us and not you directly. Have you any thoughts on it?'

I am not sure I quite like the questioning tone that he is using. There is something about it that comes across in a bad way. It is like he is a bit slimy and is hoping that there is a bit of scandal or something like that, that he can use to his advantage. That is just how my mind has jumped to that thought. I put a puzzled look on my face, before replying to him.

'I saw you talking to him, but I thought it was someone you know. I have absolutely no idea why he would be asking about us. He's probably confusing us with someone else, I imagine.'

'He seemed adamant it was you, if you know what I mean?'

I am getting the feeling that I don't know and haven't been told the full extent of the conversation. I really don't think Martin is a nice person either. He is enjoying this a bit too much.

'Well I haven't seen him before, as far as I am aware. If you bump into him again, you can tell him to come and ask us himself, next time he wants to know anything. I hate it when people talk about you to others, rather than come and talk to you themselves.'

I am about to turn away and walk off, as I think they are, when Maggie throws her spanner into the works. And what a spanner it is.

'He's invited us round for a drink on Thursday evening. We've said we will go.'

I am thrown by this. I hope my face hasn't let me down though.

'Well you can tell him then, if he asks about us again, to come and ask us to our faces.'

At that I turn away and start walking back down High Street. I don't look over my shoulder, to see if they have also gone on their way, or whether they are standing there watching me walk away from them. I don't care really, but of course I do care about what they have been talking about. The matter is at a much more critical point than I ever imagined it could be. Something is going to have to be done, or everything is going to unravel and that is the last thing that I want to happen. I need to plan something. To do that, I need to get away from here for a while.

But that is one of the good things about our relationship. We both know that sometimes we want, or need, a bit of space. We have both had time away without question. I am going to ask for some now.

Chapter 50 A Death in Wenlock

Harvey lives alone in Much Wenlock. He has lived there for many years and always in the same house. When he first moved to Much Wenlock his wife was with him, but she died a few years back. He decided that he would stay on living here. There is no point moving back to where they had moved from. Most of the people he knew had either moved away themselves, or had died. Even though his circle of friends here is quite small, he is happy here and has no desire to move. He has a son, but he lives in Australia. They haven't seen each other for years, but they do talk every week, regular as clockwork. They have a time when they speak and they haven't missed that time once since his wife died. In that way he and his son are close. But they are not close in the way of him really opening up to his son when they talk. They chat about what each has been doing since last week. They chat about whether he is well and looking after himself. He asks about his daughter-in-law and his grandchild. That is about the extent of it.

But it is a regular chat and so when Harvey doesn't take the call when it comes in, his son is worried. Harvey is normally there, ready for the face time chat. But on this occasion the ringing is not answered. His son gives him an hour, just in case he has got the time wrong. He knows he hasn't, but it is just the reason he does it. Still there is no response from Harvey.

It is hard to know what to do, when you are literally on the other side of the world and you need to find out what has happened to someone. It has always been something that he dreaded would happen one day, since his mother died. Who looks after the survivor?

Who is going to notice something is wrong, when it comes to their turn? He has asked Harvey on more than one occasion, if there is anyone he could ring if he can't get hold of him. He has always been rebuffed by Harvey, saying it has never happened. So he has never given his son the number of a friend to ring.

He has no idea why Harvey isn't taking the call. He can hardly ring the police and say that he is worried, because his father isn't answering his weekly face time. You can imagine what the response might be.

There are absolutely no names that come to mind, of people Harvey has maybe mentioned over the years. Generally he is very much one for keeping himself to himself. The only thing that does come to him, after an hour talking it over with his wife, is that he remembers Harvey talking about the vicar they have in the church at the moment. Matthew is like a breath of fresh air, he remembers Harvey saying to him.

All the time he has been trying to connect with Harvey, but with the same result. Harvey is not there to face time them. Once he has this idea, it takes him less than a minute to look up the church, on the internet. Matthew is the Team Rector and better still, there is a telephone number showing too. Without thinking, he dials the number. It is picked up soon enough and he finds himself talking to Matthew. He explains his problem, quickly and clearly. Matthew listens. He thinks he knows Harvey. He has been known to attend services sometimes. Matthew takes his name and number and also Harvey's address. He does tell Harvey's son that maybe the internet is down. There have been a few issues over the past few weeks. He is told that Harvey's telephone is just ringing out too. Matthew says he will go round straight away and then let him know what he finds out.

Matthew puts on his coat and leaves the vicarage. He turns left out of the drive and then left onto Queen Street. He gets down as far as the Bull Ring and then takes a right to go past the church and up towards the square. He goes through the arch and does a right and a left into St Marys Lane. The house is now in sight. He walks up to the front door and rings the bell. There is no answer and there is no sound coming from within. The net curtains prevent him from being able to see through the front window, so he goes round the side of the house and bangs on the back door. Still there is no response. He looks through the window. At first he can only see a part of the kitchen, but as he moves to one side, he gets an angle where he can see beyond that, presumably it is the living room there. But that is not what catches his attention. He can't see much, but he can see something and that something is a foot. It looks like the foot of someone sitting in a chair. It is that sort of angle the foot is at. The foot isn't moving, not that he really thinks it would be. It could just be at rest. He wouldn't probably have thought twice about it, if he hadn't been asked to check on Harvey, because he isn't responding to phone or face time.

Matthew tries the door, but it is locked. He goes back round to the front and tries the front door, but that is locked too. He calls at the neighbours to see if they have a key, but they don't. He dials 999 for the police and ambulance. The fire people arrive first, followed quickly by the police and ambulance. The decision is quickly taken to break the door down. The back door is chosen, as it will be easier. Once they are in, they rush through to the living room. Harvey is there in the chair, with a cushion over his face. It doesn't take long to establish that he is dead. That changes everything and they all leave the house, to minimalize contamination of the house. If he had been found just dead in his chair, then the natural assumption would be he has just died. But with the cushion over his face, it makes it look like a suspicious death.

After a time, it is agreed that Matthew can ring Harvey's son back and tell him the bad news, but just that Harvey is dead, at this stage. He is asked to say nothing to anyone else for the time being. In the meantime the police are in Harvey's house, to search for clues.

On the opened desk in the corner of the room, they find his notebook. There is a pile of papers to the left of the notebook. The detective carefully rifles through the pile. Second from the top, he finds a printed sheet of paper. Reading it makes him want to see if there is a file on the notebook computer. Surprisingly, they find it is switched on and no password is required to use it. Although the version of windows is older than the one he is used to, he easily finds the list of document files and near the top, finds the one that relates to the piece of paper. He opens the file and reads the content. It would appear the sheet has been printed recently, as the contents of both are the same.

"A Death in Wenlock"

A while after the body was discovered under the floor in my close neighbour's house, something nagged at me. I couldn't at first locate in my brain what was causing that nagging. Then I remembered about what it was. My near neighbour was in hospital at one time and while she was there, her sister came to visit her. She stayed in the house during her visit. I saw them doing some work in the extension and I seem to remember them saying that they were making the floor better and putting new floor units in the extension for her sister, for when she came home. I do get a bit confused at times, but I do seem to remember that much. But there was someone who brought her here as well and I think that is the person who did the floor and fitted the units.

I didn't think there was enough information in that to be of use to the police, but then I noticed one day while I was in the square, someone who I thought I recognized. I wasn't sure what it was that I recognized, because the person I was looking at looked different to the person I remembered. But there was something. I returned a few times and each time I was surer that this person was the same one who had done the floor.

I needed to be more certain before I went to the police, so I approached them today and asked if they had been in the town long. They seemed to be curious about what I was asking them, so I decided to invite them round for a drink on Thursday. I will take them into the garden, so they can look down to the neighbour's house from my garden and see how they react."

'He doesn't say who this is?'
'It shouldn't be too hard to find out who he talked to.'

Chapter 51 And another one or two

'The alternative is that we wait until Thursday. Then maybe whoever he was talking to will come round for drinks.'

'I'm guessing that won't happen, because in a place like this the word will be around before you take a breath outside this front door.'

'You're right! In a place like this you can learn stuff about yourself that you never knew.'

'How did they get in? Or more to the point, how did they get out again? The front door is locked from the inside and the key is still in it. The back door was locked too, until we broke the glass to get in.'

'Were the keys in both doors then?'

'As far as I am aware they were. I need to check on that with whoever was here when they gained entry.'

A few minutes later, they have the information they are looking for. The back door key was found on the floor, once the door was opened. They had just assumed that it had been in the lock and jolted out, as they battered the door open.

'But the door was definitely locked?'

'It would appear so.'

'Then they had a key?'

'Now that is interesting. Can we also assume that he knew them?'

'I think we need to start a door to door, to try to establish who knows him, who visits him and who might have a key.'

'Matthew, the vicar, said that the neighbour does not have a key. He asked there when he originally came round, after the son raised the alarm to him.'

'And the son is definitely in Australia?'

'Yes, he is definitely in Australia.'

'Are there any other relatives close by, or even in the country?'

'I don't know. I will speak to the son and see what I can find out.'

That doesn't take long to establish that, as far as the son is aware, there are no close relatives either here or close by at all. In fact there appear to be no relatives, or at least he is unaware of any. He suggests that they look in the address book. His mother had an address book she kept by the telephone in the hallway.

That takes a bit longer to go through, when they find it in the drawer by the phone. The problem being that they are listed in there with names and addresses, and not whether or not any are relatives. There is no quick way to sift through them. They run some of the names by the son, but he isn't familiar with more than the odd one. None of those are relatives either. They pass the address book onto someone else to do the donkey work and establish their relationship with Harvey.

That still leaves them with the fact that someone has a key to the back door. That in itself they find a little bit odd, in that normally it is the front door that you would give someone the key for. The other odd thing is that the back door was locked. Why would they lock it on the way out, after murdering him? The next question they ask again is, whether they are sure it is murder? Surely he wouldn't have been able to suffocate himself with the cushion. No he would not, is the answer to that one.

The door to door produces little or nothing. The row of houses in St Marys Lane only consists of a few houses. The house opposite is empty. It is a holiday let and it isn't in use at the moment. You have to move out of this part of the lane and into the main road, before there are more houses where someone might have seen anything. But then that is not the only question they are asking door to door. It may as well have been, because literally no one in the near neighbourhood knew him at all well, and that includes his next door neighbour, who is the only person they actually get to speak to, in that part of the road.

The net is spread a little bit wider, but all they really find out, is that Harvey was quite a private man. He was certainly a lot less well known than his wife had been, when she was alive.

In the meantime, the search inside his house continues too. But it would appear that the only useful piece of information to be found, is the one they have already stumbled across; the piece about the body under his near neighbour's annexe floor. It is just a shame that he hadn't been a bit more descriptive, about the person he was thinking and talking about. They find a photo of Harvey that appears to have been taken relatively recently. It might be needed to show people, so that they know who they are being questioned about.

It is the next day, armed with one of these photos, that there is a bit of progress in that direction. They have been wandering up and down the High Street, showing the picture and asking people if they have seen him in the past few days. If they hadn't made progress there, then it would have only been a matter of time before someone else also gave them the same information they get from a couple in the High Street.

They had seen Harvey on Monday morning, in the square, when they had come back from the Monday walk. It took a further minute of questioning to find out what that was.

Anyway, it would appear that this couple had come back, as one of the last people to return from their particular walk that morning. They are almost sure that they saw Harvey talking to a couple in the square, when they got there.

Do they know who this couple are? It would have been too easy if they just said yes. But they don't. But they have seen them regularly on the walk for quite a time now. They define quite a time now, being several weeks at least. They believe that the couple are relatively new to the town. Have they any idea where they might live? No, not really, but they think they have seen them walk up High Street, so maybe they live in that direction. But what they can say; is that they walk with the same people every week they have seen them. There is a group of maybe six or eight people, who walk together each week.

Do they know who any of the others are then? Well, not exactly. They think they are all relative newbies in town. None of them have been around for long, so they think. But they think they might know them in Tea on the Square. Some of that group go into there for a coffee, after the walk each week. They have seen them do that? Does that include the couple they are asking about? No, they don't think they join in that bit of the social.

The enquiries then move over to Tea on the Square. Yes they know who the police are talking about but no, they don't know where they live.

At very much the same time, armed with the latest update, one of the door knockers comes across one of that group of eight from the Monday morning walk. Yes they do know the couple. No, they didn't see them talking to anyone in the square on Monday after the walk, but then they were facing inwards and not out of the window. But they do have a phone number for David and Barbara and also for Leonard and Lucy, if not an address. They know roughly where they live. No they don't have a telephone number for the other couple. They are Martin and Maggie. They don't come for the coffee after the walk. They did the first time, but it wasn't their way, so they don't come any more. But they believe they live in a house just off the High Street.

That at last narrows it down quite a lot. The High Street finishes at the Gaskell corner. There aren't that many roads off the High Street, although the off High Street bit hasn't been specifically defined.

It doesn't take long for the team to congregate in the centre of town and start to concentrate their search in that area. Ask the right people and you will get the right answer. It doesn't take long once they start; to lead them onto the right road. Once there, it is a simple process of knocking on the right door, to be pointed to the exact address.

Chapter 52 And so here they are!

All of this is because they are trying to find out the people he was talking, to after the walk on Monday. These are the people he had invited over to his house, for a drink on Thursday. There is nothing more to this line of investigation than that, but it is pretty much all they have to work on at the moment.

Everyone they have spoken to has known about the discovery of the Harvey's body. Beyond that fact there is a varying level of truths being suggested, but none of them include the cause of death. But there is a degree of belief that the death is suspicious, rather than a natural one. That has probably been fuelled, by the police questioning going on in the town.

It is down to Andy the detective, to make the first approach. His intention is to ask about their conversation with Harvey and to try to find out how well they knew him.

There is no reply to his knock at their front door, when they get there. The house is of a modern design and the front door is double glazed. What glass there is in it is frosted and they can't see through to the hall behind the door. They have no joy at the back door either.

There is a car on the drive, so they decide they will wait around for a while. One thing that has been mentioned to them is that they both like a drink, particularly Martin. So someone is despatched to check on the drinking establishments, to see if they happen to be in there. By the time they get back, with no news on that front, Martin and Maggie have still not returned home from wherever they have gone.

Another hour goes by before a decision is taken, with permission from upstairs. They have already looked through the letter box and cannot see anything pertinent. They have shouted through the letter box too, but the house inside is perfectly still and quiet. From the little they can see, including looking through the windows, everything is in order in there. But they need to see all of it for themselves.

Like before, the decision is taken to go through the back door. This time they manage to smash a pane of glass in the back door and reach through to unlock the door. With access gained, they quickly look through the downstairs. There is not a lot to check on. Kitchen, living room/dining room, hall and downstairs cloakroom are the extent of it. All of these rooms are tidy and empty of people. That much they already knew from what they could see from outside.

One of the neighbours had come out to tell them that Martin and Maggie, funny couple in their opinion, were keen bus users. They liked to use their bus passes wherever they could, as they travelled free. No, she hasn't seen them go out today, but she is just saying they may have gone to Telford, Bridgnorth, or Shrewsbury, on the bus. Annoyingly, it is not something they had given any thought to. The fact that the car is on the drive had gone to make them assume that the couple, if they were out, were only out locally.

But they still decided that they needed to know. So from the downstairs they move upstairs. Andy leads the way and it is Andy who enters the main bedroom first. It is Andy who finds them there in the bed. At first he thinks they are asleep, but it soon becomes obvious to him that these two people aren't going to wake up again.

They have not responded to his first cough. They have not responded to his first words. They have not responded when these same words are repeated, at a much higher volume. It is carefully that he takes the next step forward, to ascertain just what their condition is, although he thinks he already knows what he is going to find out.

It only takes him a few seconds to establish the facts. Neither of these people is alive. There is a swift withdrawal, before they contaminate the scene more than they have done already.

A couple of quick phone calls bring the people he needs to the scene. It must have been quite a few years since the same team has had the need to assemble in Much Wenlock for three deaths like this. Andy doesn't know how they have died, but this is too much like a coincidence for them to have just died together in bed.

'I would put the time of death at not that long after Harvey's. Certainly not more than a few hours after, I would say at most. I will be able to tell you more after I have taken them back to the shop.'

'Is it a death pact?'

'On the face of it, it could be. But something tells me it is not. I would say that this one died first and not necessarily out of choice. Look there on the bedside table. That glass has some sort of powder residue in it. Then there are the bottles lying on the floor. They aren't all empty and that one in particular looks a bit cloudy. I will get the contents tested. My guess is, and don't hold me to this, is that one of them was killed by the other and then they took their own life. I should be able to tell you more in a bit. Is there anything more you want or need to do, before I take the bodies away?'

'Have they finished dusting and taking their photos?'

'Have you boys?'

'We have pretty much, of the current scene. We'll hang around and see if Andy comes across anything after you've gone.'

'Leave them where they are for a minute, if you don't mind. I want to get a picture in my head of what may have gone on here. The way they are laying is almost as if they have been placed.'

'I agree the one does, but as I said, I think that one went first. I suspect they were straightened up first, before they went on to kill themselves.'

'I guess you could be right. I'm just going to go downstairs to check something.'

Andy goes downstairs and stands by the front door. He looks at the door, wondering what it is that is nagging at him. Then it clicks. There is no keyhole on the inside of the door. It has a turn handle, to lock the door from the inside. It only uses a key from the outside. That sort of answers that one. There are a couple of jackets hanging on the hooks in the hall.

Without really knowing why he is doing it, he feels in the pockets. There is nothing in the first jacket pockets, but he has more luck in the second one. As he puts his hand in, he feels the jangle of keys in there. He gets hold of the bunch of keys he can feel and withdraws his hand. As he does so, he can feel a key has dropped back into the pocket. He removes the bunch of keys and then puts his hand back into the pocket. He brings out just the one key. It is older than the ones on the bunch. He opens the front door and tries the keys from the bunch in the door. One fits and another fits the back door. Another key fits the outside shed in the back garden. But the single key does not fit anything.

He pops them all in a bag and puts them in his pocket. He notices a small rack of keys on the wall in the kitchen. It looks like a spare key or two for the front or back door. One is for the front door and two for the back door.

He goes back upstairs and stands in the main bedroom, looking at the bodies lying in the bed.

'I've found a door key in the pocket of a jacket in the hall. I have a funny feeling about this.'

'Do you need more time here before I take them away?'

'No, I think I'm done thanks. I am just going to get one of the lads to go round and try this key in a certain door.'

'No prizes for guessing which door that is then?'

'I guess not' he replies smiling.

They start to move the bodies off the bed and in to their respective bags. As they move one of them, they see the edge of a piece of paper sticking out from between the pillows

Chapter 53 This is what it said in the confession

Everything stops while the piece of paper is investigated. It is between the pillows of the one they think died second.

'It's a suicide note, I'm betting.'

Andy picks it up, with his gloves still on. There is more than one sheet to this.

'There was a time when people would just scribble a quick handwritten note to quickly explain things, but these days…'

He lets the end of his sentence drift off into the ether. He does so, because he has started to read the note that has been left. It takes him a little time and no one interrupts him while he is reading it. When he has finished, he passes the papers over for the others to read them. No one says anything until they are all up to speed with him.

'Well that on the face of it, wraps up a few things. Who would have thought they were all connected?'

'I suppose we shouldn't just take it on face value.'

'Good lord no. But you know and I know; it is all going to check out.'

Andy picks up the sheets and goes downstairs, to read them through again. Meanwhile the bodies are finally removed from the house.

"It was never supposed to end like this. And now it will all be over. My partner does not deserve to be shamed like he would be, if they ever found out what I have done.

I knew it was a mistake to move to Much Wenlock. I should have been firmer in my argument against moving here. But my partner fell in love with the place and as for me, well it has been a long time and much water has passed under the bridge, since I was last here briefly. It was foolish still to think I could come back here and I would not have to pay for what I did the last time I was here. I am of course talking about the body which has been discovered under the floor, in the extension in St Marys Lane. It is Mary who lies there and not her sister Rose, but I am sure you already know that. Why is Mary there, I hear you ask?

I really don't know why I did what I did. The opportunity just came at me. It presented itself and I saw that I could help myself to what was hers, so easily. I met her as I was putting my shopping in my car. She was passing by and the bags broke. I helped her pick her shopping up and then I ran her home. She talked and I listened. She was thinking of moving to Much Wenlock to be nearer her family. She was unhappy where she was. It seemed natural to me to offer her a lift here and so I did. She'd put her house on the market and she'd told all her friends that she was leaving. No one was going to miss her. She'd even set it all up with her solicitor and the estate agent. Then when we got here and she said what she wanted to do for Rose while she was in hospital, well it was all too good an opportunity to miss.

Years later we moved here and I was absolutely certain that Mary still lay under the concrete undiscovered. I was right about that, but not for long. Someone had bought the house after Rose died and they were redeveloping the annexe at the back. So it was that Mary was rediscovered. I was convinced that I had not been seen enough by anyone locally, for them to remember me after all this time. But I was wrong about that. I have changed in the intervening time and I look different, not just older as we all do. I have changed the way I am, if you know what I mean.

We had taken to going on the Monday morning walks. We met with three other new couples to the town. Everything was going well and despite Mary being found, I still felt as safe from discovery of what I had done, as if I had been anywhere in the country. I was wrong about that and in fact if I had not moved to Much Wenlock, then I would not have been approached by Harvey.

His appearance on the scene was a shock to me, to say the least. I'd noticed for a few weeks that there was this man looking at our group, when we came back from the walk. I didn't know at the beginning that he was specifically singling me out, but he must have been just getting things straight in his head.

Then after our walk, he just walked up to us both and started asking me about when I was in Much Wenlock before. I tried to not let the shock show on my face. My partner of course was insistent that we had not been here before we moved. That is what I told him when we looked at this place in the beginning. Harvey was very insistent that he had seen me before. Before my partner got too suspicious about how tenacious Harvey was being about seeing me before, I said that if he wanted, then I could come round to his house and talk about it. He replied that we should both come round for a drink. He said Thursday and we (I) readily agreed.

I was so shaken up by this approach and how strongly that Harvey was arguing his case, that we stopped off in the Talbot for a drink, or two or three or more as it turned out. All the time my head was spinning and not just because of the drink. Somehow it was clear to me that Harvey recognized me from when he saw me working out the back of Rose's house, doing the floor and the units.

I knew I could not wait until Thursday. I was thinking that because Harvey had so readily agreed to have us round to his house, that he must have something else to back up his claim of recognizing me. The only thing that kept me sane, was the thought that if he was going to talk to us (me) about this on Thursday, then there was a good chance that he hasn't spoken to anyone else about it yet, not even the police.

Later that day, well it was almost evening, when I made an excuse to leave the house and go downtown. I realised that I could not leave it until Thursday to sort this out. I needed to talk to Harvey before then and try to reason with him that he was mistaken. That was all I intended to do when I visited him. But I was also prepared to do something different, should he for some reason not want to listen or to believe me.

No one was around when I knocked on his door. That part of the street is very quiet anyway, which is fortunate. I had taken a bottle of wine with me. I have added some crushed tablets of mine, should we get to that point. We very quickly did. There was never going to be a second when he would believe that he was wrong. Of course he wasn't wrong and what he described was the scene I had been part of. I didn't think I was going to be able to get him to have a drink of wine, but I did. I asked him to be patient and I would tell him why it could not have been me. While he went for the glasses, I added some more powder to the wine. I needed it to take hold as quickly as possible.

I was amazed how quickly he succumbed to it. Surely there must have been another factor, but I wasn't going to question it when it was so strongly in my favour. I saw him yawn and then I saw him struggle to keep his eyes open. Then he was fast asleep. I just grabbed a cushion and ran over and sat on him, pinning his arms to the chair. Funnily enough, he didn't fight very much. It was almost as if he wanted to die.

The front door was locked and the key was in there. There was also a key in the back door, but there was also one on the hook nearby. I took the key out and then locked the door with the one from the hook. I took the wine bottle with me and the clean glasses were put back in the cupboard.

There would be no undoing what I had done. I had not hidden his body like I did with Mary's. I had this thought that he may have written his suspicions down somewhere, but I didn't think to look. I needed to get back home, before my partner started to ask too many questions about how long I had been out.

It was between Harvey's house and ours, which isn't a great distance; that I decided that it was all going to come out anyway. My partner does not deserve to live through the shame of what I have done. It would break them and destroy them.

So when I arrived home, we had something to eat and we had some more wine. In fact we had quite a lot more wine. I wasn't bothered about the mess, because I knew that we would not be alive to clear it up in the morning. While we could still walk, we made our way up to bed. My partner was asleep almost the moment their head hit the pillow. I sat stride them and suffocated them in their sleep. They were too drunk to even stir while I was doing this. I then laid them tidily in the bed and prepared to take my potion that I had prepared for me to take.

It is surprising that however drunk you may be when you commit a murder, or two, as I have today, how quickly you sober up. I thought then that I should leave this explanation, so that there is no doubt that it is I who has killed these people.

M"

Chapter 54 Check it out

Andy lays down the sheets of paper. There is something niggling at him. He can't put his finger on it, but he knows it will come soon enough. In the meantime another thought comes to him.

'We should just check that the paper is not the same for these two notes. I don't think for a minute it is, unless they just happen to have bought it from the same place.'

'The other one wasn't a suicide note like this one was.'

'I know, but the question has come into my head, so we need to check. Could you also get onto the Mary side of things? We need to know what happened there. If we can, we need to find out exactly when that was. We already knew it wasn't Rose and there had been some suggestion from somewhere that it might have been her sister. But we need to establish that Mary isn't still alive and running around the country somewhere. Again I don't for a minute think it is anyone else other than Mary, but we do need to just check up and make sure she isn't still alive'

'I'm on it.'

Andy walks around the house, looking around and opening drawers and cupboards. He doesn't know what he is looking for, but he knows he will if and when he finds it. There is nothing that stirs interest in him downstairs, so he ventures up the stairs again. There are still a couple of the SOCO team working in the bedroom. That doesn't matter, as he doesn't want to go in there. He has already seen what there is to see in there. The first room he goes into is the bathroom. There is nothing out of place in there. There is just what there should be in a bathroom.

The next room is a spare bedroom. It doesn't look as if it is used very much, if ever at all. Everything looks pretty much new and there is nothing in the drawers of the bedside cabinet, or the chest of drawers. The wardrobe is empty too. That just leaves the small box room. As soon as enters, he knows he has found what he is looking for. There is a small desk and a chair. There is also a small cabinet, with three drawers.

On the desk top is a computer. It is a laptop and it is sitting open, but not on. Beside it on the desk, is a printer. He still has his gloves on, but before he touches anything, he calls one of the others through, to check if they have dusted in here. No they haven't, but it is done before he touches anything.

'I can tell you now that that is the same set of prints we have in the bedroom. They must have a scar on the thumb and the index finger. It is easy to pick out. There are just the two sets of prints everywhere we have checked and I'd lay money they are theirs. They are on all the handles and switches. Some are partials and overlays, but there are only two prints, his and hers.'

'I didn't think it would be any other way, but we need to confirm that of course. I'm just going to switch on this laptop and have a look. Hopefully it will be unlocked.'

That hope is not fulfilled this time. The password box appears as soon as he switches it on, or wakes it up from being dormant rather. He tries one or two old favourites. 0000, the original default, does nothing to help and nor does 1234 or ABCD. That would just have been too handy. He knows the tech boys will manage to get in if he doesn't. It is just he would like to know the answer now, if he could. If what he hopes he will find on there is there, then it will set his mind more at rest. Until he finds that bit of information, he isn't going to be able to rest this case. He tries a few more passwords, but the result is the same. Thankfully there would appear to be no limit on the number of wrong tries you can make, before it shuts off completely.

He sits down in the chair and surveys the scene around him. The room is quite sparse. Apart from the desk, chair and the cabinet, there isn't any more furniture. Mind you, there isn't room for much more. The walls are almost equally bare too. In fact there is only one wall that has anything on it and that is the one by the desk. And saying that, it is an odd thing to have there; well the subject of the picture is odd. It is a picture of a large packet of M & M's, peanut ones.

Andy looks to see what else there is to see. Nothing is the answer to that one, except for the two pens and a pencil lying on the desk, between the laptop and the printer. He picks up the pencil and starts tapping it on the desk, while he is thinking. The SOCO man comes back through when hearing the noise.

'Is there something wrong?'

'No, not really. I was just hoping to get into this, so I could print off something. So we could compare the print to see if it is printed on here. I'm guessing it is, and even more so now I've found you need a password to get access to the laptop.'

'The tech guys will get that open and compared. You'll just have to bag it up. I suppose you've tried the easy ones.'

'Yes I have, well the ones I can think of. Sometimes there is a clue left around for them, to remind them.'

Their eyes swing round the small room. There is only one thing for their eyes to rest on. The SOCO guy then asks a question.

'What were their names again?'

'Martin and Maggie; why?'

He smiles, as he points to the picture on the wall.

'Have you tried M&M's?'

Andy smiles and leans forward. M&M's doesn't do anything and neither does leaving out the apostrophe, which the laptop doesn't like anyway. But when he enters MandMs in the password box, the laptop springs to life. It doesn't take him long to search for the document file. It takes him less time to locate the file in there. The last use date is correct and when he opens it, he finds the stored copy of the confession he has been reading. He selects print and then waits for the printer to connect. In less than a minute he has the copy of the confession in his hands.

'I can't see any difference, but then it isn't like the old typewriters, which had their little tell-tale signs.'

'The tech boys will be able to tell you exactly.'

'I know and they will tell me they are both printed on the same printer.'

'I'll get that bagged up if you like and sent back with the other bits we have in the bedroom.'

'Yes, it all needs to be checked.'

It doesn't take that long for the first results to come back to them. Everything that has been said in the confession appears to check out. The fingerprints are those of Maggie and Martin. There are no other prints from their house. It would appear that they didn't know Harvey had written his suspicions down, but everything about his death fits too. Mary has not been recorded dead, which makes sense. Her house was sold and the proceeds invested and then disappeared, but the confession made it clear that she had been killed for her money. The investment company had long folded and there was no trace of where her money had ended up. It would appear that looking back into Martin and Maggie's history, that they did not have jobs that would have afforded them their lifestyle, not that it was that grand. All in all, there appears to be nothing more to investigate.

But of course, that doesn't mean they stop talking about things in Wenlock

Chapter 55 Back in Wenlock

I'm not sure who rang who first. It could have been Barbara who started the chain of phone calls. Not everyone was in at the first try and even then not all of the couples were at home then too. A chinwag on the telephone is sufficient initially, to release the first piece of information that is spreading like wildfire round the town. Everyone is talking about it. No matter if you are in Sheinton Street or Wilmore Street, Barrow Street or High Street, in the heart of town, there is only one subject of interest.

As yet to be confirmed, but there have been multiple deaths in the town over the past days. The exact time isn't known of course, because these are rumours flying around, ahead of any official press release. The exact names of the deceased aren't factual either and there are several people named, depending on where the source of that particular rumour began. Obviously some of the people named are still alive and kicking. In some cases, some are being told to their faces that they are among the dead, before the storyteller even realises who they are speaking to.

But over the course of the day, the inaccuracies are generally thrown out and from the most reliable sources; names very close to the truth are being bandied about. It is somewhere in the middle of this process, that it is Barbara who is the first of the four couples to hear about it. Of course one of the couples, Maggie & Martin already know, well I'm not sure that they did really, but they are part of the action, so to speak.

Of course when Barbara starts her ring round, she is not aware of that fact. And because of that, she is unable to get a response from their phone. The number just keeps ringing out, every time she tries to contact them. She doesn't think anything of it. She just thinks that they are out for the day; or something like that. She does manage to get hold of at least one person from each of the other couples.

Initially that is all she does, just to pass on the word, however inaccurate, that she has picked up on her mini shopping trip into town. Even when she still couldn't get through to Martin and Maggie later, she didn't even start to think they might be caught up in it all.

What is only discovered later by the police; is that they (that is what they assume) had pulled the telephone wire out of the socket, so that no one could interrupt them as they were dying.

Brian has cause later in the afternoon, to go down to the shops for some milk. As he walks down Racecourse Lane and across into St Marys Lane, he is directed to go another way, as the road is taped off. He walks down to the corner at the Raven and then along Barrow Street into the centre of town.

Surprisingly for the time of the afternoon, there are still quite a lot of people lingering around the square and in the High Street. Most are in little groups, talking about the latest piece of news. It is to one of these little groups that he is waved over to, by someone he sometimes chats with on the Monday morning walks. The reason he is being called over soon becomes apparent, as he is told that the latest word is that two of the dead are Martin and Maggie. The quality of the information this little group has, and now pretty much every one of them that is gathered in town does too, is very close to the mark. It is hard to ignore where the tapes are and whose properties those tapes stop people approaching. The name Harvey and who he was doesn't mean anything to Brian. He can't even recall seeing anyone at that house before. But of course he knows Martin and Maggie, as they are part of their little group on Mondays, even if they don't go for a coffee afterwards. But of course the information now circling very much points the finger at one of them, for the death of Harvey in St Marys Lane. But also that one of them has killed their partner and then taken their own life afterwards too.

The reasons for that are not known by the public at this stage, but people are already starting to put two and two together and linking this set of murders with the body that has been found under the floor in St Marys Lane.

Brian, in his haste to get home and pass on the very latest talk of the situation, almost forgets what he came down for, but remembers just in time. He doesn't think it would look good on him if Jackie thought he is more interested in what he has to tell, than to do the task he has gone to do.

Jackie speaks to Barbara first. She feels she should, as it was Barbara who had first broadcast to them about the events. It is quickly decided that a quick chat on the telephone isn't sufficient to express their thoughts, so they arrange to meet up in the George, in about half an hour. Leonard and Lucy are both at home too and they readily agree to the meet.

When they get there, the George is rammed. It appears that a lot of people have the same idea, about having a drink while discussing the goings on of the town. The six of them retreat through to the back, where they manage to grab a table and then decide that it would be a good excuse to eat out too. It is as well that they got there when they did, as soon the back is full too. The place is buzzing with conversation and there is only the one topic.

All of them appear to be shocked that it is a couple from their walking group who is involved in this and that one of them is a murderer. No one knows at this stage which one it is. It could have been Martin or Maggie.

It is Brian who makes the remark that is quite obvious really, but also brings the stark reality of what has happened home to them all.

'You just don't know what lies behind a closed door. You just don't know what goes on in someone's head, if they don't want to let you in there. I wonder if Martin and Maggie knew that their partner was capable of doing what they say one of them has done. It is quite scary really. You just really don't know.'

His words are received soberly by the other 5. They are also overheard by the people at the next table and they wholeheartedly agree with the sentiment of his words.

Food is eaten and copious quantities of wine are consumed. Eventually the conversation turns to other things, but nothing is able to really take the place of the murders that have been committed in Wenlock and apparently swiftly solved too.

Part 5
Chapter 56 When I went away

I know I needed this time. I also know that my partner won't question it. We never do, as it something we agreed on at the very beginning. We are allowed our secrets from each other. That is something that came out very early on in our relationship. Neither of us had planned the relationship, or any relationship for that matter. We just happened and it took both of us by surprise I think. Because of that, we both have areas, that for varying reasons (none were discussed); we don't want to relay parts of our personal histories to the other. Some people may find that odd and even not a good basis for a healthy relationship. But we didn't and we started as we meant to carry on. What lay behind stayed behind with that person.

I pack a few special clothes in a small bag. I am not expecting to be away for long. Neither of us ever wants or needs to be away from the other for long; just long enough to do what we need to do, for our sanity or whatever.

I drive away. I need some time to think and I need some time to plan, before I put anything into action. The initial problem I have to work out; is where am I going to stay? I need a base and it would be good if it was close by, but then on the other hand the further away the better. I also need to work out how I am going to make my way back into Wenlock. I drive about twenty miles and stop off for a cup of coffee at a roadside café. I sit drinking my coffee, with the map book on my lap; and decide where I am going to make for to stay. I decide on a place I have used before. It has its uses for that reason for one, and also because it has outside rooms, where no one necessarily sees you come and go. It also benefits from the fact that it is a place that can be accessed, without having to go on the main arteries. It is far enough away to be good for that purpose, being on the outskirts of Leamington Spa. My excuse for doing this; is that I use country roads as a way to unwind. I suppose, looking back, that I have always chosen places and ways that avoid the main glare. I am comfortable with it and that is all that matters, although I do need, on this particular occasion, for me to be as invisible as possible.

The other advantage of this place; is that there is a car rental place not too far away, where I will be able to rent a fairly non-descript vehicle, but it will be reliable. The last thing I need is a vehicle that will let me down at the wrong moment. The rental costs a little more than usual, but there is no paperwork as such and therefore there is no record of my use of one of their vehicles. I found this place purely by chance on the internet.

I make my way to the guest house, if that is what you want to call it. I check in and leave my stuff in my room. I will be staying here tonight. I drive off smartly and make for the car rental place. It is on a farm. The cars are kept in the barns and that is where my car will stay, until I return it later. All I have to do is swop vehicles over when I get back. I don't need to see anyone. I don't see anyone when I get there. All transactions are completed through a hatch in the porch of the farm house. They do have CCTV, but it is wiped when the car is returned. I said it is slightly more expensive, but that is untrue; it is a lot more expensive, but very handy.

I find a quiet place on the road back to Wenlock. I have to change into my protective clothing. I am relatively short of time, but this is a necessity. I am soon on my way again. I still have to find time to write the file I need. It is only as I near Much Wenlock that I get the first bout of nerves. I cannot afford to be seen by a soul, other than the ones I have come to see. To that end, I wait until dusk before I venture the last few miles into the town, approaching from the Broseley direction. I use the time to write the file on my notebook. It is now all ready to download when I need to. I have it stored on my memory stick and with my multi wire; I can download it pretty much onto any device when the time comes.

Barrow Street is quiet and no one is walking along the pavement as I drive slowly along. I turn left at the Raven and after about one hundred yards I turn left into Racecourse Lane. I find a place to park, as near to the bottom as I can find. As I walk away from the car I look back, but there is no one around. I get to the bottom of Racecourse Lane and cross the road without being seen. Then I am into the side part of the lane. I decide to chance a knock at the front door, while the coast is clear. No one lives opposite. That is a holiday let. No one really overlooks the front of his house at all. I rap sharply on the door and then stand back a single pace, to wait for him to answer, always assuming that he is in.

I have given it nearly thirty seconds and am getting a little anxious that someone may walk along this way and see me. I am about to turn back and go round the side of the house to try the back door, when I hear the key turning and the door opens. To say that Harvey is surprised to see me standing there; is an understatement. His mouth drops open a fraction and I see his brain start to work. I do not intend to stand here on the doorstep, debating why I have come to see him. I hold up the bottle of wine I have brought and then say.

'I think it best I come in to talk to you. I hear you have been talking about me to friends of mine.'

I don't think he expected for one minute for me to say anything like that. It wasn't something I had planned. This part of the task was always going to be off the cuff reactions. Surprisingly he steps back and I quickly climb the step and follow him in. I shut the front door, as he has moved into the living room. I also turn the key while I am at it. The last thing I want is for him to have a visitor.

He has walked over to where his computer is at the far side of the room. He picks up a piece of paper and turns to me.

'I have written down what I suspect and what I have done. It was you wasn't it?'

'I have no idea what you are talking about. When they told me earlier I was puzzled, as I haven't been here before, until we came to look at properties and then bought one. That is all recently.'

He looks over at me. I can see the cogs turning. I can also see that he is not convinced by that.

'I have brought a bottle of wine. I thought it might take a bit of time to explain to you why that couldn't have been me. If you will give me the chance to tell you, then it will become clear why you are wrong.'

I know that he can take that one of two ways. Thankfully he appears to relent. I am guessing he is not 100% sure, otherwise he would have gone to the police straight away and I am convinced he hasn't, yet.

He goes to the dresser in the kitchen and brings out 2 glasses. I stand up and walk through.

'Shall I pour?'

He nods and walks past me back towards the living room. I fill both glasses; his from the bottle and mine from a small bottle I have in my pocket. I take the two glasses back through and pass him his. We say "cheers" and as I sit down, we take the first taste of our wine.

'It's a bit drier than I normally drink, but it is alright.'

That is probably the powder I think, as I sip my wine that is not spiked. Thankfully he appears to like the wine enough to gulp down most of it before I have even started to spin him my yarn. I go and get the bottle and top his up. I haven't drunk enough out of mine yet to need a top up. It would have been awkward to do that anyway, now we are back in the living room.

'When was this event you are mistaking me being here for?'

'Is that so you can twist your story to fit?'

'Oh, no, not by any means. My story fits for the last thirty years.'

I can see that has got him puzzled. I also see him looking a bit confused. I decide I will just hit him with it.

'I was in a mental institution for twenty five years. I did not leave that place once in all that time. It was in Kent. I was released just over two years ago, when a judge ruled that I was well enough to integrate back into society.'

He is just sitting there listening to me. I haven't made my story long and boring. I have made it short and punchy. It will be hard for him to question it. I have a bit more if I need it, but somehow I don't think I will. I have seen some familiar reactions. I am surprised, because I thought I would have to wait a lot longer than this for it to take effect.

'I was convinced you were the person' he says and then closes his eyes.

I wait a minute, to see if he is just thinking, but it dawns on me that he is not. The tablets have taken effect. I get up and walk over to him. I grab hold of the cushion and then I cover his face with it and then more or less sit on it, awkward as it is. He doesn't struggle and when I judge I have held it in place for long enough, I remove the cushion and check for life signs. There are none. I replace the cushion over his face.

I walk quickly over to his desk and pick up the piece of paper he showed me. I read it quickly. I see that he has literally finished this before I came round. It needs a little alteration though, to fit a bit better. I flick on his laptop, with the intention of searching for the file. No need, as it is still up. I make the changes to it I need, to make the story more fitting. I use a pen to hit the keys as I type. I then print off another copy. I then save the file and check that he has no other files on the subject, he hasn't.

I fold his original and put it safely in my zipped pocket. I put the new copy just down from the top, in the pile of papers by the printer. I wash the glasses and put them away and take the bottle with me to the back door. There is a key in the lock, but I see some keys on a rack. One of them is also a back door key. I take the key out of the lock and put it on the floor and use the other key to let myself out and lock up after me. This key will come in useful at the next stage of my plan.

Chapter 57 I am still away

I am still all alone as I make my way back to the car for some more wine. I can't believe my luck in having the streets to myself. I retrieve the rest of the bottles of wine from the boot of the car. Back down to the bottom of Racecourse Lane, then a left and a right, as if I am going into the car park. It doesn't take me long at all and I am at my next port of call, the house where Martin and Maggie live. It is now properly dark and the streetlights that there are around, are not close enough to be able to make me out, not that anyone appears to be looking out anywhere. I ring the bell and again have to wait a while. I know they are in. The lights are on and there is music playing; quite old fashioned music. I hear the music stop and a few seconds later, the door is being unlocked.

Martin is standing there, looking out to see who it is. He hasn't switched on the outside light either, which is good for me, but it doesn't help his cause in identifying his visitor. I can see straight away that he is a bit worse for wear with drink. His nose and cheeks have a red glow to them.

'Oh, hello' he says, as he recognises me.

'Can I come in' I reply, as I want to get off the door step as quickly as possible.

I show him the bottles and that makes up his mind for him. He steps back and I step in.

'We've already had some, I have to admit. We started earlier in the Talbot and well it has become a session. Come on through.'

'Look who has come to see us and they've brought more wine, Maggie.'

Maggie is sitting, more slumping in the chair. She has had a good drink too. There are a couple of empty bottles on the floor and their glasses are nearly empty.

'Where do you keep the glasses?' I ask, as Martin has gone to sit down where he was sitting before I came.

'They are in the kitchen, in the cupboard by the sink. Help yourself.'

I take my opened bottle with me and find and fill a glass from my hidden bottle. I then return and top up their glasses to the top, from my open bottle. They raise their glasses to me and then take a big slug of wine. It is not pretty to look at. I think they had stopped drinking before I came and I have just revived them.

'It's a nice house. How many bedrooms have you got?'

I need to get my questions in, before they ask why I am here. Thankfully in the state they are in, they are not too bothered at this second. They have nearly finished the glass of wine I poured them. A top up is necessary before they answer. They have made no comment about the taste of the wine.

'Three, but we use the little one as an office. You know desk, chair, computer and printer. That is it just about, oh and a picture on the wall, our password hint.'

I know what I need to know now. I just need to get to the stage when I am going to be able to use it. I have to open the next bottle and pour another drink before Martin shows signs of reaction first.

'I just need to go to use the loo' he gets unsteadily to his feet and walks towards the door.

'Is he alright' I ask Maggie.

She doesn't answer straight away, as there is the sound of something from on the stairs.

'He always goes upstairs like that when he has had a drink.'

'The toilet is upstairs then?'

'Well there is one downstairs, but he goes upstairs and then he'll just flop out on the bed. I hope it wasn't him you came to see?'

'It was both of you actually.'

I don't get to say any more, as there is a thump on the landing. I get to my feet. Maggie sits forward and sniggers.

'He's fallen onto the landing' she slurs.

'Will he be alright?'

'Don't know.'

I am excited about how this is working out for me. I am not going to let this situation run away from me.

'I think we had better take a look.'

I can see she is not keen, but I go over and pull her to her feet. She gives me a nasty look, but doesn't resist my pull. I push her towards the door and she makes it through to the hall and looks up the stairs. I give her another push and she starts climbing the stairs.

'Are you alright Martin?' I ask up ahead of us. There is no reply. That is because we can see when we get to the top of the stairs, he is asleep.

'Come on' I say 'let's put him to bed.'

Again I get that nasty look from Maggie, but she does grab his arm and between us, we manage to manoeuvre him into their bedroom and onto the bed. I get the covers back and lay him out, before covering him. I'm betting it is not the first time he has gone to bed dressed, when he is drunk. Maggie lets me do this last bit on my own. I don't know where she is and she hasn't said a thing since we put Martin on the bed. I turn to see where she is and she is half on and half off her side of the bed. She has dropped off too. The powder seems to have worked really fast today on all three of them. But these two are not done yet. I decide to do Martin first, so I leave Maggie where she is and deal with Martin. He does struggle, but he is so far out of it, that it is just a gesture of resistance, before he succumbs to the lack of air. Rather than disturb Maggie and risk waking her reactions up a bit, I gently lower her to the floor. She is the type who will come out of it and fight. I don't give her a chance. I leave her where she lies, as I then put the next part of my plan into action.

I go into the small bedroom, their office. It is as they said; other than they missed out to mention the small set of drawers. I switch on the laptop and it asks for a password. My biggest fear was this, but they have given me the answer already. I look up at the picture on the wall. I am initially puzzled. It is a picture of a large packet of peanut M&Ms. I pick up a pencil in my gloved hand and tap the keys with it. I try peanut and then I try peanut M&Ms, as it is written and then with no gap. Nothing happens. I don't need this problem. I stop to think. The clue is there, but I am just not seeing it. Then I get a light come on in my head. Martin & Maggie is M & M. That is about their level I think, not quite as bright as they would want folks to think they are. But M&Ms won't have enough letters. Then I get it; replace the & with and. Bingo I am in.

It takes only a few seconds to plug in my memory stick and download the file and save it. I send it to the printer and print it off. I switch everything off and go back to the bedroom. All is still quiet in there. Well it would be as they are both dead. I slip the papers I have printed between her pillows and put her in the bed and cover her up. I go and fetch their glasses, adding more powder to Maggie's one, as I want that to be easily noticed. I leave them by the bed, along with some bottles lying on the floor. Once I am satisfied with the scene, I leave and go to finish off downstairs.

I spill some wine on the carpets from a new untampered bottle and swill the last of it down the sink. I move into the hall and put Harvey's key into a coat pocket. I then take a key off the rack in the kitchen and open the front door to try it. It works. I switch off all the lights and after checking the coast is clear, I leave and lock up the house.

My short journey back to my car is uneventful. Someone walks across the bottom of the road as I cross St Mary's Lane, but they don't look up the road and they are too far away anyway. That is the only person I see. I drive up Racecourse Lane and out the top onto the Bridgnorth Road. I take a left at the crossroads and then make my way along the quiet roads, all the way back to the car rental place. I do stop on the way at one spot, to dispose of the key in a ditch and I burn the paper at another point.

It is late when I get back to the guest house in my own car. I leave in the morning after having breakfast. Mine host makes no comment about me being out late, even if they noticed; which I doubt.

I arrive home to my partner just before lunchtime.

Chapter 58 Is this the end?

Life in Much Wenlock remains interesting over the next few days. There is still a police presence at both of the scenes of death (or murder scenes as we know them as). Checks are done and about a week later, an official statement is made, announcing the timing of events and who was responsible.

Brian and Jackie, Leonard and Lucy, David and Barbara are all again having a meal at the George. Today the police have released their official statement regarding the deaths in Wenlock. They discuss this as they drink and eat. The gist of the statement is this:

The police are satisfied that after full investigations that all of the recently discovered deaths in Wenlock; namely Mary, Harvey, Martin & Maggie, that they are not looking for anyone else regarding these deaths. It has become clear, with the evidence they have found, that Maggie was responsible originally for killing Mary, for her money. This she appears to have spent, as there is little left other than their property. But she and Martin have taken lavish holidays and cruises and they think that they have spent beyond their means. Maggie then killed Harvey, when he recognised her in the square after the Monday Walk. Harvey approached Martin and Maggie and then she visited him and murdered him. Not wanting to bring shame onto Martin, or have him find out about her past, she got him drunk and then spiked his drink and killed him before taking her own life. She left a full confession.

And that just about wraps up the entire episode.

The six of them discuss the findings and as usual it is Brian who speaks out with his words of wisdom.
'Well you would never have known that about them. I have said it before, but you just don't know what goes on behind closed doors and you don't know what goes on in someone's head and what secrets they might be holding.'

They clink their glasses and have a drink on that.

"I wonder what you all would think if you knew the truth; that you are sitting and eating with a murderer. Even my partner doesn't know."
'Cheers' says Lucy as she thinks this and looks round at the faces of the other five.

The end

It's Murder in Wenlock Copyright © 2019 William (Bill) Stenlake

It's Murder in Wenlock By Bill Stenlake

All rights reserved. No part of this book may be reproduced, distributed or transmitted in any form, by any means without the prior consent of the author.

All characters in this publication are fictitious and any resemblance to persons, living or dead is purely coincidental. Some places named in the book exist and are real and some do not exist and are not real. The placement of all things geographical is relevant to this story only and as such should be deemed fictional.

Book Cover Photo: © Esben Hansen/Dreamstime.com

Other books by Bill Stenlake:
HOLLOW MILL
THE KEEPER
KENAN'S LEGACY
CORNERSTONE
THE GRAND MASTER
DETECTIVE BRAMLEY BOOK 1
RANDOLPH
VOICES IN MY HEAD
LOWARTH TOLL
THE CORIDAE KEY
BRAMLEY BOOK 2
THE MANNACHS
DIMENSIONS
THE ROOTS
A PAIR OF SHORTS
THE WATCHER
THE KEEPER TRILOGY
IT'S DARK IN WENLOCK
RODDY JOHNSTONE

Printed in Poland
by Amazon Fulfillment
Poland Sp. z o.o., Wrocław